In *Mozart's Shadow:*

HIS SISTER'S STORY

In Mozart's Shadow:

HIS SISTER'S STORY

Carolyn Meyer

Harcourt, Inc.

Orlando Austin New York San Diego London

Copyright © 2008 by Carolyn Meyer

All rights reserved. No part of this publication may be
reproduced or transmitted in any form or by any means,
electronic or mechanical, including photocopy, recording,
or any information storage and retrieval system, without
permission in writing from the publisher.

Requests for permission to make copies of any part
of the work should be submitted online at
www.harcourt.com/contact or mailed to the following address:
Permissions Department, Houghton Mifflin Harcourt Publishing Company,
6277 Sea Harbor Drive, Orlando, Florida 32887-6777.

www.HarcourtBooks.com

Library of Congress Cataloging-in-Publication Data
Meyer, Carolyn, 1935–
In Mozart's shadow: his sister's story/Carolyn Meyer.
p. cm.
Summary: In eighteenth-century Europe, Anna "Nannerl" Mozart, a musician
whose talent and dedication is overshadowed by that of her gifted younger
brother, Wolfgang, struggles to win the notice of her father and patrons
who might further her career, despite her gender.
1. Berchtold zu Sonnenburg, Maria Anna Mozart, Reichsfreiin von, 1751–1829—
Juvenile fiction. 2. Mozart, Wolfgang Amadeus, 1756–1791—Juvenile fiction.
[1. Berchtold zu Sonnenburg, Maria Anna Mozart, Reichsfreiin von, 1751–1829—
Fiction. 2. Mozart, Wolfgang Amadeus, 1756–1791—Fiction. 3. Musicians—
Fiction. 4. Brothers and sisters—Fiction. 5. Sex role—Fiction. 6. Mozart,
Leopold, 1719–1787—Fiction. 7. Vienna (Austria)—History—18th century—
Fiction. 8. Austria—History—1740–1789—Fiction.] I. Title.
PZ7.M5685In 2008
[Fic]—dc22 2007037450
ISBN 978-0-15-205594-3

Text set in Requiem Text
Designed by Lydia D'moch

First edition
A C E G H F D B

Printed in the United States of America

In Mozart's Shadow is a work of fiction based on historical figures and events.
Some details have been altered to enhance the story.

Remembering my parents, Vic and Sara Meyer,
who loved music—especially Mozart

In Mozart's Shadow:
HIS SISTER'S STORY

Prologue

Papa steps into the salon brilliantly lit by chandeliers that blaze beneath the painted cherubs on the ceiling. Our papa is tall, handsome, a commanding presence. The audience—the highest nobility—seated on carved and gilded chairs, falls silent. My brother and I wait behind heavy velvet draperies, out of sight. Papa launches into his pretty speech: "It does us great honor," et cetera, et cetera.

Wolferl fidgets with his little ceremonial sword. He is exquisite in a suit of lavender satin trimmed with gold lace. Our hairdresser adjusts Wolferl's wig, rearranges the ribbons in my elaborate curls, and dabs a bit of powder on my nose.

Papa's rich baritone rises to the pitch that signals my entrance. "Now it is my privilege to present to you my daughter, Maria Anna Mozart," he trumpets, "just eleven years old with talents that, you will surely agree, are a gift from God."

Papa always has me go first. I glide out from among the folds of the draperies and offer my hand to Papa, who bows and kisses it. Then, gathering my voluminous silk skirts, I honor the bejeweled audience with a deep curtsy. I love this moment, when all eyes are upon me!

"Another inch lower and you'll fall on your face, Nannerl," my brother whispers from behind the curtain. With a secret smile I sink down one more inch. I don't fall.

The audience applauds politely.

Arranging my skirts, I seat myself at the harpsichord and wait, my hands calm in my lap. This, according to Papa, will focus the attention of the audience. Then I lift my hands and begin to play. Papa chose the piece to show off my skill: fast, accurate, brilliant. I love to play, love to perform. The applause rises, warm and admiring. Papa smiles.

After two more bravura pieces I step aside, and Papa plunges into his Wolferl spiel, pronouncing my brother's full baptismal name: "Johann Chrysostom Wolfgang Gottlieb Mozart. My son will astonish you, esteemed ladies and noble gentlemen, with his incredible displays of keyboard virtuosity. And he is only seven years of age!"

Papa is lying. Wolferl is eight, going on nine, but so small no one doubts Papa's word. I'm thirteen, still without noticeable breasts; Mama dresses me to look younger. I wish Papa would be truthful about my age, but he insists the little deception is necessary.

My brother struts in, grinning impishly and exuding endearing charm. Papa makes a show of helping him up onto the chair on which a thick cushion has been placed; Wolferl's tiny feet dangle several inches above the floor. He looks like a precious doll. But in the next moment his little fingers are skimming expertly over the wooden keys. His per-

formance is breathtaking. When he finishes, I can hear the gasps of astonishment.

Papa enthralls the audience with one trick after another. "Next, our little Wolfgang will play with just one finger!" And he does so, precisely and at unbelievable speed. Amazed murmurs rustle like a breeze. "Now, dear friends, Wolfgang will play with the keyboard completely hidden out of sight beneath this black cloth!" The rapt listeners lean forward, their chairs creaking. They've never seen the like!

He's got them in the palm of his hand. Smiling, Papa invites members of the audience to offer challenges to the prodigy. A gentleman with some knowledge of music comes forward and picks out a line of melody. Without hesitation Wolferl repeats the line, adding a bass and harmonies, altering the rhythm, embroidering the tune, turning the simple melody—nothing more than a nursery song—into a sonata.

The audience is spellbound. At last Papa calls for me to join my brother at the keyboard, and we begin a duet. Playing together like this is as natural to us as our breathing. Then Papa tucks his violin under his chin, and we perform as a trio. For nearly three hours we hold the audience captivated. When Papa signals the end, the ladies rush forward excitedly. Wolferl not only endures their kisses but wants more. He loves being loved! He gets more attention than I do, but Papa says that's because Wolferl is so young, so adorable!

Afterward they lavish us with gifts: watches, gold rings, snuffboxes, toothpick boxes. Papa hopes for ducats, thalers, florins, louis d'or. Sometimes he collects a fat purse for our performances. Sometimes it's just another crystal snuffbox.

———

MANY YEARS HAVE passed since those heady days. My life is much different now—not at all what I expected then, when we were *Wunderkinder*—"wonder children"—Wolfgang and Nannerl Mozart, the toast of Europe. This was our life, when we had mostly each other, before we grew older, before things happened that drove us apart. Now I sit in the gathering darkness, and I remember it all.

Part 1

WOLFERL
1756

Chapter 1

WONDER CHILDREN

IN THE BEGINNING, when I was four, Papa sat beside me at the clavichord, the music book open to minuets and other short pieces he had prepared for me, and he taught me how to play. I loved these lessons with Papa. In the next room Wolferl, a newborn babe, mewled and howled. I ignored him. Every day I practiced—an hour at first, then two, then three or four. By the time I was seven, I had mastered Johann Sebastian Bach's inventions and sinfonias and moved on to the preludes and fugues.

My talent dazzled everyone. "The child is a wonder," they said.

Papa and Mama were delighted. Their musician friends—Herr Schachtner, the court trumpeter; Herr Adlgasser, the court organist; and many others—often visited our little third-floor apartment. These men took for granted that I was musically talented—as the daughter of Leopold Mozart, second violinist and composer at the court of the prince-archbishop of Salzburg, how could I be otherwise?

"She has a great future, has she not?" Papa said.

"You have only to look at those long fingers!" Mama exclaimed, and everyone agreed that my hands were, indeed, extraordinary, the hands of a gifted performer.

But I hadn't long to bask in their pride. When my little brother was just three, he clambered onto the bench by the clavichord, peered at my exercise book, and quickly figured out how to do what I did. It would not be long before he, too, would be playing Herr Bach's most challenging compositions.

Mama and Papa watched him, openmouthed, and hugged each other. "A true prodigy," Papa whispered, tears of joy glistening in his eyes. "You see, Nannerl?" he said, turning to me. "Your brother is surely blessed by God!"

"I am, too!" I said, glaring at Papa. "Aren't I, Mama?"

Mama put her arms around me and pulled me close. She always smelled sweetly of lavender. *"Ja, mein Liebchen,"* she crooned. "Of course you are."

At four Wolferl began to compose simple tunes. Papa wrote down the notes as Wolferl played.

When he was five, Wolferl decided to write down the notes himself. He presented the ink-smudged manuscript to Papa, explaining, "It's a concerto." He proceeded to play it, reading the blots and squiggles on the paper. Papa, chest swelling with pride, showed him how to write it properly.

I practiced and practiced—always Bach, and more Bach—and Papa praised my keyboard technique. I worked even harder to please him. Sometimes I made up little songs—I put words with mine—and pretended to write them down. Papa was too busy to teach me to do it properly. "I'll show you how," Wolferl offered. When I later presented my efforts to Papa, he said only, "Very nice indeed." His cool response brought me to tears.

But Wolferl far exceeded anyone's expectations. He was making amazing progress as a clavier player. He had a perfect sense of pitch and could instantly name any note that was played. He could detect when an instrument was tuned a quarter tone off. He taught himself to play the violin. At first he was awkward with the bow, but he insisted upon joining Papa's trio rehearsing in our front room; he was good enough that they allowed him. And he kept making up "concertos" and writing them down.

I practiced even more diligently, to show that I was as good as Wolferl. Mama always said I was. "You must not be jealous of your brother," she said. "God gives each of us different gifts."

Wolferl had not yet reached his sixth birthday on the twenty-seventh of January—I had turned ten in July— when our father decided that Salzburg was not a large enough stage for his two brilliant children, his *Wunderkinder,* as he always called us. Papa made plans to take our family to Munich, to play for Elector Maximilian, the prince of Bavaria.

I became half sick with excitement as our parents prepared for the journey. Wolferl could hardly sit still, racing up and down the narrow stairs, prancing through the cramped rooms, crawling under the furniture on his hands and knees until Papa made him stop. His antics made me even more nervous.

"Come, play chess with me," I coaxed, thinking it would soothe my queasy stomach. Papa had taught me the game years ago, and I'd taught Wolferl. Chess was the one thing besides music that calmed him. He was good, but I was better. It pained him to lose to Papa, but he seemed not to mind when I won. Sometimes, though, he simply wanted to use the chess pieces to make up a story in which he was the king and I was the queen.

Our friends the Hagenauers, who were also our landlords, promised to look after our apartment on Getreidegasse and to take care of Bimperl, our little terrier, while we were gone. Mama ordered us each a new dress from our seamstress. I made my two best friends, Viktoria Adlgasser and Katherl Gilowsky, envious with our plans.

"Show us your dress," begged Katherl, a barber-surgeon's daughter who loved ribbons and laces, the more the better. Viktoria, who dreamed of a singing career, listened solemnly while I played the pieces I'd been practicing until

I thought my fingers would drop off. I had added a sonata by J. S. Bach's son, Carl Philipp Emanuel Bach, to my repertoire.

"The elector is sure to be impressed," said little Viktoria. "You're talented, and lucky, too. I hope someday my papa will give me such an opportunity." She was the daughter of the court organist. We always spoke of her as "little Viktoria"; she was two years younger than I and small for her age but solemn as a judge.

"It's not Nannerl her father's showing off," said Katherl, holding up my new red velvet dress in front of her and admiring her image in the looking glass. "If it weren't for Wolferl, she'd be stuck here with the rest of us."

I snatched the dress out of Katherl's hands. "It's both of us!" I insisted.

Katherl shrugged. "He's a *boy*," she said, drawing out the word. "And that makes all the difference."

"And I'll prove you wrong," I said, throwing the dress on the bed.

IT WAS MIDWINTER and very cold when we left Salzburg for Bavaria. Several times the rented carriage bogged down in snowdrifts, and each time Papa and the driver had to dig it out. Even wrapped in furs, I complained about my freezing feet.

Once we arrived in Munich, though, everything went off splendidly. Elector Maximilian's Residenz was very large and sumptuous, but I didn't think it was any nicer than the Residenz of our own archbishop Schrattenbach. Our little apartment on Getreidegasse would have fit into just one of the halls of either palace.

The elector, himself a musician, was delighted with us. To begin, I played one of Bach's dance suites. My favorite was the gigue, the fast part coming after the stately sarabande, and it brought the elector to his feet, crying, "Her fingers fairly dance!"

But it was the musical tricks Papa had devised to show off Wolferl's amazing skill that brought gasps from the audience. My little brother easily sight-read difficult pieces he'd never seen before, and he could improvise endless variations on a simple line of melody. To demonstrate Wolferl's perfect pitch, Papa called for someone in the audience to ring a bell, and Wolferl immediately named the note. "That's an A-sharp," he said, and he did the same with crystal glasses filled with water, chiming clocks, tinkling pocket watches, always accurately identifying the tone. He didn't have to think about it; he just *knew.*

We loved all of it—playing before an admiring audience, hearing the applause, being called back for encores. Wolferl promptly fell asleep afterward, but I lay awake for a long time, going over the entire evening in my mind, reliving the attention showered on us—both of us. *Katherl is wrong,* I thought contentedly before I drifted off.

OUR VISIT was a great success. At the end of three weeks the elector rewarded Papa with a purse bulging with money. We slogged home to Salzburg, shivering in the carriage, our backsides sore from bumping over a frozen road creased with deep ruts. Bimperl greeted us, running in joyful circles, Papa resumed his duties at Archbishop Schrattenbach's court, Mama went back to keeping house, and Wolferl and I settled down again to our routines of studying and practicing hour after hour.

About this time Wolferl thought up a new game. "We could play duets," he said.

We had no duet music, so we improvised, using one of Herr Bach's preludes. At first I played the treble with my left hand and Wolferl played the bass with his right, to keep out of each other's way, but it quickly got boring. Wolferl solved that by making up variations on his bass part, and I tried doing the same with the treble. Then we switched places. We enjoyed our "duet game" as Wolferl called it, but only when Papa was out, so he wouldn't say we were wasting time.

But this ordinary life didn't last long. Papa was already talking about our next journey. "We shall go to Vienna," he said, "and play for their imperial majesties, Emperor Franz and Empress Maria Theresia."

Mama and I at once began discussing the dresses and cloaks and shoes and gloves we would need, and I rushed to tell little Viktoria and Katherl the news. My friends had news of their own: The archbishop was sending Magdalena Lipp, Maria Brauenhofer, and Anna Fesemayr, daughters of court musicians, to Venice to study singing.

"Maria is only thirteen," Viktoria said. "But the archbishop believes she has a great future. I'm hoping he'll do the same for me."

"I wonder if the archbishop also sends keyboard players to Italy," I mused idly, the idea first entering my mind that this might be my future as well.

"He does. He sent my papa to study there when he was young."

"Wolferl stands a good chance," Katherl said pointedly. "But how many women keyboard players do you know?"

Her question stung. "None," I said, my chin lifting defiantly. "But who is to say that I could not be the first?"

Katherl must have realized she'd hurt me, for she reached for my hand and squeezed it. "Oh, Nannerl," she said with a sigh, "it's just that I don't want to see you disappointed."

"You won't," I replied, truly believing I was right.

WE LEFT FOR Vienna in the autumn of 1762: Papa, Mama, Wolferl, and I, with a servant to look after our mountains of baggage. We made our first stop in the city of Passau, where we were kept waiting for several days before the prince-bishop decided if and when we might play for him. Papa's patience stretched thinner and thinner, like Mama's pastry dough, but Wolferl and I didn't mind. We amused ourselves making up stories with our chess pieces. The only time we argued was when I, as queen, pretended to defy the king, and Wolferl wouldn't tolerate it.

At last Papa burst into our room at the inn and announced, "Wolferl is to play tonight." There was a hurried discussion of what to wear and what to play.

"And I, Papa?" I interrupted. "What shall I play?"

Papa barely paused to answer. "You will not be needed, Nannerl."

"Why am I not needed? I always play when Wolferl does."

"Not this time," Papa said impatiently. "Only Wolferl."

I stamped my foot and burst into tears. "But I want to play!"

"Nannerl!" Papa exclaimed. "For shame!"

Wolferl stared at me, openmouthed. But Mama touched my cheek and said, "Never mind, *Liebchen*. Your time will come."

I threw myself, sobbing, into her arms. I wanted to believe her, but I suspected otherwise: I was not a six-year-old *Wunderkind*. I was already eleven. Lots of eleven-year-old girls played well, even brilliantly, although I knew that few were as accomplished as I.

Wolferl's time had already come. That night, for the first time, he played without me.

———

THE NEXT DAY we boarded the post-boat on the Danube bound for Vienna, making several stops along the way. In Linz, Wolferl and I gave several concerts at which a number of Viennese noblemen were present. This pleased Papa. "Surely these important people will return home and tell their friends about us," he said. Farther downriver at Ybbs, Wolferl played the organ at the Franciscan monastery, astounding the monks who heard him.

"From triumph to triumph," Papa gloated when we were again on the post-boat.

Even the torrents of icy, wind-driven rain didn't dampen Wolferl's spirits. He pulled out his small violin and began to entertain the passengers, who chuckled and clapped.

"Can't you just be still?" I grumbled.

He looked at me, surprised. "What's wrong, Nannerl? I was just having a little fun with music."

I realized then, for the first time, that I *was* jealous.

Chapter 2

VIENNA

WE ARRIVED IN VIENNA in early October—there was already snow in the air—and settled in a room that Papa described as "one foot wide and a thousand feet long." Mama and I shared one bed; Papa and Wolferl slept in the other. Almost immediately we received an invitation to perform for the emperor and empress at Schönbrunn Palace.

Empress Maria Theresia had inherited her title from her father and wielded enormous power throughout the Holy Roman Empire that covered much of Europe. She was married to Franz I and had given birth to sixteen children, eleven of them still living. (My own dear mama had given birth to seven, but only two of us had survived.) All their daughters, the archduchesses, had the first name of Maria, and each had a second name by which she was called: Kristina, Elisabeth, Amalia, Johanna (who was betrothed to King Ferdinand of Naples), Josefa (eleven, like me), Karolina, and Antonia. The oldest son, Archduke Josef, was married to pretty Isabella of Parma. Archduke Leopold was eight years old, and the youngest child, Maximilian, was six, the same age as Wolferl.

The entire imperial family and many of their friends were present that day. Papa had arranged for Wolferl to play a concerto written by the court composer, Herr Wagenseil, who was also the music teacher for the empress and her children. But the composer was nowhere to be seen as our program began. My brother turned to the audience and asked, "Is Herr Wagenseil not here?"

His tone was so haughty that I feared our hosts might take offense. I glanced at Papa, who had half risen from his seat. Mama leaned forward, trying to catch Wolferl's eye. Wolferl paid no attention. Archduke Josef offered to fetch the tardy composer and soon returned with him. "I'm going to play one of your concertos," Wolferl informed Herr Wagenseil, who was smiling condescendingly at my audacious little brother. "Be so kind as to sit here beside me and turn the pages for me."

Herr Wagenseil looked too surprised to object and did as he was ordered, perhaps because the empress seemed amused. I felt myself blush deeply, and Mama pressed a handkerchief to her lips, but the others merely smiled and nodded. When Wolferl began to play, the patronizing smile left Herr Wagenseil's face and was replaced by a look of awe.

At the end of Wolferl's performance, the composer lifted him up and carried him around the hall to great applause.

Then it was my turn. I sometimes felt a little nervous before our performances, and that day I had been unable to eat a thing. But as soon as I was seated at the keyboard, I forgot about my brother's spoiled behavior and the favoritism shown him. My nervousness vanished as I struck the opening notes of the Scarlatti sonata I had learned for this occasion. I forgot everything else and lost myself in the music that had become as much a part of me as my daily prayers. The emperor and empress praised my playing so generously that I promptly gave my heart to the whole royal family.

The moment our concert was finished, while everyone was still exclaiming over our brilliant performances—mine just as much as Wolferl's—my brother climbed up on the empress's lap, threw his arms around her neck, and planted a loud, smacking kiss on her powdered cheek. I could hardly believe my eyes. Such behavior would not be tolerated in many places, but the empress seemed unperturbed—maybe, with so many children of her own, nothing surprised her. Emperor Franz, a kindly man with a dimpled chin, called Wolferl the "little wizard" and signaled the servants to bring refreshments.

We sipped thick, frothy chocolate from delicate china cups and nibbled little cakes made with marzipan. Archduchess Johanna, enchanted by Wolferl's charms, took him by the hand and led him off for a tour of the royal apartments. I trailed along behind them with several of the archduchesses, past silk-covered walls, gilded furniture, and marble statues. My little brother was prattling away giddily when he slipped on the highly polished floor and fell down. Seven-year-old Antonia rushed to him and helped him to his feet.

"You are so kind," Wolferl told the pretty little archduchess with a courtly bow. "When we're grown up, I shall marry you."

"I would be honored, Herr Wolfgang," she said with a sweet smile, sweeping him a curtsy.

Later the empress arranged for us to be presented with court costumes originally made for her children. Wolferl's was a suit of lilac-colored cloth, the waistcoat richly embroidered and the coat trimmed with wide gold braid. I received Johanna's splendid dress of white taffeta brocade with lots of lace on the sleeves and around the neck. The gift giving continued with all sorts of costly items, and finally Papa was presented with a purse bulging with silver thalers.

We climbed into our carriage, Papa on one side with his arm around Wolferl, Mama and I seated opposite, our fingers linked. "Another triumph for the Family Mozart," Papa said contentedly as we rode back to our room—the one that was one foot wide and a thousand feet long.

————

WE STAYED ON in Vienna, performing as often as we were invited, nearly every day. At each concert Papa had me present a solo or two that I had rehearsed thoroughly, Scarlatti or one of the Bachs. Sometimes I sang as well, which I enjoyed then nearly as much as I did playing. My brother always led the applause for me, and the effect of a little six-year-old on his feet and clapping enthusiastically always encouraged the audience. Then I shared the keyboard with Wolferl to play two or three duets. Our four hands on one keyboard were no longer a game; Papa supplied us with proper duet music, and we'd grown so closely attuned to each other that we scarcely had to think about it.

But it was Wolferl, performing alone, who claimed the center of attention. Not only did he dazzle with his musical abilities, but the "little wizard" spoke out impudently, kissed the ladies, and charmed everyone. I smiled and learned to flutter a fan while engaged in chitchat, although it did not come easily to me. I was shy and reserved as a young girl—unlike my brother!—and it would be several years until I learned to enjoy these social occasions.

Papa wrote often to Herr Hagenauer, our Salzburg landlord who now also served as our banker. He composed these letters in stages, over several days, naming the wealthy and famous people for whom we had played and describing the purses of money and the gifts showered on us. One day I found an unfinished letter lying on the writing table.

Mama and Papa had gone out, and Wolferl was practicing on one of the claviers that Papa had borrowed for us. I was supposed to be practicing, too. But I stopped long enough to read what my father had written. The words flowed across the page in his clear script: *Wolferl amazed everybody. His talent knows no limits. And my little girl performed very well, too.*

I sat on the bed I shared with Mama and thought about what Papa had written: *And my little girl performed very well, too.* I was still sitting on the bed when Wolferl left the clavier and came to stare at me, his small features puckered in a frown. "Is something wrong, Horseface?" That was his latest teasing name for me.

"Not a thing," I said sharply. "Go back to your practicing, Wolferl," I added impatiently. "Otherwise, you may not continue to amaze everybody."

He shot me another puzzled look and within half a minute I heard the clavier again.

When Mama and Papa returned, we went to the eating house across the street for a meal. Bent over my plate of goulash, I tried to put Papa's words out of my mind—tried, but failed. *Perhaps it's all true,* I thought. *Wolferl's talent has no limits, but mine does. Then I must work harder. It's as simple as that.* I stood up and asked permission to return to our room.

"Are you ill, Nannerl?" Papa asked.

"*Nein,* Papa," I said firmly. "I'm fine. I must go and practice."

Chapter 3

THE NEW CARRIAGE

WOLFERL COUGHED and coughed and burned with fever. "He's suffering from a catarrh in his chest," Mama dithered. "It's the foul weather that's done it."

My brother was a fragile child, and the constant performances tired him. A day or two after we played a second time for the empress at Schönbrunn Palace, he'd fallen ill. Papa dosed him with the usual remedies: black powder as a cathartic and margrave powder to sweat away a fever. When those medicines failed to cure Wolferl—he'd developed a rash of red spots—Papa sent for a physician.

"Scarlet fever," pronounced the doctor, a portly man with a thick black beard. "Caused by the change in air." His diagnosis was a great relief, for we were afraid it might be smallpox. All over Vienna people were coming down with the terrible disease, and many deaths had been reported.

Sometimes those who recovered were horribly scarred or even went blind or deaf.

For two weeks Wolferl lay in bed. Papa paced the length of our room, muttering about the money he was losing because of the missed opportunities to perform for the Viennese nobility. In the next breath he insisted that nothing was as important as the health of his children. "Anna Maria! Nannerl! Fall on your knees and pray fervently for God's mercy and Wolferl's restored health!" Papa commanded.

Of course we had already done so. We didn't need Papa to tell us that Wolferl's life was in danger. I was so afraid we might lose him that I found it difficult to think about anything else, or even to practice. What would I ever do without Wolferl?

On October 31, the Feast of St. Wolfgang, my brother's name day, he seemed a little better. A few days later, when the doctor allowed Wolferl to leave his bed for the first time, Papa dressed him warmly and prepared to take him out for a stroll in the park beyond the old city walls.

"Do you think this is wise, Leopold?" Mama asked, frowning. "He's still very weak. It might be best to keep him inside for another day or two." She twisted a handkerchief, as she did when she was worried.

Papa dismissed her fears. "It's important for everyone to see that the boy is quite well again and able to perform." But what everyone saw were the remains of Wolferl's rash, and they avoided him. Mama turned out to be right—my brother was still weak, and soon he was back in bed again.

Slowly the spots faded, and Wolferl seemed stronger. Our concerts resumed. It may not have been a good idea. "He is so tiny!" people remarked. "So frail! Is it right that his father should exploit him for the sake of a few ducats?" If Papa heard the remarks he shrugged them off, as he did Mama's fretting.

Mama didn't argue. No one argued with Papa. "After God comes Papa," Wolferl said wisely. Mama agreed, and I, too, believed it. Papa knew best.

THE WEEKS PASSED, and the frigid Viennese winter tightened its iron grip. I shivered, even with thick petticoats and a knitted shawl. It was hard to practice when my fingers were stiff with cold.

"When are we going home to Salzburg, Papa?" I asked.

"In time for Christmas," he told me, patting my shoulder in a way meant to be reassuring. But one thing after another caused him to change plans and postpone our return.

I lay awake at night, listening to our parents' murmured conversations. Mama timidly brought up the notion that perhaps we should leave for home as soon as possible.

"What will happen to your position at court?" she asked. "You've already overstayed your leave of absence, and the archbishop will not be pleased."

"Don't worry, Anna Maria," Papa said. "I've taken in more money on this little junket that I earn in two years in Salzburg. Wolferl's growing fame brings honor to the archbishop's court."

The discussion ended. Papa knew best.

But after Wolferl's illness the number of invitations to perform dwindled to almost nothing. We continued to go out to lunches and suppers and to attend the opera and other public entertainments—"To keep the Mozarts in the public's eye," Papa said—while we waited for more opportunities to play. None came. My hopes rose that we would soon go home. Then Herr Hagenauer wrote that two of his daughters, Ursula and Franziska, had come down with smallpox. Papa, fearing we might catch it, decided again to postpone our return.

About this time Papa received several requests from noblemen in the city of Pressburg, the capital of Hungary, not far from Vienna on the Danube. One night as we ate supper in our room, Papa laid out his new plan between bites of bread and sausage. "Enough of rattletrap rented coaches," he said. "We shall go to Pressburg, the children will give concerts there, and I shall purchase a fine new carriage."

Mama threw up her hands. "But Leopold, think of the cost! The generous people of Vienna have always sent their carriages for us. Wouldn't it be more prudent to continue to accept their kindness?"

Papa dismissed her objection with a wave of his fork. "And every time they send a carriage, I have to pass out tips to the drivers and the lackeys. I've often thought it would be cheaper simply to rent a coach than to accept the goodwill of our patrons. How much better still to *own* the carriage!"

So instead of going home for Christmas, we spent most of the month of December in Pressburg, giving concerts and allowing Papa time to place an order for a carriage.

"Twenty-three ducats!" Mama gasped when she learned the price. "You paid twenty-three ducats?" Our mother was from a poor family and never could get used to the way Papa sometimes spent money, although at times he could be painfully tightfisted. It depended on the situation and what he wanted to do.

Papa smiled and patted her hand. "It will more than pay for itself, my dear," he assured her. "We will travel far and wide in this carriage. A new life is beginning for the Family Mozart!"

Wolferl let out a cheer—"Bravo!"—and I grinned proudly. How grand to be part of Papa's great plans!

Several days and several concerts later, we drove out of Pressburg in our handsome new carriage, the seats lined with sheepskins and a brazier at our feet to warm us. We somehow made it across the rough and snow-clogged roads without damage and arrived in Salzburg just as the year 1763 was beginning. We had been away for nearly four months.

We were glad to find that the Hagenauers' daughters had survived their smallpox, although poor Ursula, a homely girl to begin with, was badly scarred. But then the sad news reached Salzburg that Archduchess Johanna, whose beautiful white brocade dress I now wore for concerts, had died of the disease two days before Christmas.

THE DAY HE turned seven Wolferl spent his time practicing the violin. He'd been "fiddling," as he called it, since he was five, but now he concentrated on it and had entirely mastered the instrument by the time we were invited to play in celebration of Archbishop Schrattenbach's birthday a month later. I accompanied Wolferl on the harpsichord when he gave his first public performance as a violinist. Afterward the archbishop came to lay his hand on each of us. "God has well and truly blessed you both with great talent," he said, smiling particularly at me. "And blessed all of us here by sending us your beautiful music."

My spirits soared. I had made a good impression on the archbishop. Surely he would someday send me to Italy to study!

For a few weeks the Family Mozart seemed content. Papa was named vice-Kapellmeister, conductor of the court orchestra. Mama was glad to be back in her own kitchen, preparing her special liver dumplings and braised calf's tongue. Bimperl leaped and licked, and Wolferl and I did what we always did under Papa's vigilant direction.

Papa had taught us reading and writing and as much arithmetic as he thought we needed. He pulled down volume after volume from the shelves of his large library and instructed us in geography and history. We became proficient at drawing.

Most important, though, we studied music and practiced, practiced, practiced—never less than three hours every day and often more. We devoted mornings and evenings to learning new pieces and playing together. We soaked up music through all our senses. It was everything to us. I could not imagine any other kind of life.

"You must learn all there is to know about music while you are young!" Papa admonished us. "The world will teach you the rest."

When we weren't practicing separately, we were together. We had our own secret language, our own particular whistle call, our private jokes. But the best part was playing together. It was as though we were not two separate people playing, but just one. Our hearts beat in the same rhythm, making it easy to agree on the tempo.

My keyboard technique was already excellent, and I worked diligently to improve it even more. There was a difference, though: I worked hard, always pushing myself, but music poured effortlessly—almost magically—out of my brother's mind, heart, and hands.

"How I do envy you, Wolferl!" I cried one day when I'd

had to slave over an especially difficult passage and my brother mastered his part on the first try.

"I'm sorry, Nannerl." His apologetic look turned mischievous. "I can't help it if I'm brilliant."

"And an odious brat in the bargain," I said, and kissed his forehead.

WHEN PAPA allowed me a little time away from the apartment, I rushed off to find Katherl, and together we went to fetch Viktoria. Even on the coldest winter days we walked along the Salzach River, wrapped in our furs, teasing Viktoria about her nose that always got red and dripped. We stopped at one of the shops in our street or around the corner at Café Tomaselli to sip steaming cups of chocolate and talk about fashions. Viktoria tried to convince us to take the steep, zigzag path up the Mönchsberg to the Fortress Hohensalzburg that loomed over the town. I resisted—I hated any sort of exercise—but when the weather warmed and the trees behind our apartment began to show a little green, I did like to cross the river to stroll in the gardens of the Mirabell Palace. Our favorite spot there was the Dwarfs' Garden, the marble sculptures of dwarfs said to be from a former archbishop's court. We each found our favorite dwarf—mine was the one wearing eyeglasses.

I had exciting news I'd been saving to tell them.

"We're going on a long journey. Papa is arranging it."

"Really? To where?"

"Everywhere," I said, exaggerating only a little. "All over Europe."

"When?" the girls asked, their eyes growing large.

"This summer."

Papa's contentment after our return from Vienna hadn't lasted, and he had soon grown restless again. Mama and I guessed—correctly—that he was thinking of a new plan.

In May he informed us, "Next month we shall leave Salzburg for a grand tour of Europe, the largest ever undertaken. The children will perform in every great city on the continent, and every person with a love of music will know of them and their genius."

Papa had said it clearly: *will know of them and their genius.* He meant both of us, Wolferl and me. I would dazzle audiences just as my brother did. And when we came home at the end of the tour, I would be old enough to study in Italy. I had the talent. The archbishop could not fail to send me!

Wolferl and I had clapped hands and danced around the table, Mama wore a look of anxious pride, and Papa puffed out his chest. Preparations had already begun.

"Here's the best part," I told my friends as we left the Dwarfs' Garden and resumed our leisurely walk. "Papa is hiring a friseur to dress our hair and take care of our clothes while we travel."

I was sure that would impress them. Only very aristocratic people had a servant to maintain their perukes, the powdered wigs that Papa and Wolferl wore for every dress occasion, and to arrange the women's hair in elaborate coiffures that were the fashion of the day.

"Oh, Nannerl," Viktoria sighed, "you're so fortunate! My papa never takes us anywhere."

"You'll write to us, won't you?" Katherl asked.

"Of course I will!" I promised. And we hurried back across the river to our favorite café in the brightest of moods.

Chapter 4

THE GRAND TOUR

WE ROLLED OUT OF Salzburg in our gleaming black carriage with red-painted wheels, drawn by four coach-horses, in June of 1763. Herr Hagenauer and his wife and several neighbors had gathered to call out, "*Auf Wiedersehen!* Good-bye!" and sent us off with a blessing. Our valet and friseur, Sebastian Winter, traveled with us. He was a small man with long, delicate fingers and a mouth that always seemed ready to smile.

We were headed west to Bavaria, but before we had traveled even half a day, one of the back wheels of our carriage flew off and smashed to pieces. It was past midnight when we limped into the next town with a borrowed wheel, Papa and Sebastian walking the whole way to lighten the load. By then, even Sebastian was not smiling.

The expense of this mishap plunged Papa into a dark

mood. He had to buy a new wheel and was forced to feed the rented horses while the repairs were made. He had to pay the hired driver and put him up at the inn for two extra days, and the five of us, counting Sebastian, had to be accommodated as well.

"*Basta!*" Papa cried, as he did when he was irritated, which was often. "Enough!"

While we waited for the carriage to be fixed, Papa took us to a church to see the great pipe organ. On our way to Vienna Wolferl had first played on an organ, using only the keyboards, of which there were several. Now Papa showed him how to work the pedal board with his feet to produce low notes. Unable to reach it from the bench, Wolferl hopped down and *stood* on the pedals, playing the instrument with both his hands and his feet. He looked as though he were dancing.

I yearned to try it, too, but that was out of the question. "It is not a woman's instrument," Papa claimed.

"Not at all a wasted stop," Papa said with satisfaction, once we were again on the road to Munich. Now he could boast about still another of Wolferl's amazing accomplishments. I felt sure I could have done at least as well on that organ—maybe better—because my legs were longer.

PAPA EXPECTED a warm welcome from Elector Maximilian, who had been so kind to us on our previous visit to Munich. But the elector wasn't in residence when we ar-

rived at the Residenz; he'd moved his court to Nymphen-
burg, the summer palace outside the city. Papa told our
driver to take us there, and, when we arrived, he paraded
us back and forth beneath the palace windows.

"If the elector looks out and sees us," Papa said as we
paced slowly, "we shall surely be invited to play."

"Mama, *must* we do this?" I whispered as we made our
third turn. "I feel ridiculous."

"If Papa wishes it," Mama replied serenely.

Wolferl managed to make it into a game, walking backward, or swinging his arms and mimicking the march of
the soldiers we'd seen, until Papa ordered him to stop.

The plan worked. On our fifth or sixth turn a servant
was dispatched with a request for us to perform for the
elector in the grand salon at eight o'clock that evening.
Papa sent an acceptance, as if the whole thing were a
happy accident.

Wolferl appeared dressed in his elegant lilac-colored
suit. I had outgrown the archduchess's beautiful white
brocade gown, but Mama and her seamstress had managed
to salvage it, adding to the skirt and letting out the bodice.
I waited quietly as Wolferl performed on both violin and
harpsichord with such brilliance that he was called back
again and again. The hour grew late, and the elector declared the evening at an end. I had no chance to play.

I loved to perform as much as my brother did, and I
struggled to conceal my disappointment in front of the

elector. But then, to my surprise—and pleasure!—Elector Maximilian said to Papa, "I should have liked to hear your daughter as well," and Papa assured His Excellency that it would be no trouble for us to stay on in Munich a little longer. But because the elector was a very busy man, occupied with hunting parties and French plays, we had to wait, and wait some more. "*Basta!*" Papa muttered as the days passed with no word from the royal court.

At last I was called to play. I had prepared a Scarlatti sonata and a short Bach fugue, and I'd practiced a song to sing with either Wolferl or Papa accompanying me. But at the end of the sonata Elector Maximilian rose and applauded. "Lovely, lovely," said the elector. "A very pretty performance, Fraülein Mozart." My little concert was over. He gave Papa a purse of money and sent me a dainty gold watch.

"A nice enough payment," Papa informed Mama tersely when he'd counted it, "although most of it must now be paid over to the innkeeper."

"But the elector was pleased, Papa," I said. "He praised my playing."

"We need money more than praise," Papa said.

This time Papa was only *half* right. He needed the money, but I needed the praise.

WE LEFT MUNICH for Augsburg, the city where Papa was born. His brother, a bookbinder, still lived there in a fine

house near the cathedral. We called on him and his wife
and their only child, Maria Anna Thekla. Wolferl seemed
quite taken with our cousin, a mischievous little thing,
four years old and quite spoiled by her parents. Wolferl
called her "the *Bäsle*," dear little cousin, and the two of
them played together more wildly than I thought was
proper. I tried to join in their fun—running, hiding, seeking, finding—but I felt too grown-up to enjoy their childish play. It was only a short visit, and I wouldn't have given
the *Bäsle* another thought, had not Wolferl tediously chattered on about her for days afterward. It annoyed me that
he seemed to enjoy something—and someone—so silly.

Papa bought a little clavier on which we could practice,
rather than having to borrow one at every stop, and we
headed north. Every other minute Mama exclaimed over
the beauty of the countryside, the magnificence of the
castles reflected in the calm waters of the Rhine. Wolferl
and I were soon bored with the scenery that so enchanted
Mama. On one of those long days of tiresome travel
Wolferl invented an imaginary world, which he named the
Kingdom of Back.

"The Kingdom of Back? That makes no sense," I told
him wearily. My body ached from the bumpy, rutted road;
no matter how many pillows I piled on the hard carriage
bench to cushion it, my backside was the only "back" I
could think about.

"Of course it does!" he crowed. "Perfectly nonsensical

sense! I'm the king, you're the queen, Nannerl, and"—he turned to our patient servant, Sebastian Winter—"you, sir, are the grand knight." It was an elaboration of the stories we used to invent with chess pieces.

Sebastian smiled. "As you wish, Your Highness."

"The king commands you to draw a map of my kingdom," Wolferl ordered in an imperious tone, and the grand knight obeyed.

As we journeyed through one city after another in the weeks that followed, sometimes traveling by boat, sometimes rattling along in our carriage, Sebastian produced an elaborate map of imaginary towns and country villages, decorated with dozens of little drawings that brought Wolferl's make-believe world vividly to life for us.

IN EACH PLACE we stopped, Papa arranged concerts. Wolferl always astonished audiences with his virtuosity. People could speak of nothing else. But no matter how diligently I practiced and how brilliantly I performed, I could not match him. It didn't really matter then, because the thrill of playing was enough. Music was nothing more than black marks on a page until I brought it to life with my own two hands, and then it was everything.

Though Wolferl received more attention than I did, I refused to blame *him*—as he said, he couldn't help it. But I did begin to blame Papa. What had started out equal was shifting in Wolferl's favor. "Papa doesn't give me a fair chance to show what I can do," I complained to Mama.

"Papa does what he knows is best," she said. "In the end it all works out."

And people were always kind to both of us, showering us with gifts. I added another little gold ring to my collection; Wolferl acquired another toothpick case.

IN HONOR OF my name day, July 26, and my twelfth birthday four days later, Papa and Mama ordered a special dinner of Rhine salmon. All I really wanted was a nice piece of boiled beef the way Mama prepared it. I was not the only one yearning for the food of our home region. Papa complained, "What's wrong with these people in the north, who never eat *Spätzle?*" Mama promised that as soon as she could get into a kitchen again, she would make the tiny dumplings he craved.

We visited Mannheim, where Wolferl and I set them all astir with our playing at the prince's summer palace. "A handsome city," I wrote in the leather-bound journal Papa bought me. In Frankfurt, Papa wasn't satisfied with the number of invitations we received and put up notices around the city: *With incredible skill a girl of twelve and a boy of seven will play concertos, trios, and sonatas.* At least for now he had stopped lying about our ages. He added a few lines about "the boy," who would perform on both violin and harpsichord, and ended with the warning that there would be only one concert, *inasmuch as immediately afterwards they are to continue their journey to France and England.*

Twice more he posted notices, cautioning each time that an opportunity to hear the young virtuosos was *absolutely, positively* at an end. But he collected only a few coins, and as our carriage rumbled out of town Papa complained that it was scarcely worth our long stay.

Summer ended, and heavy autumn rains pummeled us day after day. In Koblenz Wolferl came down with a catarrh, and Papa decided we must rest a little before continuing on. But each delay cost money, and Papa fretted.

"Perhaps, Leopold, we should take less costly lodgings," Mama suggested tentatively.

"No, Anna Maria," Papa replied. "For the sake of the children's health we must stay in refined places. Our accommodations must reflect well on my position at the archbishop's court. And if we wish to receive the respect of the aristocracy, then we must live and travel like aristocrats."

I had begun to understand that Papa loved the idea of being an aristocrat. So we continued to lodge in inns Papa said he couldn't afford, and Mama and I continued to sleep in one bed, while Papa shared the second bed with my brother.

We traveled to Bonn and Cologne, finally crawling stiffly from our carriage in Aachen in October. Many times those aristocrats we were trying to impress didn't give us any money for our playing, or else they made us wait so long to be paid we'd spent the money before we received it.

But they certainly fussed over us. After every concert the ladies rushed forward, nearly smothering us with compliments and kisses. Wolferl never seemed to get enough of these displays of affection, while I simply endured it. "If the kisses the princess and the duchess gave to the children were all gold coins, I'd be a happy man," Papa grumbled as we drove out of Aachen two weeks later.

In Brussels we waited for an invitation to play for Prince Karl, the brother of Emperor Franz. To fill the time, we gave a few concerts and collected a few more fancy snuffboxes and toothpick cases, and Wolferl acquired two more ceremonial swords. We went sightseeing, visited churches, and gazed at paintings, but I was more interested in the ordinary people in the street. I wrote to Katherl and Viktoria, "Here women dress in hooded cloaks, and people clatter through the cobbled streets in wooden clogs."

Wolferl was mad to have a pair of those clogs, but Papa refused. "They are the footwear of common people. Gentlemen wear leather boots," Papa said, and ordered them each a fine pair.

Time passed slowly. Sometimes Wolferl and I argued— he could behave very childishly when he was tired—and

Sebastian would have to intervene. Finally, when Papa had all but given up—we had waited for nearly a month—Prince Karl summoned us to perform. Everyone praised us to the skies, and Papa counted a rich booty of silver thalers and louis d'or. The compliments and the money were a nice reward, of course, but I was vaguely dissatisfied. I wasn't sure our aristocratic audience truly understood the richness of my performance. They seemed more interested in musical tricks than in true musicianship. I was growing impatient to prove I was as worthy as my brother.

In mid-November we climbed back into our carriage with Sebastian Winter and our mountain of luggage. We had four fresh horses and a new postilion to crack the whip.

"Bound for Paris!" I wrote in my journal. Maybe in that glamorous city I would have an opportunity to distinguish myself.

Chapter 5

PARIS

PAPA HAD TALKED about Paris for months. "Once our
reputation is established there, we'll give as many public
performances as possible. Hundreds of louis d'or will pour
into our pockets."

He found a place for us to live in the home of Count
and Countess van Eyck, friends originally from Salzburg,
and before we had finished unpacking, he set out to make
our presence known to the music lovers of the city. He
presented a letter of introduction to another Salzburger,
Baron Friedrich Grimm, who had lived in Paris for many
years and was highly placed in the French court. The
baron offered to arrange concerts—"And I shall introduce
you to King Louis!" The king of France! I was surely on my
way to making my mark in Paris.

But the death of King Louis's granddaughter, Isabella of

Parma, brought those plans to a halt. I remembered pretty Isabella, the wife of Archduke Josef, at our concerts at Schönbrunn. Smallpox had struck again, and the court was in black with no entertainments allowed until the mourning period was over.

While we waited, Wolferl composed every day, keyboard sonatas pouring from his pen. I added the works of French composer François Couperin to my repertoire, sure that would attract attention. When we weren't working, Papa made sure we took in the sights. I jotted notes in my journal about French women with brazenly painted faces and delicately painted chamber pots on marble pedestals.

At the start of the Christmas season the mourning ended and the gaiety of the French capital resumed. We gave one of our first performances in the stately mansion of Madame de Pompadour. At first I didn't understand that madame was the king's "great friend"—his mistress— and had enormous influence in the French court. Although Papa was a devout Catholic with high moral standards, he decided to overlook this immoral situation.

"It is not for us to judge," he told Mama, who must have been scandalized. (More surprises were to follow: It turned out our friend Baron Grimm also had a mistress, the elegant Madame d'Épinay.)

Madame de Pompadour was a handsome woman, not young but still good-looking with a lovely oval face and beautiful eyes. I admired her gown, a delicate green taffeta that set off her coloring, the neckline cut very low to display her powdered bosom, the waist drawn tight. Great quantities of lace and silk flowers had been lavished on the skirt and sleeves. She invited us to play on her fine harpsichord, lacquered and painted and embellished with gold leaf. When she kindly helped my brother onto the chair by the keyboard, he reached up to embrace her and to receive the kisses he expected her to give him, like every other lady he had met and charmed. But Madame de Pompadour was a rather reserved person, and she stepped back from his embrace without kissing him.

"What!" Wolferl cried to all who could hear. "She didn't kiss me! Who is this lady, not to kiss me? Even the empress Maria Theresia kissed me!"

Mama uttered an embarrassed "Tch! Tch!" Even Papa looked dismayed—this was much worse than Wolferl's temperamental outburst at Herr Wagenseil, the Viennese court composer. But Madame de Pompadour seemed unruffled. "Perhaps," she said with a sly smile, "you would prefer to kiss *me*, Herr Wolfgang," and she held out her soft white hand.

If the king's mistress didn't offer Wolferl the kisses he expected, the king's wife made up for it when we arrived at the royal palace at Versailles outside of Paris. Queen Marie, the daughter of the king of Poland, had grown up speaking German, and it pleased her to converse with my saucy brother. I was never sure what would come out of his mouth, but whatever it was seemed to amuse her. I felt content to stay in the background, wanting only to let my music speak eloquently.

We stayed in Versailles for two weeks. Papa hired costly sedan chairs to get around, and we dressed stylishly, "because," Papa said, "it would not do to appear otherwise." He bought Wolferl a handsome little black suit and a tricorne, a three-cornered cocked hat (and one for himself, too), in which my brother looked quite splendid. Naturally, Mama and I had to have new dresses for our appearances at the royal court—not so many ruffles and laces and silk roses as Madame de Pompadour's, but they made us feel fashionably turned out. Sebastian convinced Papa to buy new perukes for himself and Wolferl and took Mama's coiffure and mine to new heights.

Madame de Pompadour kept an apartment at Versailles furnished with thick carpets and rich hangings. When we weren't playing for her, we performed for Queen Marie. I did wonder how the queen felt about having her husband's mistress living in the same palace. Queen Marie was a deeply religious woman who also loved to play the harpsichord—and, it appeared, to eat. Baron Grimm told us that the queen was known for her appetite.

"It's nothing for her to devour fifteen dozen oysters at a single sitting and wash them down with two great tankards of beer," the baron reported. The queen was very fat, as were her son, the dauphin, and her four daughters, always referred to as *"les Mesdames."*

"None of *les Mesdames* has been allowed to marry," the baron explained.

I felt sorry for these four royal ladies, a dour lot all past marriageable age, but Queen Marie seemed amiable. Our friendship with the queen resulted in lots of invitations for us to play. The ladies and gentlemen of the court made it a point to do whatever the royals did, and they kept us busy running here and there to give private concerts. Papa appreciated the presence of a paying audience, but there were problems.

"They ignore us!" Wolferl complained. "They keep on eating and drinking and talking while we play! They listen with only half an ear, if that."

This had never happened before.

"*Ja,* they are rude," I agreed, for I, too, was vexed. What did it matter how superbly I played, if no one listened?

"I know how to get their attention," Wolferl whispered to me when our audience burst into loud laughter during one of our most intricate duets—not at us, to be sure, but at some private joke. "We'll stop playing, and I'll stand up to take a bow, turn my back, and let out a loud fart."

I suppressed my own laughter and persuaded him not to do it.

———

BARON GRIMM AND Madame d'Épinay were in the audience when a lady in expensive silks and jewels suddenly rose and asked if my brother would accompany her while she sang her favorite Italian song. Wolferl cheerfully agreed, and as the lady warbled, fanning her large bosom with a lace handkerchief, Wolferl invented a bass accompaniment for her quavering voice.

"My dear madame," Wolferl said when she'd finished, "be so good as to sing it once again. I'm not satisfied with what I've provided."

Bosom heaving and handkerchief fluttering, she sang again while Wolferl added the right hand. The third time he improvised variations and embellishments, stunning his listeners, who burst into sustained applause. Naturally, the lady kissed him.

"Every day God performs fresh miracles through this child," Papa said piously as the singer finished taking her bows and, face flushed, returned to her seat. *I wonder if God ever takes notice of what a brat he is,* I thought, remembering his plan for catching the audience's attention.

These "miracles" convinced Baron Grimm that the Mozart family was worth his time and enthusiasm, and he and Madame d'Épinay became our greatest champions. The baron told everyone I played the harpsichord brilliantly, and I adored him for that. (He also claimed I was eleven and Wolferl seven, because Papa had again fallen into the habit of making us out to be younger than we actually were.) Mama was appalled that our dear friend flaunted his mistress in public, but when Madame d'Épinay presented her with a red satin dress, a painted fan, and an amethyst ring, Mama chose to regard their arrangement more tolerantly.

I could scarcely wait to write to Viktoria and Katherl about all of this—not just the splendid clothes but also the splendid mistresses. What fun it would be to shock them!

WE ENJOYED MANY luxuries in our daily life on the grand tour, but there were always discomforts and illnesses to endure. By the end of the day we were ready to drop from exhaustion, especially Wolferl. All I wanted was to go to bed.

Every night, from the time my brother was a tiny child, the same ceremony had to be performed in exactly the same way: Wolferl stood on a chair and sang the first part of a little song he'd made up. After Papa sang the second part, Wolferl kissed Papa on the tip of his nose, and Papa carried him off and placed him in his bed. Only then did Wolferl surrender peacefully to sleep. In the midst of the most difficult travels, the most demanding concerts, this ceremony could not be omitted.

Mama and I had our nightly ritual, too. She rubbed my hands with a special cream she had prepared and reminded me of the special powers I held in each of my ten fingers. "Beautiful hands, skillful fingers, wonderful talent," she repeated.

But family rituals and ceremonies didn't cure everything. Wolferl and I both fell ill easily, sometimes upset by the food, sometimes contracting catarrhs or fevers that sent us to our beds. Papa dosed us with his powders. At times the illness was deadly serious. Everyone in Paris feared smallpox. As more people fell victim to the ravages of the disease, a French doctor urged Papa to have Wolferl inoculated.

"A simple matter," the doctor explained. "Your son would be exposed to a mild form of the disease, become briefly ill, and recover quickly with no harm done. English royalty have been doing this for years with good effect."

But Papa opposed the procedure. *"Nein,"* Papa said firmly, when Mama hopefully questioned him. "It is up to God. All depends on His divine grace whether He wishes to keep this prodigy of nature in the world, or to take it to Himself."

There was no inoculation for Wolferl, and—to my relief—no one suggested it for me. I believed that Papa was right: Death was all around us, its long shadow cast over our lives from the moment we were born. Whether we were to endure for many years or be taken early was all in God's hands, not ours.

THE DEPARTURE OF OUR beloved servant and friseur, Sebastian Winter, shattered us. In March of 1764 Sebastian decided to return to his home in Bavaria. If we'd been pay-

ing attention, we might have noticed how much he suffered from homesickness. Somehow my brother and I
were convinced Sebastian would always be with us, involved as deeply as we were in our make-believe world of
the Kingdom of Back.

"What could you possibly do in Donaueschingen?"
Wolferl demanded, petulant and tearful, as he often was
when things didn't go his way.

"I want to go home," Sebastian explained simply, but he,
too, was tearful. "I have been offered a position as friseur
to Prince Josef Wenzeslaus von Fürstenberg. I believe I
will be happy there."

"But surely you'd be happier here!" Wolferl insisted, and
he continued to argue with our loyal servant nearly every
day until Sebastian said good-bye. Wolferl took Sebastian's departure as a personal betrayal and threw himself on the ground, sobbing dramatically. I, too, wept—I
couldn't imagine there would ever be another friseur able
to pile my hair in such an attractive arrangement of curls
and rolls and waves—although I lacked Wolferl's gift for
theatrical display.

Papa hired a replacement, Jean-Pierre, an Alsatian who
spoke both German and French—a great help, for Papa
felt we were always being cheated by the French because
we didn't know their language. Despite this advantage,
Papa complained about the expense of having to purchase
new suits of livery for Jean-Pierre, who was much bigger

than Sebastian, and all of us complained about our hair, our clothes, everything. We surely made Jean-Pierre's life miserable.

Much deeper sorrows lay ahead. Countess van Eyck, the kind friend who had given us a lovely place to stay, fell ill and died unexpectedly. We had just finished having lunch with her when she took suddenly to her bed and expired. Only a few weeks later Madame de Pompadour succumbed to a congestion of the lung, another sad day that brought us all to tears.

WE GAVE CONCERTS, but they were no longer well attended, and Papa decided it was time to move on. "To England," he said.

Mama objected in her quiet way. "There is still so much for the children to see in Paris," she said. "And they've both learned to speak French rather well. Surely, it would benefit them to stay here longer."

It was true that Wolferl and I had quickly figured out how to make ourselves understood. But Mama never did learn any French, and she was probably frightened of being confronted by another incomprehensible language.

Papa dismissed her objections and began to prepare for the next part of the grand tour. He arranged to store some of our luggage in Paris and to leave our carriage at Calais. He hired a second servant, Porta, an Italian who claimed to speak some English. He wrote to Herr Hagenauer, asking him to have a Mass said for us as we made our first journey by sea.

Before we left Paris, Baron Grimm sent an artist to paint a family portrait: Wolferl was seated at the harpsichord, Papa posed behind him with his violin, and I stood half hidden by the harpsichord, holding a sheet of music as though I were singing. (Mama was not included, because she didn't perform with us.)

"But Papa," I reminded him, "I don't often sing at our concerts. Shouldn't I be shown sitting next to Wolferl?" I wanted the painting to match the dream I had of my future as a keyboard performer. I enjoyed singing, but playing was my passion.

"It doesn't matter, Nannerl," he replied.

"It does to *me*," I said.

"Nannerl, you have developed a very unpleasant habit of questioning my decisions," Papa said, frowning.

When the painting was finished, Papa had an engraving made of it, to be used in posters and calling cards. It was a pretty watercolor, but I never liked the way I was portrayed, as though I were fading from the picture, while Wolferl occupied the center of attention and Papa loomed over us both. That portrait seemed to reflect my role: I didn't stand out. I wondered if I ever would.

Chapter 6

LONDON

I TURNED TO A fresh page in my journal and labeled it *England.*

Papa had hired a private boat to take us across the English Channel, and as we waited to go on board, I wrote, "I shall never forget my first sight of the sea. In Calais I saw how it runs away and comes back again."

Wolferl peered over my shoulder. "Your journal is dreadfully dull, Horseface," he said. "Shall I write in it for you?"

"Absolutely not!" I said and snapped it shut.

We chattered excitedly as the boat left the shore. After a time, though, the sea began heaving up and down, and my stomach tossed as wildly as the waves. We spent most of the crossing hanging over the rail in utter wretchedness.

But once we'd arrived in London, we quickly forgot our misery. Papa found three small rooms in which to live and soon arranged for us to play for the court of King George III and Queen Charlotte. We enjoyed playing for this audience. The English understood music, and they were very courteous and actually paid attention—unlike the French! They were used to having fine musicians at court: Queen Charlotte had brought Johann Christian Bach, youngest son of Johann Sebastian Bach, to be the music master. Every evening after dinner the king played the flute, and Herr Bach accompanied him on the harpsichord.

One night the king arranged to have a second harpsichord brought to the salon. Wolferl and I were to play a double concerto on two harpsichords. I loved playing duets with my brother, but a duo on two instruments was much more difficult. We spent hours practicing together, determining which melodic line should dominate, the precise tempo, the meaning of the subtle glances that passed between us. Papa supervised the tuning of the two instruments. The results thrilled everyone who heard us. The audience that night went mad with joy—I'd never heard such sustained applause—and Papa was even more joyful, because he took in one hundred guineas within three hours. It seemed to us that everyone in England was rich, and Papa was determined to make as much money as he possibly could.

WE LOVED ENGLAND! When we discovered that the French were looked upon with disfavor, we realized our

Paris clothes would not do. We acquired an English wardrobe, and Mama and I bought broad-brimmed hats trimmed with a glory of ribbons and flowers. The next time I wrote to Viktoria and Katherl, my letter to be included with Papa's to Herr Hagenauer to save postage, I attached a little sketch of my hat.

"Mama and I adore our hats and wear them every chance we get. No woman crosses an alley without a hat on her head! Papa says if we were to wear such things in Salzburg, people would come running as if a rhinoceros were loose in the streets." Then I added, "Please write to me, dear friends! You say nothing interesting happens in Salzburg, but I know it cannot be true!" But as I wrote those words, I recognized that, compared to my life, it was true indeed.

The king and queen waved and called out to us from their carriage whenever they passed by on the street, so friendly it was possible to forget they were the monarchs. But Papa hadn't realized the court and all the nobility would leave for their country manors late in the spring. Nobody of importance stayed in London through the summer. Our audience had suddenly vanished.

When everyone flocked back to London in June to celebrate the king's birthday, Papa quickly arranged a concert. King George handed Wolferl compositions by J. C. Bach and George Frideric Handel, difficult pieces my brother had not seen before. Wolferl played them as though he'd practiced them for weeks. He performed on the king's organ and accompanied the queen, who had an agreeable singing voice. As usual, my brother's extraordinary talent amazed everyone. And, as usual, I was proud of him, but my pride was soured by my belief that I should be getting as much attention as he did. After all, I played Bach and Handel, too, although not without hours of practice.

Papa still advertised Wolferl as "a boy of seven," when in fact he was now eight and a half and I was approaching my thirteenth birthday. Papa often boasted that his daughter was one of the most skillful keyboard players in all Europe, but only my brother could still claim the title of *Wunderkind*. "Our little genius," Papa called him.

I never spoke to Papa of the sharp pangs of disappointment—and jealousy—I often felt. But I did sometimes bare my rawest feelings to Mama. "I know I play as well as Wolferl," I said to her one day when I could no longer hold it inside. "I sing well, and I even compose a little. Why don't I please Papa more?"

"Ach, Nannerl," she said, "I know Papa believes in you and your great talent. He often tells me so! But he also believes that, because Wolferl is a boy, he will bring us more fame and fortune than a girl can."

This was just what Katherl had said. I looked into Mama's calm gray eyes. "If I were a boy, then it would be different?"

She glanced away. "Who can say, exactly? All of us must

suffer disappointments. Your life can still be good, but you must make it so."

"But how can I make it so without Papa's help?" I demanded in a voice clogged with tears. "Can't you speak to him about it? Maybe you could change his mind."

"He will not listen to me, Nannerl," she said. "We must all do as Papa thinks best."

I turned away, disappointment making a bitter taste in my mouth. I would get no help from my mother either.

WE HAD BEEN away from home for a full year, twelve months of traveling, performing, meeting new people, and observing new customs, some—such as women smoking pipes—that caused Papa to throw up his hands in dismay and me to scribble a note in my journal. Most days I was the complete English girl, chattering in my new language, wearing my flowered hats, admiring the beautiful gardens in full bloom. On other days thoughts of Salzburg overwhelmed me, and I longed for home.

I thought of how sweet it would be to stroll again arm in arm with Viktoria and Katherl among the marble dwarfs in the Mirabell Gardens, talking and laughing and sharing secrets. When I mentioned my yearning to Wolferl, he seemed perplexed.

"I don't understand, Nannerl," he said. "Home is wherever we are with each other and Papa and Mama. What else could you wish for?" And he turned back to his composing and left me to my discontent.

THE ENGLISH SUMMER slipped by pleasantly. Then an alarming thing happened. Unable to find a carriage to take us to a private concert one hot summer evening, Papa hired a sedan chair to carry Wolferl and me, while he followed along on foot. Papa became overheated, took a chill, and came down with what the English people call a "cold," a common complaint there. His cold worsened, and when his usual remedies did no good, Papa took to his bed. A doctor prescribed purges and bled him, but nothing helped.

It frightened us to see our strong papa suddenly as weak and helpless as an infant. *What if he dies?* I worried. How would we live, so far from home in what suddenly seemed like a very strange country? What would happen to us? Mama and I took turns going to church to light candles and pray.

Papa always made the decisions and the arrangements for everything we did, but now that became Mama's responsibility. Mama, who always deferred to him in even the smallest matters, took it upon herself to move us away from the bad air of the city to Chelsea on the outskirts of London. There she found rooms in a house with a lovely garden and devoted all her time to nursing Papa. He was a difficult patient, and she had to put up with his endless complaints.

Mama insisted Wolferl and I stay absolutely quiet. We were not allowed to touch the clavier, so I couldn't practice. This didn't bother Wolferl as much as it did me, for my brother didn't *need* to practice. Instead, he turned to composing, which he could do entirely in his head. No longer satisfied with sonatas and concertos for one or two instruments, he had begun to write symphonies, music for a whole orchestra.

The two of us worked together. We sat quietly at the writing desk, and as Wolferl imagined the music, mentally hearing every note played by each instrument, he dictated the notes to me to write down.

"Remind me to give something good to the trumpets," he said.

"You used to be terrified of the sound of a trumpet," I reminded him. "You fainted if someone blew a trumpet anywhere near you."

"Because they were out of tune and hurt my ears. They're necessary in this piece, though. And the kettledrum, too—I have a great fondness for the kettledrum!"

After a while I found the dictation tedious. I would have preferred to use the time of enforced quiet to do some composing of my own, but Papa grew agitated when I suggested it. So I continued writing down Wolferl's music, and the weeks of Papa's illness passed.

From the day of our arrival in England we'd complained about the food. Breakfasts, for example, consisted of a cup of weak tea further diluted with milk, and a pile of cold toast. No omelets. No pancakes with jam. Now that we were settled in our new rooms, Mama gladly took over the cooking. She hired Clara, an English maid, to help with the chores and do the shopping for her. Wolferl and I laughed at Mama's poor attempts to explain to Clara just what she wanted.

"How do I ask for a half dozen eggs?" she asked us. "Some flour, and sugar? A little butter, but not too much, and coffee, and good, thick cream?"

I came to her rescue, but Wolferl, the scamp, carefully taught her to say "horse turd" when she thought she was asking for beefsteak.

As difficult as it surely was for Mama in her new role as acting head of the household, I experienced a freedom I'd never known before. Wolferl had always been my closest companion, and with the exception of Viktoria and Katherl I had few good friends. There was neither time nor opportunity, for I was always studying or practicing or traveling, and always under Papa's strict eye. But in Chelsea I met Davey, Clara's nephew, who came to work in the garden. He was fourteen—a year older than I—with orange-red hair and green eyes. He knew nothing about music, but he called me Nannie and taught me the name of every flower that bloomed there and every bird that sang in the bushes. He showed me the hedgehog's burrow and the den of a red fox. And he talked about one day going off to sea.

I found ways to spend a little time in the garden, explaining to Mama that this was an excellent chance to practice my English. I prayed she wouldn't tell Papa about Davey, and she didn't. But when Papa at last gathered the strength to leave his bed and looked out of his window and into the garden, he saw the two of us together.

"No more of that," Papa said sternly when I'd come upstairs again. "I have no idea who that boy is, but you will not waste any more of your time in idle conversation with him. I'm afraid you've fallen far behind with your practicing. Haven't you, Nannerl?"

"If I've fallen behind, it's because I didn't wish to disturb you," I said, feeling resentful. I saw a window close firmly in my life, the bit of freedom I'd experienced was gone, and at that moment I disliked my father intensely.

I resolved to have one more meeting with Davey.

"I must stay inside to help my parents," I explained to my friend when I was able to go down to speak to him again.

He stayed silent, studying the tip of his shoe. Then he dug in his pocket and produced a marvelously curving seashell. "It's a whelk. I've been meaning to give it to you. I found it on a beach." He held it to my ear and told me to listen. "Hear the roar of the sea? It'll remind you of me." Then he turned and walked away.

I hid the shell in an old stocking. Many times after that I took it out and listened to the sound of the sea, remembering red-haired Davey and those rare moments of freedom.

ONCE PAPA HAD regained his health, he moved us back to London to rooms above a corset shop and immediately began searching for opportunities for us to perform.

Wolferl composed all the music we presented at a concert in February. Papa had twice postponed this concert, hoping for a larger audience, but he was disappointed. We all were. The king and queen hadn't invited us to play for months. In the beginning it was surely because of Papa's illness, but now there was no explanation for it. Once so friendly, they seemed to have lost interest in us. "The way of royalty," Papa grumbled.

Later that spring Papa devised a new scheme for earning money. Every day from noon until three o'clock the public was invited to come to our rooms and pay half a guinea to hear us play. For a couple of months there was not a day when a few curious souls did not stop by to be entertained. I hated it.

Protesting to Papa was useless, and so I complained to Mama. "Wolferl says he doesn't mind," I told her. "He loves to play anytime for anybody. But these people don't know a thing about music! They're worse than the French! They just come here to stare at us as though we're freaks of nature."

"If your father thinks this is the right thing to do, then it is surely the right thing to do," she said. Mama always took his part, no matter what, and that annoyed me, too.

There was no break from these ridiculous performances. Papa could not fail to notice that Wolferl, the family treasure, the source of virtually all the money that was coming to us, was increasingly tired and listless, as was I after spending the entire morning practicing. Grudgingly, Papa reduced the hours during which we were available to public gawking; he also reduced the price of admission by half, warning in the posters he put up around the city that the "two young prodigies" would soon be leaving the country.

But he would not give up. He arranged for us to perform every afternoon at a large room in a public house, the Swan and Hoop, hoping to wring a few more shillings from the curious. Wolferl and I played together on one clavichord with the keyboard covered by a cloth, a trick I had also mastered. This always impressed a naive audience.

After a *final* final concert in May, Papa realized that all possibilities of earning our fortune in London had been exhausted and announced our next move: "The time has come to leave England. We'll collect our belongings in Paris and set out immediately for Salzburg."

Home! At last! I wrote the good news to Viktoria and Katherl, and just before my fourteenth birthday at the end of July we started to pack. But then Papa had a change of heart; he still wasn't ready to go home—not just yet. "First we shall travel to Holland," he said. "I'm told many people there are eager to hear the prodigies of Salzburg perform."

Wolferl was thrilled. His listlessness vanished. He was perfectly willing to keep on traveling forever. And I had heard so much about the dikes that held back the sea, the canals, and the windmills with their creaking sails that for the time being I forgot my impatience to go home.

Chapter 7

BLACK ANGELS

WE MADE OUR WAY toward Holland by carriage and by boat, arriving in The Hague in mid-September. Papa and Wolferl were both suffering from colds, and the heavy catarrh had been passed on to me. We planned to perform Wolferl's two clavier concertos, accompanied by a full orchestra for Princess Karoline of the royal house of Holland. But hours before the concert I was seized by a chill, followed by a raging fever. I recall that Wolferl performed something else without me that night; I remember only imperfectly what happened in the days that followed.

Papa's worried face floated above mine like a pale moon as he peered into my swollen throat. I could eat nothing and drank only a little, although Mama pleaded with me to swallow a spoonful of this or that. "Look how thin she's gotten," she fretted to Papa. "Every day there's a little less of her."

Sleeping and waking were all the same to me. A doctor came and bled me. Mama and Papa prayed over me, and Wolferl hovered nearby, gazing at me with tears in his big, sad eyes. Through my fever I observed with slight interest the bristling gray eyebrows of an old man. A pair of large, pale hands swooped down over my face, brushing against my eyes, nose, ears, and lips, and pressed something on my tongue.

When the eyebrows and hands had disappeared, Mama and Papa sat by my bedside. Far away I could hear someone—it must have been Wolferl, but I suspected angels— playing the clavier. "Am I dying?" I asked my parents.

"If God so wills it," Papa replied. "But you are now prepared. The priest has just given you the last sacrament." Mama wept softly, and Papa spoke in a comforting voice about the vanities of this world. "A greater place awaits us, Nannerl, when we pass to the arms of the Heavenly Father."

So I am dying, I thought, but the notion didn't trouble me.

Mama managed to stop her weeping long enough to try to console me. "Children are blessed with a happy death, *Liebchen*," she said. Her fingers were gentle as teardrops on my cheek.

"You must not be afraid," Papa said in a tone meant to

console me. "We must be ready to accept our fate, whatever the Lord God may have in store for us."

I became aware of the presence of a pair of large birds with black iridescent wings. Maybe they weren't birds but angels—I couldn't be sure. *Not ordinary angels,* I thought; *angels are white.* The creatures opened their great black shining wings, and I knew they were angels of death, surrounding me and singing tenderly to me in voices clear as church bells and inviting me to join them.

I was preparing to go with these black angels wherever they were taking me when my brother stole quietly to my bedside and laid his little hand on mine. "Dear Nannerl," he whispered close to my ear, "what language are the angels singing? You're speaking to them in English and French as well as German, and I wonder how they answer you."

I emerged from the dream and opened my eyes. The angels vanished. I smiled at Wolferl. His presence made me glad, and I experienced a sublime moment of feeling that my brother and I were two parts of just one person.

When Princess Karoline learned of my illness, she sent her royal physician, who instructed Mama to feed me strong calves' broth with well-boiled rice. Mama immediately put a pot on the stove. When the broth was ready, Papa propped me up, and Mama spooned a few drops at a time between my dry, parched lips. Wolferl did his part by playing his newest composition.

Gradually I returned to life. The angels did not sing

again, in any language. In an odd way I missed them. Though I did not want to die, I no longer feared death.

Then it was Wolferl's turn. Just as I was able to leave my bed for the first time in several weeks, Wolferl fell ill.

He lay unconscious, his small body ravaged with fever. His lips turned black and peeled; even when he awoke from his fever, his tongue was so stiff that he couldn't utter a word. For thirty terrible days this new dread gripped us. The calves' soup that had restored me didn't seem to help my brother.

"Patience," Papa admonished. "What God sends must be endured."

I stayed by Wolferl's side, keeping a close watch for the shimmering black wings and listening for the ominous rustle of their feathers. If the angels of death came for him, I resolved to send them away. It was up to me to protect him, as I believed he had protected me. I decided to sing to him, softly at first, barely above a whisper, then with more assurance, a little prayer we both knew: *Dona nobis pacem*—Give us peace—repeated over and over.

The crisis passed. After three more weeks Papa lifted Wolferl from his bed and carried him to a chair; in another week my brother was able to take a few shaky steps. Yet even while Wolferl slowly regained his strength, he managed to spend hours working on two new symphonies. By Christmas he felt stronger, and the symphonies were nearly finished. Mama, who had not dared to leave us for even an hour in the course of three months, hurried out to the market for the luxury of buying a few pastries without fearing that one of us would die while she was gone.

"I always wanted to see Holland," I wrote to Viktoria and Katherl. "But it was nearly the end of us! I do hope and pray we'll soon be coming home."

MAMA, TOO, BEGGED to return to Salzburg, but Papa said no. "It would not do to expose the children to the rigors of winter travel, after all they've been through." I suspected another, more compelling reason: During the months of my illness and then my brother's we had not earned a single Dutch gulden. Papa was determined to make up the losses.

Just before Wolferl's tenth birthday in January we gave our first concert together for a Dutch audience in The Hague. Both of his new symphonies—one in the key of D, the other B-flat with its unusual andante movement— were performed as well. Weeks later we arrived in Amsterdam. It was Lent, when ordinarily no entertainments were permitted. But we were no ordinary entertainers, and the authorities made an exception for us, declaring, "Miraculous gifts serve to praise God."

Our "miraculous gifts" included the new symphonies, duets for four hands, and duos using two harpsichords. Then, for a formal court occasion honoring Prince Willem van Nassau, Wolferl composed "Seven Variations for Keyboard" based on the Dutch national anthem, one variation for each of the Dutch provinces. His quodlibet, a suite for orchestra, made clever and charming use of familiar tunes and ended with their national anthem. The usually stolid Dutch audience was on its feet, cheering and waving hand-kerchiefs.

Before we left Amsterdam Wolferl announced that he'd started working on an opera. "As soon as we get home to Salzburg, I'm going to finish my opera," he told me as we watched our possessions being packed one more time. "We'll perform it with our friends."

Papa approved. "There's a fortune to be made in opera." He began calling Wolferl "our little composer."

More important than the giddily enthusiastic response of our audiences was Papa's growing conviction that Wolferl's future lay as a composer as well as a performer. Wolferl's compositions were no longer childish exercises but had become original in concept and fluent in execu-tion. But there were some skeptics who insisted Leopold Mozart was the *real* composer. This was not true, though he was in some cases a close collaborator.

Papa often dreamed out loud of the future he saw for the Family Mozart. Fame, of course—that was already a reality. And fame would surely lead to wealth as we were offered highly paid positions in one or another of the great courts of Europe. Wolferl would certainly receive large sums for his compositions as well as his performances. We would live like aristocrats every day—not just occasionally.

These dreams led Papa to think about changes that would be necessary when we returned to Salzburg. Wolferl must have a place of his own to study and work. Papa wrote to our landlord, Herr Hagenauer, asking to have a special bed built for me in a corner of our small apartment and enclosed by curtains. I would have some privacy, and Wolferl would have more space.

As Papa sketched the great future that lay ahead for his son, there was no mention of *my* future. I would soon be fifteen. Would we continue to travel and give concerts together? Would Papa propose to Archbishop Schrattenbach that I be sent to Italy? I had never thought of a future apart from Wolferl's, but now I wondered if Papa saw it that way.

IN MAY WE WERE back in Paris to collect the trunks and boxes of books and music we'd left in storage. We gave a few concerts for nobility, although there were no glamorous visits to Versailles, and just as I thought we were indeed homeward bound, Papa again changed course. Due to the high expenses that had piled up while Wolferl and I were ill and unable to earn money, Papa decided it would be prudent to look for ways "to fatten the family's purse." Wolferl reacted as he always did, happy for a new adventure. Mama reacted as *she* always did, agreeing with Papa. I was the only one weeping silently as he ordered our carriage to Dijon.

We stayed in Dijon for a month, giving concerts, before moving on to Lyons and allowing time to order new clothes made of the finest silks and trimmed with the most expensive ribbons and laces and buttons. We would arrive back in Salzburg splendidly turned out.

After we'd traveled eastward through Switzerland, stopping in cities where we could give public concerts, Papa turned his eye south, to Italy. "It makes good sense," Papa reasoned. "Just look at the map, and you will see."

This time Mama *did* protest, pointing out my brother was not strong, I was not strong either, and we both needed to have time to recuperate. She pleaded with him to return at once to Salzburg.

"*Ja, ja,* of course," Papa sighed, reluctantly putting away his map, "we're going home."

Anyone could see Papa didn't *want* to go home. Back in Salzburg he would again be a lowly court musician in service to the archbishop, no longer an aristocrat accustomed to luxury and the admiration of the crowned heads of Europe. Anyone could see we would continue the grand tour for as long as Papa could make it happen, no matter how Mama protested it was time to go home.

Then Papa offered an irresistible temptation: We would stop at Donaueschingen, at the castle of Prince von Fürstenberg. Our former servant, Sebastian Winter, our beloved chronicler of the Kingdom of Back, awaited us.

We all wept when Sebastian rushed out to greet us,

shaking Papa's hand, kissing Mama's cheek, bowing low to me, and scooping up Wolferl in his arms. For twelve days we played for the prince and resurrected the Kingdom of Back with Sebastian. When the time came to leave, Wolferl begged, pleaded, and demanded that Sebastian quit his position with the prince and come with us. It did no good. I realized, as Wolferl did not, that the Kingdom of Back belonged in the past, part of a childhood that, at least for me, was over.

WE HAD ONE MORE stop to make before we really, truly headed home: Munich, to play for Elector Maximilian, as Papa had promised the elector at the beginning of our journey.

"Look how big my children have grown!" Papa boasted, and the elector smiled and nodded politely.

I *was* a bit taller and much fuller in the chest, but Wolferl had not grown at all and his illnesses had left him thinner. Papa convinced only himself.

And then, thanks be to a gracious God, our carriage, hard used after so many miles on so many terrible roads, rolled into Salzburg on the twenty-ninth of November 1766. We had been away from home for three and a half years.

Chapter 8

AMONG FRIENDS

THE MOZARTS WERE famous—some said the most famous family in Europe. People could not stop talking about
us. Herr Hagenauer had saved newspapers reporting
our successes on our grand tour. One writer said I played
"with more art and fluency" than my brother but praised
Wolferl for having "far more refinement and more original ideas." People were astonished at his brilliance as a
performer and now as a composer, too. "As skillful as any
Kapellmeister," they said.

Art and fluency, I reminded myself; I play with *art and
fluency.* Nice words, but there was no mention of refinement or originality, of brilliance or amazing skill. I read
the articles over and over, absorbing an undeniable truth:
It counted for nothing what Papa said about my playing, or
the elector of Bavaria or the queen of France, or anyone

else who wished to compliment me. My brother had soared past me, and no matter how many hours I practiced, I could never catch up. As this sank in, my feelings were a painful mixture of disappointment and anger—at Papa and at the writer of the hurtful words, but not at Wolferl.

Papa unpacked the dozens of gifts we'd accumulated and put them on display in new cabinets that now covered every wall of our small apartment. Viktoria and Katherl were among the first to come to visit. We greeted each other with hugs and kisses and exclamations about how each of us had changed. Viktoria was now plump with dimpled cheeks, and Katherl had grown tall and rather gawky.

"But just look at you, Nannerl!" Katherl exclaimed. "You've become a beauty!"

I felt myself blush, but I knew what she said was true: I'd left Salzburg a child and returned a young woman with a graceful figure, skin as smooth and white as porcelain, my father's bright blue eyes and finely arched brows, and my mother's generous, smiling mouth and thick, fair hair that I considered my best feature.

"The newspaper listed your treasures," Viktoria said when we'd finished exchanging compliments.

"But we didn't believe it," Katherl interrupted.

"Look for yourselves," I told them, and led them to the cabinets.

Katherl, the barber-surgeon's practical daughter, began to count: nine gold pocket watches, a dozen gold snuffboxes, several gold rings set with precious stones, numerous earrings, necklaces, knives with golden blades, bottle holders, toothpick boxes. "One would have to spend hours doing nothing but *look*," Katherl said.

"It's like a church treasury," said Viktoria, wide-eyed. "The newspaper said the value of the collection was twelve thousand florins."

"The writer underestimated the value," Papa told my friends, beaming. He was pleased to have his riches attracting so much interest.

He didn't recognize that some people would be put off by our good fortune. No one we knew had ever traveled as far, as widely, or for such a long time as we had. For over three years I had lived the kind of life Viktoria and Katherl could hardly imagine. Our collection was a reminder of all we had experienced and they had not.

"Where did you get *this*?" Katherl would ask, pointing out a gold ring or a snuffbox, and I described the scene for her. Or I'd mention the palace at Versailles or the canals in Amsterdam or the tides in the English Channel, and I'd see it was all too much for my friends. I sensed their growing resentment. I'd open my mouth to tell them about something and then close it again; or if I did speak of it, I regretted it when one of them dropped some slighting remark. I soon stopped mentioning anything at all about our grand tour. And I didn't show them the marvelous whelk shell. Once in a while, when I was alone, I took it from its hiding place, held it to my ear, and thought of red-haired Davey.

PAPA BASKED IN the attention, encouraging a steady stream of visitors to climb the stairs to view our treasures. Wolferl ignored it and concentrated on his music. Mama yearned for a little peace and quiet in her home. But no matter what else was going on, Papa insisted I keep up a demanding regimen.

Six days a week I rose early, went to Mass, practiced for two hours, ate breakfast, attended to my studies that now included music theory, ate lunch, and practiced alone for two more hours: scales, arpeggios, keyboard exercises designed to extend my reach beyond an octave, piles of sonatas and concertos—more Bach, more Scarlatti, more Couperin, more Handel. Later, Wolferl and I practiced together for another hour or two. It was grueling, but I didn't mind. I felt most truly alive when I was playing. I believed music would always be my life's work.

We would travel again—surely to Italy this time—and Wolferl and I would play again for royalty and wealthy nobility. He would wear beautiful clothes. I would have my own friseur. We would live in splendid apartments. Wolferl would be the most famous composer in Europe, and I would be the most acclaimed performer of his music. Papa would be proud of us both. So much could happen!

Practice hard, I told myself, *and soon the archbishop will send you to Italy to study.* The girls who had gone to study in Venice had long ago finished their training, and all now held well-paid positions as court singers—they were known around Salzburg as "the Three Ladies."

I was nearly sixteen. Time was growing short. There was no encouraging word from His Serene Highness, Archbishop Schrattenbach. But it was unthinkable that I would go to him myself.

ON MY ONE free hour each afternoon, my friends sometimes fetched me to go off with them to drink chocolate with clouds of whipped cream, to gossip about people we knew, and—this was the main topic—to discuss the eligible young men in Salzburg and what our friends' matrimonial possibilities might be. Katherl reported that Magdalena Lipp, one of those who had studied in Venice and was now a court singer, was engaged to marry Michael Haydn, concertmaster and composer in the archbishop's court.

"Another good prospect, snapped up just like that." Katherl sighed. "If it keeps on, all the best ones will be taken."

I laughed. "Are you so worried, Katherl? You're only sixteen!"

"Just you wait, Nannerl," she said darkly. "You'll find out for yourself."

"Madderl is so much in love with Haydn it's almost laughable," Viktoria said, forking into a slice of *Gugelhopf*, a rich cake. "She couldn't wait to come home from Venice. They met when he came to Salzburg, and the archbishop had just approved her training in Italy. They wrote so many letters back and forth I don't know when they found time to make music."

"It sounds very romantic," I said. Michael Haydn was much older—almost thirty—but my friends said he was quite handsome. I thought of red-haired Davey and wondered what it was like to be in love. "But what about you?" I asked. "Are you both in love, too?"

Viktoria and Katherl exchanged glances, and Katherl blushed a little. "*She* wants to be in love," Viktoria said mischievously, pushing the *Gugelhopf* toward me. "All she talks about is finding a beau and turning him into a husband."

"That's not true!" Katherl protested.

"Well, you do have someone in mind," Viktoria reminded her.

"Please tell me about him!" I begged.

"His name is Franz von Mölk," Viktoria answered for her. "You surely know his family—"

"But you must say nothing to anyone about this!" Katherl interrupted passionately. "It's true I find Franz very at-

tractive and interesting, but"—she bit her lip, nearly drawing blood—"I'm afraid he doesn't know I'm alive."

"Well, then, we must show him you are!" I said brightly,
as though I were some kind of expert in the art of romance.
Together we finished the cake, every golden crumb.

PAPA DIDN'T FORBID me to spend time with my friends,
but he made it clear he'd rather I wouldn't. "It's important
that you not waste time, gazing out the window! And you
should leave the house as little as possible," Papa lectured.
"Time lost with idle chatter and drinking chocolate is
never found again."

"Papa," I asked, suddenly finding the courage to pose
the question, "what have you planned for me that requires
so much practice? Are you hoping, as I am, that the archbishop will send me to study in Italy?"

"Send you to study in Italy? My dear Nannerl, there is
no chance of that. You were sent by God to play beautiful
music with the Family Mozart. Sometimes you may play
solos, sometimes duets with Wolferl, sometimes trios with
your brother and me. You will have many opportunities,
and you must be ready. That means constant preparation
here, with us—not study in a foreign city! In a word, Nannerl, practice!" Papa was very tall, towering over me. His
voice carried authority, even when he spoke quietly. His
powerful presence was intimidating. He stared down at
me. "Do you understand? Practice, practice, practice!"

"*Ja,* Papa," I said. "I understand."

"Good. Now, to work! Follow your brother's example!"

Papa strode away, and under my breath I muttered angrily, "Practice, practice, practice!" after his retreating back.

Papa could say whatever he liked, but I was unwilling to give up my dream so easily. I took up pen and paper and started to compose a letter to the archbishop.

Most Worthy Prince of the Holy Roman Empire, I wrote, unsure if this was the correct way to address him. *I come to you as your most humble and obedient servant, Maria Anna Mozart, daughter of Leopold Mozart, with an urgent request. It is my desire to serve our gracious Lord God as a musician in your court. For this I am in need of additional training in the art of performance upon the clavier, such training as has been made available by excellent teachers in Italy. . . .*

I stopped and read what I had written. What else should I say? The archbishop already knew who I was. He'd heard me play and said I was talented. He also surely knew my father had already decided not to ask to send me to Italy. It was useless. I dropped the letter into the stove and watched the flames consume my dreams.

OUR LIFE SETTLED into an ordinary pattern. Papa had resumed his duties as vice-Kapellmeister, a sharp fall from the life of an aristocrat, and he chafed under the demands of such a mundane existence. One important commission after another came to Wolferl, and Magdalena Lipp sang several of Wolferl's songs at a concert in the archbishop's Residenz. People who had once claimed peevishly that one so young could not possibly compose such complex works and Papa must be passing his own compositions off as Wolferl's now had nothing but praise for my brother.

"We belong in a larger, more worldly city," Papa said. "Where people have more cultured tastes. Not Salzburg."

The summer after our grand tour ended, Salzburg learned of the coming marriage of Empress Maria Theresia's daughter, the archduchess Josefa, to Ferdinand IV, king of Naples. Josefa's older sister, Johanna, had first been pledged to Ferdinand. I remembered how kind Johanna had been to us when we'd visited Schönbrunn Palace several years earlier. Just weeks after our visit Johanna had died, and now sixteen-year-old Josefa was to take her dead sister's place as Ferdinand's bride.

"If the empress learned we were in Vienna," Papa said, "I am absolutely certain she would send for us to perform during the wedding festivities."

"Leopold," Mama asked hesitantly, "does this mean that we're going to Vienna?"

"Indeed it does, my dear Anna Maria!" But he left the room without hearing her heartfelt sigh.

Wolferl, naturally, adored the idea. I loved to perform; I had even learned to enjoy mingling with the nobility. "We won't be gone long," I assured Katherl and Viktoria.

Just ten months after we'd returned from our famous grand tour, the carriage was packed, and in September the Family Mozart set off for Vienna.

COURT ETIQUETTE dictated that we could not play for any of the empress's courtiers before we had played for the empress herself. While we waited, we attended every opera and play and concert that Vienna had to offer. "Keeping ourselves in the eye of the public," Papa said. But Maria Theresia, who had welcomed us so warmly a few years earlier, had since then suffered heavy losses: First her twelve-year-old daughter Johanna and then her husband, Emperor Franz, had died while we were on our way to Holland.

The grieving empress had cut off her hair, dressed entirely in black, and stopped wearing cosmetics or jewels. She gave up holding private concerts at Schönbrunn Palace and no longer went out to plays and operas. She named her oldest son, Archduke Josef, to rule with her; he was now titled Emperor Josef. Our invitation depended upon him, but, to make matters worse, Emperor Josef himself was in official mourning for his second wife. I felt sorry for Archduchess Josefa. Who was planning the poor girl's wedding?

Papa threw up his hands. "I am determined to be patient," he declared, but Papa was not a patient man. He paced nervously, waiting for the important royal invitation. But there was no word from the emperor.

Without knowing it, we had driven straight into a virulent outbreak of smallpox. All anyone talked about was the terrible scourge.

Then, on the very eve of her wedding, Archduchess Josefa died. God had taken the second princess bride, and yet again King Ferdinand was cheated of a wife. Once again the whole city went into mourning. For six weeks there would be no operas, no plays, no concerts. The next victim was Archduchess Elisabeth. When the royal physician told the young woman the cause of her fever, she called for a looking glass in order to bid good-bye to the face that would no longer be beautiful, if God allowed her to live.

We learned that the family from whom we rented rooms was infected with the dreadful disease; three of their children had fallen ill. Papa searched for safer lodgings, but when he could find nothing to accommodate our entire family, he decided to take Wolferl and move to a different quarter of the city. Mama and I and our servant would have to stay where we were.

"Leopold, what is to become of *us*?" Mama cried fearfully, one of the rare times I ever heard her raise her voice to question Papa's decision.

"Our lives are in God's hands," Papa reminded her. "Nannerl is much stronger than Wolferl. Besides, she may have already had a mild form of the disease. We must trust that she is safe."

Mama submitted quietly, but Papa's words struck me as hard as a thrown rock. After Papa and Wolferl left and the shocked numbness wore off, I grew furious. "Why?" I shouted at Mama. "Am I worth less than Wolferl? Are we not as deserving as they are? Papa could have found something for us all, even if we were crowded. He doesn't care! And why did you not speak up?"

"He cares, Nannerl," Mama said wearily. "As much as I do. Your papa knows best—you must always believe that." But I had begun to doubt it. And I promised myself I would never be as submissive as Mama.

No place was safe. Death stalked every street corner. Once Papa realized that, he decided we must flee to another city. Olmütz, three days' journey to the north, seemed a likely destination. "I know people there," Papa said. "You and Wolferl can give concerts and earn a thaler or two. In time the deadly disease will run out of victims and the princess bride's mourning period will come to an end. Then we'll come back to Vienna."

Eight days after the death of Archduchess Josefa, we left the city. We heard later that Archduchess Elisabeth did survive. She chose to enter a convent, hidden away where no man would see the ruin of her once-lovely face.

Chapter 9

THE SCOURGE

OLMÜTZ WAS CROWDED, and rooms were scarce. The one Papa found was damp, and the stove belched smoke that had us all coughing. Within hours Wolferl was feverish, his face burning red and his hands icy cold. By morning he was raving.

Papa dispatched a messenger to Count Podstatzky, a friend who held an important position at the Olmütz cathedral, and the count sent us his own physician. The doctor shook his head. "Smallpox."

Papa, Mama, and I fell on our knees and prayed for a miracle, and our prayers were answered: The count invited us to move to his official residence, despite the danger of infection we carried with us. He was courageous, maybe even foolhardy, to do that. "The count says Wolferl is a gift from God," Papa told us, "and everything must be done to save him." We wrapped Wolferl in furs, and Papa carried him to the palace. The count's servants must have been terrified when they saw what lay curled inside that bundle of fur.

Wolferl's body was swollen, covered with pus-filled pocks as hard as peas. Even his eyes were covered, and he seemed to be blind. I couldn't see or hear the beating wings of death's black angels, but their dark presence was unmistakable. I remembered the little prayer I'd sung when he'd been so ill the last time, *Dona nobis pacem.* Wolferl reached for my hand. "Someday I'll write a mass," he whispered. "That will be part of it."

I kept singing *Give us peace* over and over and over.

Nine days passed. Then a second, greater miracle: Wolfgang regained his sight, and slowly he regained his health as well. Soon he felt strong enough to work on his symphony. My brother's sweet face was deeply scarred with dozens of the telltale pits, but—thanks be to a gracious God!—he lived. I sobbed with relief. "What would I do without you!" I cried. "I was afraid this time you really were going to die."

Within a month I, too, fell victim. As I lay suffering from fever and headache, I wondered if I would survive this illness. And what if I did survive but became blind? Or deaf? What if I could no longer see a musical score, or hear it? Would I even want to live if music were no longer part of my life? I had another worry: the scars I might have to endure for the rest of my life. I was sixteen and aware of my looks. Until now, my skin was fresh and smooth. What if I lost that? Many afflicted women wore veils to cover their disfigurement. Young girls sought refuge in convents. If I were hideously scarred, would I have to give up performing in public? And what about finding a husband? I wasn't like Katherl, already thinking of marriage, but I did assume it would someday be a part of my life, as it was for nearly all women.

I couldn't confide those fears to my parents—Papa would surely lecture me about vanity—but I did whisper to my brother, sitting by my bedside, "I don't want to be ugly, Wolferl. What man will ever love me?"

"You will never be ugly, dear Nannerl," he murmured. "And I shall always love you best."

As it happened, I was one of the fortunate ones. The illness passed quickly, and scarcely any marks remained.

"Surely it was God's will that led us into the caring hands of Count Podstatzky," Papa said. "And now the time has come to return to Vienna. I'm told the scourge has run its course."

We traveled by way of Brünn, where we arrived on Christmas Eve. Even though I was still feeling a bit shaky, Papa arranged for us to give a concert that included the premiere performance of Wolfgang's first full symphony in four movements—he'd begun it in Vienna and finished it in Olmütz while he was recovering.

"I wasn't sure we'd be alive," Wolferl said when it was over. "But we are."

Alive, but exhausted. We clung to each other, grateful we'd been spared.

SHORTLY AFTER the dawn of the new year of 1768, six horses dragged our carriage through drifting snow and the icy blasts of winter, all the way to Vienna.

Empress Maria Theresia sent for us at once. She greeted us gowned entirely in black, still in deep mourning for her husband and daughters. With her were her son, Emperor Josef; her daughter, Princess Maria Kristina; Kristina's husband, Prince Albert of Saxony; and the two archdukes and four surviving archduchesses, including twelve-year-old Maria Antonia, the youngest and most beautiful. Only the imperial family was present that day—no one else.

This time, instead of fussing over Wolferl, Maria Theresia gave her full attention to Mama. Taking Mama's hand and tenderly stroking her cheek, the empress whispered to my mother about the sufferings of women who must watch their children die, and Mama wiped away the empress's tears with her own handkerchief.

I watched and listened as the others spoke. Because Papa and the impudent Wolferl always did the talking, I had not become skilled in courtly conversation. My skill was all in my fingers! At times throughout the afternoon I was aware of Archduke Ferdinand's gaze flickering over

me. Just once our eyes met and held, and I thought I de-
tected the hint of a smile. Ferdinand was a little younger
than I, and something about him—maybe his half-smile—
reminded me of red-haired Davey. For a moment I wished
we could talk together, the way I had once been able to
talk with Davey in the garden in England. But then I felt
the color rise in my cheeks and stared down at my hands.

The empress asked us to play for her, and for over an
hour we entertained her and her family. Later, as we drove
back to our rooms, Papa grumbled, "Doubtless Emperor
Josef believes he has paid us handsomely with his most
gracious conversation. The empress leaves such matters
up to her son, and His Imperial Highness is notoriously
tightfisted."

Even if it turned out we'd receive no financial reward
for all our efforts, I remembered Archduke Ferdinand's
almost smile and thought our time well spent.

ONCE THE EMPRESS had officially received us, we were
free to perform for whomever invited us. But no one did.
Fear of smallpox still gripped the city. Freezing tempera-
tures made Wolferl's pockmarks flame a bright red, and
the sight of him frightened people away.

There were no invitations, and Papa was incensed. "The
scourge is not the real reason we're being ignored," he said
darkly. "It's jealousy! These small-minded Viennese are
consumed by envy of Wolferl's talent."

He found other reasons to explain why we were being ignored. We were getting older and had less appeal to audiences more impressed by child prodigies than by grown-up musicians. Although Wolferl was still quite small and Papa routinely subtracted a year or two from his age—he was actually twelve—Papa could no longer easily pass him off as "a child virtuoso," an outspoken little genius who could perform all sorts of musical tricks. Some people even claimed Wolferl was a fraud and Papa had made sure my brother was thoroughly familiar with the difficult music he was handed to display his astonishing gift for sight-reading.

There was also the matter of Viennese taste. "These people are interested only in foolish frivolity," Papa complained. "There is no appreciation of serious musical performances."

THE NEWS FROM Salzburg was not good. The archbishop sent a terse message: He would no longer pay Papa's salary unless Papa was actually present in Salzburg and earning it. Mama fretted over this. "Leopold, perhaps we should go home."

Papa wouldn't hear of it. "Things will work out—you'll see!" he said. Mama pressed her lips together and said no more.

Then one night at the opera we encountered Emperor Josef. During the usual polite exchanges, the emperor asked casually, "My dear Wolfgang, have *you* considered the composition of an opera? I believe you might well provide us with a charming entertainment."

It was all Papa needed to hear. "I told you things would work out!" he crowed when we were back in our rooms. "Our Wolferl shall compose an opera, at the request of the emperor himself." He tossed his peruke onto the wig stand. "And he'll conduct it from the harpsichord, as well."

"Have you forgotten that the emperor hates to pay for anything at all?" Mama asked mildly. "Wolferl's opera won't cost him even a ducat for the price of admission."

"Must you always see only the dark side?" Papa rebuked her. "Think of it, Anna Maria! This opera might well bring Wolferl an offer of a permanent paid position in Vienna. And perhaps for me as well! We'll move here from provincial, small-hearted Salzburg, where no one truly appreciates us!"

He must have forgotten that only recently he had complained about the musical taste of the Viennese and their lack of appreciation of serious music.

IN THE SPRING of 1768 the imperial palace announced that Archduchess Karolina would step into the shoes of her two dead sisters and marry King Ferdinand. *How must she feel?* I wondered when I heard of this latest engagement. I wondered, too, how *he* must feel, or if it made no difference to him. When I put my questions to Mama, she merely smiled and shook her head.

"Royalty does not marry for love," she said. "They marry for duty."

"Then I'm glad I'm not royalty," I said. I'd sometimes envied the archduchesses their great luxury. Imagine living in an enormous palace, all marble and silk and gilding, instead of four small, stifling rooms! But I was sure I would never marry out of duty, not even for a marble palace.

The official announcement of Karolina's wedding brought us a flurry of invitations. We provided dinner music for the imperial court before the ceremony in which the couple was married by proxy. The Russian ambassador later asked us to perform. The attention encouraged Papa.

"Now, Wolferl," Papa said, "it's time to begin work on your opera, as the emperor suggested."

The text of an Italian comic opera, La finta semplice—"The Pretend Simpleton"—was chosen by the manager of the Vienna Burgtheater, a certain Signor Affligio, who would be in charge of the production. Wolferl immediately set about composing the arias. My brother wrote even the most complicated music as easily as a cat catches a mouse, pouring out a score of 558 pages. When he was composing, he lived in his own world and shut out everything else. He ate when someone brought him food and slept when Papa sent him to bed. He often looked at me as if he didn't recognize me, or perhaps didn't see me at all. And he never rewrote anything; it was all there, complete, in his head.

But one thing after another seemed to go wrong. Not everyone wished to acknowledge Wolferl's talent. Postponement followed postponement. Doubts and criticisms piled up. Some people insisted Wolferl could not possibly have written the score. Singers didn't want to perform the music of a child. Musicians refused to follow the direction of a twelve-year-old boy they considered nothing more than a clever trickster.

Signor Affligio wanted to delay the project. "The work will be booed and hissed," he argued. "It will be a disaster! An embarrassment!"

Everyone was angry with everyone else. Papa dwelled on what he saw as plots against us. Wolferl ignored the tempest swirling around him and kept working. By July he had finished the opera.

The weather turned hot, and we sweltered in our heavy winter clothes. Papa wrote to Herr Hagenauer, asking him to send our summer clothes, the silk suits made in Lyons, and some patches to fix outfits that were wearing out. The patches reminded Papa that we weren't earning any money.

Papa's temper frayed. He suspected that Signor Affligio, "the thieving Italian," was a cheat and a scoundrel who had no intention of producing the opera, and there would be no pay for my brother's efforts. He fired off an angry letter denouncing Affligio to the emperor, who passed the letter on to the empress, who directed her anger not at

Affligio, but at Papa. She accused the Mozarts of "running about the world like beggars." Papa raged, Mama despaired, and even the usually high-spirited Wolferl was downcast.

I hated the shabby way he was treated. We resumed our chess games. I coaxed him out for walks without our parents. He was still my best friend and closest confidant, and I was his—we had no other.

At exactly the right moment Papa made the acquaintance of a physician named Franz Anton Mesmer, who invited us to his splendid home. We were fascinated by Dr. Mesmer's glass harmonica, the invention of an American, Benjamin Franklin. It produced tones of ethereal beauty; Wolferl was invited to play it, but I was not. Before the evening was over, Dr. Mesmer asked Wolferl to compose an operetta to entertain friends of his wealthy wife.

Wolferl dived into this new project, *Bastien und Bastienne.* The operetta was a much less ambitious work with only three singers—a pair of rustic lovers and a shepherd-wizard—plus a handful of musicians. He finished it in a few weeks. That autumn we had the pleasure of seeing the operetta performed in the doctor's private theater.

This success restored our spirits, and Wolferl rushed on with his next composition, a solemn mass for the consecration of a new church. He conducted it himself in December, and Empress Maria Theresia attended with her family. Her displeasure melted away when she recognized how much Wolferl's talent had matured. Here was a small twelve-year-old boy, doing the creative work of a man three times his age! But the moment Wolferl stepped away from the harpsichord, he acted as impish and irrepressible as ever, scrambling to kiss the hand of every lady within reach.

Still no one offered Wolferl a position in Vienna. We had been gone this time for more than a year, and Archbishop Schrattenbach threatened to suspend Papa if he did not return to Salzburg at once. Our arrival back in Salzburg in the dead of the winter of 1769 didn't produce nearly the excitement of our return from the grand tour two years earlier. The mountains surrounding Salzburg gleamed white against a heavy gray sky. The streets were quiet, almost empty compared to Vienna. As I ran up the stairs of the house on Getreidegasse, Bimperl appeared at the door and growled. She seemed to have completely forgotten me.

Part 2

AMADEO
1769

Chapter 10

A NEW JOURNEY

I LOST NO TIME before getting in touch with Viktoria and Katherl. Bundled against the cold, we walked along the frozen Salzach. In the sixteen months I'd been away this time, gawky Katherl had become elegantly graceful. Little Viktoria was still as round as a dumpling, but her usually rosy cheeks looked pale, and her eyes had lost some of their sparkle.

Katherl gossiped about engagements and weddings. Viktoria mentioned concerts in which she'd sung and spoke longingly of the dream she'd once cherished of a musical career. "I've given up praying that Archbishop Schrattenbach will send me to study in Italy."

"But why, Viktoria?" I asked.

"I couldn't go, even if the archbishop should decide to send me," she said sadly. Her stepmother had died recently, and Viktoria was now in charge of a younger half brother, Josef, and a little half sister, Anna. "I love the children dearly," she said, "and Papa says I'm needed at home."

"But what about you, Nannerl?" Katherl asked. "Surely your father can persuade the archbishop to send you."

"I've given up the idea. Papa is set against it."

"You are a superb musician!" Viktoria said loyally. "Everyone says so. Your father must not deny you this opportunity."

Their enthusiasm encouraged me. Maybe I could convince Papa that the training would enhance my role in the Family Mozart.

The sun had already dropped behind the looming gray rock of the Mönchsberg. Darkness was settling in when we passed a café with lights glowing invitingly. "It's a new place," Katherl said. "Come on, Nannerl, you must try it!"

We sat at a little marble-topped table, each of us with a steaming mug of chocolate, and shared a plate of pastries. The talk turned to balls my friends had attended, who had danced with whom, flirtations and courtships, couples who were planning weddings. Magdalena Lipp had just married Michael Haydn, and I had to hear all about their wedding. I was eager to know if Katherl had succeeded in attracting the attention of Herr von Mölk. "What about Franz?" I asked at last.

"She's still hoping," Viktoria answered for her, spooning up whipped cream.

Katherl cast a withering glance at Viktoria. "He's cordial enough when we meet. We've even danced a few times. But he hasn't called upon me."

"I think she should forget about him," Viktoria said. "It's not as though he's the only fish in the sea." She licked her lips, leaving behind a faint, creamy mustache. "But Nannerl, tell us about you. Have you met anyone exciting?"

I shook my head and steered the talk to rumors that Emperor Josef, widowed twice, might be contemplating matrimony for the third time.

I couldn't deny that marriage was on my mind. Papa had remarked more than once that I was of marriageable age—I was seventeen—and I had begun to think about the kind of man I might wish to marry. Someone to whom music was everything, as it was to me. But at the same time I often dreamed of my life continuing just as it was, with my brother and me playing music together for the rest of our lives. I could not imagine that someday we might be separated, by marriage or by anything else. The Family Mozart would have to include my husband as well. Whoever he was, he'd be marrying all of us, not just me.

"You're very quiet, Nannerl," Katherl said mischievously, interrupting my thoughts. "Tell us the truth, now—did you meet some fine young gentleman in Vienna who set your heart aflutter?"

I said nothing but smiled mysteriously, to tease them.

"Oh, you did—I can tell!" Katherl said with a giggle. "Is he a musician? A nobleman, perhaps? Wait—!" She paused dramatically. "I know! The archduke Ferdinand! I've heard he's intelligent—a bit young, perhaps, but quite good-looking. Is that who it is, Nannerl?"

"I did once look at the archduke," I confessed, "and he did look back at me. But that was the beginning and the end of it."

"That's all?" Katherl pressed, disappointed.

I shrugged. "What more could there be? He's an archduke and I'm a musician. Besides," I added, "Papa was always there."

AFTER OUR RETURN to Salzburg, Papa swallowed his pride and went back to work in the archbishop's court as a violinist. "I'm nothing more than a lackey," he complained. One day in spring he rushed home from the Residenz with surprising news: The archbishop wished to arrange for the premiere performance of *La finta semplice,* the opera written in Vienna but rejected by the scoundrel Affligio. "It will take place at the Residenz without scenery. The archbishop has promised us the court orchestra and chorus as well as the seven soloists."

Rehearsals began at once. The Three Ladies took the female roles: Magdalena Haydn in the main soprano role of Rosina, a girl pretending to be naive in order to snare

Cassandro; Maria Brauenhofer as Giacinta, Cassandro's sister; and Anna Fesemayr in the part of Ninetta, Giacinta's chambermaid. Viktoria was thrilled to be part of the chorus.

On the first of May 1769, the night of the performance, we dressed in our best costumes, Wolferl in a new green silk suit, Mama in the red satin dress given to her by Madame d'Épinay, I in my best blue velvet. I was nervous when we took our seats in the ornate Guard Room of the Residenz, worrying that perhaps Affligio had been right— Wolferl was too young, stretched beyond his limits. Wolferl, of course, wasn't at all nervous; he never was.

The court orchestra, with Papa as first violinist, and the chorus were already in place when Archbishop Schrattenbach entered, smiled benevolently, and took his seat. The singers stepped onto the improvised stage. The "little composer" entered, bowed to the audience, flipped his coattails out of the way, sat down at the harpsichord, and plunged into the music.

The libretto was one of those complicated plots in which lovers are sent off in the wrong direction in Act I, confusion reigns in Act II, and everything gets sorted out and ends happily in Act III. But the music! "Total dramatic and harmonic assurance," Michael Haydn remarked afterward, when everyone was talking about the scene between Rosina and Cassandro in which the two spoke only in gestures. No one minded that the composer was a boy of only thirteen or the conductor was that same young boy—after all, he was a Salzburger! If only the Viennese knew what they had missed.

Mama beamed as friends came to congratulate us, Papa walked with a swagger, and I shed tears of joy. Wolferl took it all in stride, enjoying the admiration heaped on him. He'd come to expect it.

After that success, Papa could endure his role of court musician for only so long. The subject of Italy and the benefits of such a journey came up again and again. Imagine the excitement, then, when Papa announced, "The archbishop has promised to finance a tour of Italy to continue Wolferl's musical education. We have his official blessing and a purse of a hundred and twenty ducats."

Papa seized Mama's hands and twirled her around. He pulled me into their dance, and Wolferl stopped composing long enough to join the celebration. Mama produced a bottle of good Riesling and filled our glasses. "To the brilliant future of Wolfgang Gottlieb Mozart!" Papa exulted, proposing a toast. "To Italy!"

What about me? I thought. *Wolferl's* musical education? *Wolferl's* brilliant future? What of mine? Papa had said nothing about *my* musical education or *my* brilliant future. I still sometimes dreamed of studying, but it was only a dream—I had not found the courage to bring up the subject with Papa since I had burned my letter to the archbishop. Numbly I raised my glass and pretended to drink, waiting for him to say more. He did not.

As soon as Wolferl left the room, I placed myself in front of my father. "Does the archbishop wish me to study in Italy, too?" I dared ask, barely able to control my trembling voice.

Papa looked at me, his head to one side, smiling quizzically. "You, Nannerl?"

"*Ja,* me, Papa!" I struggled to appear calm, rational. "It's what I dreamed of for years and years! I hoped that when the time came, you would petition him to send me for training, as he sent Magdalena Haydn and Anna Fesemayr and Maria Brauenhofer—all the ladies singing in Wolferl's opera."

"But they are singers, Nannerl. There is a great demand at court for female singers. The archbishop has sent no girls to train as keyboard players."

"It's true, I'm not a singer—that's not my gift. Maybe the archbishop has sent no girls to train as keyboard players because none are as talented as I am!" I couldn't stop now, though I knew I no longer sounded calm and rational. "I want to study with new teachers and learn new things, Papa. You used to boast of my talent. Doesn't it matter anymore? I want to have a future, too!"

"Enough, Nannerl!" Papa said sternly. "We have already discussed this, have we not? Your future is as a part of the

Family Mozart. I will teach you all you need to know. Now let us hear no more about this."

I subsided into wounded silence, Papa's words hammering in my ears.

The next time I saw Viktoria and Katherl I told them the news. "We're leaving soon for Italy," I said. "The archbishop has given Wolferl his approval."

"How wonderful!" Viktoria exclaimed sincerely. "I'd give anything in the world to be going away."

Viktoria's life had recently taken another unfortunate turn. Only six months after the death of his second wife, her father had wed his third, Anna Fesemayr, one of the Three Ladies. But Viktoria didn't get on well with this new stepmother, who left the care of little Josef and Anna entirely up to her.

"Don't envy me too much," I said. "I won't be studying there. Just Wolferl."

"Oh, Nannerl!" Katherl cried. "How sad for you!"

I had nearly persuaded myself I was glad for the opportunity to visit Italy, give some performances, perhaps even attract some notice on my own. "There still might be a chance!" I said brightly. "Things can always change, can't they?"

"Of course," my friends agreed. "There's always a chance." But I could see they didn't believe it.

———

EVERY DAY the conversation at our table was about Italy. "When we're in Milan," and "When Wolferl performs in Bologna," and "Our opportunities will surely be great in Rome," and "We'll need to spend ample time in Naples, the center of Italian music." Wolferl excitedly interrupted Papa every other minute with questions.

I assumed, naturally, that "we" meant the four of us, as it always had. At lunch one day I asked Papa if he'd chosen the music he wanted me to learn for the journey.

Papa chewed a bite of veal and followed it with a swallow of beer. He laid down his fork and folded his hands. "*Nein,* Nannerl, that won't be necessary," he said. "You and Mama will remain here while Wolferl and I are gone."

I stared at him, thinking I must have misunderstood. "Mama and I are not going with you?" I asked as this new truth began to sink in.

Papa didn't try to sugarcoat the pill he was forcing me to swallow. "Listen to me, dear ones," he said, pretending not to notice my distress. "It is not that I don't wish to have you both with us—if only that were possible! But it's a matter of money. The money the archbishop is giving me to take Wolferl for training is not enough for four of us. Only for two!"

I blinked back tears. Mama twisted her handkerchief around her finger. I wondered if she already knew Papa's decision or if she was as stunned as I was.

"All of us went on the grand tour," I ventured. "And to Vienna as well."

"*Ja,* of course you did! It was a great pleasure to have you with us, and it cost a great deal of money. But this is not the same situation, Nannerl. Sacrifices are sometimes required for the good of all. Wolferl's future is at stake, and *his* future is the future of the Family Mozart."

"Wolferl and I could play duets again," I persisted, refusing to give up. "I can give concerts with him, as I always have."

Papa continued as though I hadn't spoken. "You will have plenty of opportunities here, Nannerl. Keep up your practicing, and you'll be in demand as an accompanist and invited to give private concerts. How nice that would be, eh? You're sure to attract a few pupils. And," he added with a sly wink, "I'll wager that any number of fine young gentlemen will come courting. You're certainly old enough."

"I don't care about being courted!" I was almost shouting. "I want to go to Italy!"

Mama leaned forward and touched my arm—my outburst must have shocked her. "Shhhh, *Liebchen.*"

But I would not be silenced. "I want to play music with Wolferl as I always have," I said stubbornly. "That's all I've ever wanted."

There was seldom any discord in our household, and Wolferl had been following this exchange uneasily. "I want us all to go, Papa!" he said, his voice breaking.

"Quiet!" Papa roared.

We fell silent. But that was not the end of it.

PAPA INTENDED to leave in early autumn, but commitments to the archbishop's court delayed him. I was secretly glad. And I was not ready to admit defeat. It was pointless to talk to Mama. Wolferl was no better. When I asked if he would help me persuade Papa, he said, "It's no use, Nannerl. He has made up his mind."

So I tried one last approach. When I managed to find Papa alone and in a good mood, I said sympathetically, "Papa, I know you worry about money, and I understand that traveling with four is terribly expensive. But there may be a compromise. Perhaps Mama would prefer to remain at home, and I could travel to Italy with you and Wolferl. Surely it wouldn't cost that much to take me along. I eat very little, and I would earn my own way as part of our trio."

I felt disloyal to Mama as I made my proposal; I had betrayed her with my suggestion. And it didn't work. Papa refused to listen to a selfish daughter's callous disregard of her own mother, and he angrily erupted. "Nannerl, I cannot tolerate any more of your yammering! This is not a trio performance, or a duo, but a solo! You will stay here with your mother and do as you are told!"

I clapped my mouth shut and vowed I would not bring up the subject again. It was a hard vow to keep.

———

"OH, NANNERL," Wolferl murmured as the time drew near, "I'm going to be horribly lonely without you."

"I'll miss you, too," I said. "How long will you be gone?" I felt my brother's mind was already far away. I began weeping, as I did every time the trip to Italy was mentioned. All anyone had to do was say "Italy," and the tears began to fall.

"I don't know," Wolferl said. "That's for Papa to decide. But it won't be long—not even a year. And I'll write to you as often as I can. Now stop your crying, or I'll have to give your behind a great kick!"

On a lovely evening in late autumn we drove to the Hagenauers' country home in Nonntal, just outside of Salzburg. On the way Papa revealed his latest good news: The archbishop had awarded my brother the title of *Konzertmeister.* "Titles are important!" Papa crowed.

Mama was more practical. "Titles are only titles. Will Wolferl be paid?"

"*Nein,*" Papa admitted, "but it will surely give our son much higher prestige in Italy."

Italy Italy Italy! I was sick to death of hearing about it. But, predictably, most of the conversation that evening was about the coming journey. All through Frau Hagenauer's roast pork and potato dumplings I tried to conceal my feelings. "I hear the weather is simply vile in Rome," I said, "and my friends tell me the roads are much worse than anything we've yet experienced." I pushed aside my plate after only a few bites. "I'm not the least bit unhappy to be staying in Salzburg!"

After supper, while the others sipped cups of coffee and little glasses of schnapps, Wolferl and I played duets for the Hagenauers and their guests. For an hour or so I lost myself in the music and forgot my misery. But as we acknowledged the warm applause of our dear friends, I could not help wondering when my brother and I would make music together again.

Chapter 11

FRANZ

SNOW SWIRLED thick as eiderdown from a feather bed as the carriage rumbled away over the slick cobblestones. Clutching each other tightly, Mama and I waved and blew halfhearted kisses until Papa and Wolferl vanished from sight. Then we tucked our damp handkerchiefs into our sleeves and climbed the stairs to our silent apartment. Mama set a pot of coffee on the stove and arranged little marzipan cakes on a china plate.

"To bring us some cheer, *Liebchen*." She attempted a smile while tears rolled down her cheeks. I tried to smile back at her. It had been a sad parting. Wolferl, who had been in a state of overexcitement for weeks, was suddenly subdued, clinging to me in the last hour. Now Mama and I made our best effort to console each other, but in my heart I knew there would be no real consolation until Papa and Wolferl came home again.

They left two weeks before Christmas of 1769, and Mama and I prepared to endure the holidays alone. We accepted the Hagenauers' invitation to their Christmas Day feast of roast goose and cabbage. We attended Mass every morning. We both tried to put on a brave face.

We bought a large map and prepared to follow their progress as though we were with them—Papa's idea. Within hours after Papa and Wolferl had gone, we'd begun our first letter to them. It lay open on the round table by the window, and each day we added a few lines to "our travelers," as we began to call them. Twice a week on post days I hurried to the post office to inquire if a letter had arrived and to send off one of our own.

In one of his first letters, sent from Innsbruck, Papa enclosed the key to our clavichord, explaining that he'd carried it away with him "in a fit of absentmindedness." Then he added, unnecessarily, "Take care not to lose it."

I hadn't touched the clavichord since they left and hadn't even noticed the key was missing. "What did he expect us to do with it, swallow it?" I asked sourly. I was quite angry with Papa. I felt as though I were getting even with him by not playing, although of course I hurt only myself by depriving myself of my greatest joy.

Mama pursed her lips and flung the key with its green

silk tassel into the drawer of Papa's writing table. She said nothing, but I knew she was angry, too.

Our travelers crossed the mountains in heavy snow and arrived safely in Italy. Letters arrived from Verona, from Mantua, from Milan. Mama read the letters aloud while I followed their route on the map. Because mail could take two weeks to reach its destination, our letters inevitably crossed, and it seemed we were continually asking the wrong questions or giving the wrong answers. Papa's always ended with the same phrase: *We kiss you both a thousand times.* Wolferl sent even more kisses, plus some affectionate insults for me: "Dear little Nannerl," he wrote, "I send you a hundred kisses on your hands or smackers on your marvelous horseface." This made me smile. It was the first time we'd ever been apart, and I missed my impish brother a great deal.

"Is Nannerl practicing regularly?" Papa inquired from Milan.

"If my practicing is so important to him, he should not have left me at home." I bristled. In truth I was playing— but not the grueling exercises he demanded, the endless scales and arpeggios. I played whatever I liked, purely for my own pleasure, knowing Papa would not approve of my self-indulgence.

Mama sighed and shook her head, refusing to be drawn into another useless discussion. But she broke down weeping when she received a letter that began, "I kiss you and

Nannerl, but only once, because you do not write." Then Papa upbraided her for being lazy, because our letters didn't arrive when he expected them. He threatened not to write for a few weeks, to give us "a taste of our own medicine." As though we weren't already being forced to swallow enough!

Papa complained—as he had when the four of us were traveling—of the high costs of the journey. "I thank God that I left you at home," he wrote. "You would not have been able to endure the cold. And it would have cost us a great deal of money, so that we couldn't have lived as well as we do now."

"I'm very good at enduring the cold!" I cried, flinging aside the letter. "And I'm sure Wolferl wouldn't mind doing with a little less stylish comfort if we could be there!"

"Listen to me, *Liebchen,*" Mama said soothingly. "We are not there; we are here. But who is to say we can't accompany our dear Wolferl and your loving papa in spirit? With our map and guidebook we can imagine ourselves with them without enduring any of the discomforts."

I blessed Mama for her good humor, but I was still resentful of being left behind. I envied Wolferl for having the opportunity I'd been denied. But when I read Wolferl's little messages bubbling with pleasure at his musical successes, I naturally rejoiced with him.

He'd composed his first string quartet. He'd written two

motets to be sung in Latin by a couple of boys aged fifteen and sixteen. Both boys were *castrati,* he explained, their testicles removed before they were eight years old.

"Can you imagine it?" he asked. "Many boys here have been altered in this way, so they can continue to sing in the highest range and have successful musical careers as sopranos."

Wolferl's once sweet singing voice had recently broken and was now more like a donkey's bray. "I can't even sing my own music!" he grumbled.

THEY TRAVELED TO Bologna, then to Florence. Papa described the miserable weather, days of rain broken by cold so fierce they had to buy foot bags lined with wolf fur, and the wretched inns and dreary food with nothing to eat but brussels sprouts and eggs. But I didn't believe for a moment that we were "better off," as Papa insisted. I doubt that Mama did, either.

Wolferl was learning Italian. He addressed his postscripts to *Cara sorella mia*—"dear little sister"—and signed them *Amadeo,* explaining, "That's what they call me here." He added notes to Papa's letters in a mixture of French, Italian, and German with Salzburger dialect tossed in, sometimes all in the same sentence. He often sang, *Tra-la-la-liera! Tra-la-la-liera!* and included puns too outrageously vulgar to explain. He enjoyed trying to shock me with crude language and ribald jokes that boys of fourteen seemed to think were hilarious.

MY PARENTS HAD MANY friends who did their best to cheer us: Michael Haydn, the composer; Viktoria's father, Anton Cajetan Adlgasser, the organist; Johann Schacht-ner, the trumpeter; Dr. Barisani, the court physician; Felix Anton von Mölk, the court chancellor; and others as well. Mama and I dressed in our best gowns, remnants of our wardrobe from the grand tour, called in a friseur to dress our hair in the current fashion, and accepted invitations to evenings of coffee and music.

Mama tucked Papa's latest letters into her purse, and when someone asked, as someone always did, "What news have you from your travelers?" she proudly read out loud those parts describing Wolferl's musical triumphs, his meetings with important people, and his extraordinary adventures. Information about matters that Papa didn't want made public, written at the end of the sheet, had been cut off per Papa's instructions. He intended the let-ters to be passed around.

I was glad when that part of the evening ended. It was painful to be reminded in front of everyone of the way my brother was living out my most cherished dreams.

On one such occasion I sat alone, sipping coffee, in a cor-ner of Chancellor von Mölk's parlor. Viktoria and Katherl, who had been anticipating this evening, had both fallen ill at the last moment, and Katherl had sent a message begging me to keep an eye out for the chancellor's son, Franz. I was supposed to observe to whom he spoke, with whom he danced (if there was dancing), and whether he seemed happy or gloomy. "Be prepared to give a full report!" she ordered.

But so far I had noticed nothing worth mentioning. Then the subject of my report approached me with a friendly smile, bowed courteously, addressing me as Fräulein Mozart, and attempted to begin a conversation. I was not used to engaging in the banter that came so easily to other girls. I, who had been in the company of kings and princes, emperors and archdukes, could think of scarcely a single word to say to this fellow with the light blue eyes who was trying to capture my interest.

"My brother, Albert, is a student in Rome," said Franz.

"How nice," I responded, and noticed that my coffee had grown cold.

"I understand that your father and your brother may have an opportunity in the near future to visit Albert."

I nodded. A clever girl would now find an opportunity to say something complimentary about her friend, Katherl, but my mind was a blank.

"Have you visited Rome, Fräulein Mozart?" he asked.

"*Nein,*" I muttered. Suppose I said, *Katherina Gilowsky is a fine-looking girl, don't you think?* I opened my mouth, but nothing came out.

"Perhaps one day you shall have the opportunity," said Franz, trying again. "To visit Rome," he added.

"Perhaps," I said, thinking, *Katherl was supposed to be here tonight. Perhaps you should call upon her.* I remained silent.

Given a little more time, I might have managed to say a few words about Katherl. But Herr von Mölk gave up, bowed, and excused himself. I considered how to report this nonconversation to Katherl.

The following Sunday, without my doing a thing to bring it about, the situation changed. Franz asked permission to walk home with Mama and me from Mass at Dom St. Rupert. Two days later he saw us at a concert and begged leave to sit with us. Both times Mama was so charming that I could see why Papa had fallen in love with her. I'd surely done nothing to invite Franz's attention.

In a town the size of Salzburg, word of these two incidents soon reached the ears of Katherl. My friend appeared at our apartment, her face pinched in a scowl and her beautiful eyes glistening with tears. I braced myself for what I knew was coming.

"False friend!" Katherl hissed.

I tried to explain. "I have no interest in Franz," I said, "and I'm sure he has no interest in me. He's just trying to be kind to Mama and me because Papa and Wolferl are away and he knows we're lonely. Please believe that I would do nothing to betray a dear friend."

At last I convinced Katherl that I was not trying to steal her heart's desire, and we walked with linked arms to a café. Not long after, her interest shifted to a young school-teacher, and she forgot about Franz von Mölk. This change prompted another: My tongue became untied, and I was able to carry on a pleasant conversation with Franz the next time we met.

Everyone turned out for Carnival, the festive season that began on Twelfth Night and lasted until the start of Lent, with masked balls nearly every night. Mama and I attended several of these balls, eating and drinking and dancing, sometimes until nearly six in the morning. Franz was there, too, but he was only one of several young men with whom I danced. I wrote a lively description of these gala parties to Wolferl, who would surely show my letter to Papa, and he would surely respond with another lecture about not wasting time.

Then in February Franz invited me for a drive in his father's handsome sleigh. Franz was careful to include Mama, but this time she refused. "You are young. You must learn to enjoy life. You don't need me to go with you."

My friends began to give me heaps of advice. "Franz is a good catch," Katherl said. "He has a promising position at court. He's not what you'd call handsome, but he's not bad-looking, either."

"He can even sing rather decently, after he's had a stein or two of beer," Viktoria added approvingly.

And so I consented to go out with Franz. Several times we went ice-skating, and twice we took sleds into the hills with his sister Barbara, whom we called Waberl, and other young people. I found myself laughing for the first time in months. My heart began to soften.

With that softening, other changes occurred: I begged for a new dress, pretty ribbons, a bit of fur on my cloak, another appointment with the friseur. I sometimes dabbed a touch of color on my cheeks and lips. My friends encouraged me. "You're like a butterfly emerging from a cocoon," Viktoria said, marveling.

"And high time, too," added Katherl.

Conversations with Katherl and Viktoria took a more serious turn. "He loves you, Nannerl," Katherl said. "Everyone seems to know it but you."

"He hasn't spoken to me about it," I protested.

"He will," she said airily.

I hoped he wouldn't, because I wasn't at all sure how I felt about him. A softening heart is not the same as love.

PAPA WROTE THAT Wolferl had been asked to compose an *opera seria,* a dramatic opera, for Milan's next Carnival season, almost a year off. He planned to leave shortly for Rome, arriving in time for Easter. From there they would go to Naples, such an important music center that they might remain there for several months, returning to Milan by the start of Advent to begin work on the opera.

"That means we can certainly get home via Venice within a year," Papa wrote.

Another whole year! My head began to throb, and I went to lie down on my bed, unable to think of anything but the endless string of days stretching out before me.

I had by then resumed practicing for several hours every day, although it was not the same without Papa's direction and discipline. I sorely missed those precious hours at the end of the day when Wolferl and I always played duets and Papa often joined us for a trio. But I had returned to music, even more deeply than before. Music took first place in my life, not only the joy it had been in the past but, now that I was older, a consolation for my disappointments. Nothing, I believed, could ever take the place of my music.

FRANZ DECLARED HIMSELF at Easter. "I love you, Nannerl," he said, his voice cracking nervously. "And I want you to be my wife. May I hope that you'll accept me?"

I blushed and stammered. I didn't say "I love you" or any of the things a girl might be expected to say to a suitor. "I do care for you, Franz" was the best I could manage, but my tone was so lacking in passion I'm sure I offered him little hope.

When I told Mama about Franz's intentions, she asked,

"Why have you not given him more encouragement? Do you not love him?"

"Music is my first love, Mama, and it always will be," I confessed. "Franz is not likely to accept second place. I'm sure Papa is already thinking of another journey. He says he's taken in a lot of money so far—certainly he won't insist it's too expensive for us to join them the next time, and I'll perform again. But if I'm pledged to Franz, he won't want me to go. I won't be able to advance my career as a musician." I seemed to have endless reasons for not encouraging him. To say *Ja* to Franz was to say *Nein* to myself and to my dreams.

Mama shook her head sadly. "Have you understood nothing, Nannerl? Your father doesn't intend for you to have a career. You are enormously talented, but your talent isn't half as important as Wolferl's. I can see plainly, even if you won't, that Papa is pouring all of his efforts into making sure the world recognizes Wolfgang's genius, not yours. Far better for you to accept that nice young man and make a different kind of life for yourself."

I stared at Mama. Now my anger rose against *her.* "You want me to be like you, to do the bidding of a domineering husband. I will never do that," I declared.

She turned away without replying, and I knew I'd hurt her. I apologized, telling her I was deeply sorry for my harsh words. "I understand, Nannerl," Mama said sorrowfully. "Believe me, *Liebchen,* I do."

I continued to put Franz off, waiting for Papa and
Wolferl to come home, hoping my life would still turn out
the way I wanted: Wolferl and I would again make music
together, and there would be more journeys to include all
of us. And I had not completely given up the idea of studying in Italy—miracles did happen!

Meanwhile, Franz continued to court me patiently—
more patiently than I deserved.

Chapter 12

JOACHIM

LIFE ON THE THIRD floor of the house on Getreidegasse was much different without Papa and Wolferl. I had more space to myself. Papa was not constantly reminding me to practice or demanding this or that. We didn't hear his complaints about the burdens placed upon him by Archbishop Schrattenbach. Mama and I missed our travelers, but we'd also begun to enjoy our freedom.

Now that we had only each other, we grew closer. As she rubbed my hands with her special cream, our old ritual, Mama sometimes told me about her life, growing up in the village of St. Gilgen, the daughter of an impoverished public official, and later meeting Papa, the son of a bookbinder, who left the university where he was studying to be a priest in order to pursue a career in music. "We met and fell in love almost at once," she said with a shy smile. "But we had to wait years until we'd saved enough to marry. When at last we did, everyone said we were the handsomest couple in Salzburg!"

Her voice trembled when she spoke of the pregnancies ending in stillbirths and the deaths of newborns. "Ach, *Liebling*," she sighed, "may God grant you the joy of a large and healthy family and only a small share of heartache."

I didn't tell her that a family was not what I yearned for, as other girls did. What I desired was the life of a musician—just as Papa once had.

Franz continued to call on me, despite my lack of encouragement. At about the same time I had begun to enjoy the flattering attentions of a certain Johann Baptist Josef Joachim Ferdinand von Schiedenhofen zu Stumm und Triebenbach. Who would not be impressed by a man with such a name! I'd met him the previous winter at a Carnival ball, where we danced to minuets composed by Michael Haydn. "And is music your greatest love, Fräulein Mozart?" inquired Joachim, the name he asked me to call him.

"My *only* love," I replied as we moved through the formal steps of the dance.

"Mine as well."

Later, while others danced, we talked, discussing Haydn's musical themes. I felt I'd met someone who truly understood me. My interest in Joachim, and what I perceived as his interest in me, was partly responsible for my fading interest in Franz. I don't even remember if Franz was at the ball that night.

IN MAY LETTERS ARRIVED from Naples, where Papa and Wolferl had gone to escape the summer fevers that plagued Rome. They'd called upon Princess Karolina, the arch-duchess who'd married King Ferdinand after the death of her two older sisters. But neither the king nor his Viennese wife had invited Wolferl to play for them.

"Everyone agrees that Ferdinand is a dolt," Mama re-marked when she'd read Papa's letter. "But I expected bet-ter from Princess Karolina. Do you remember how kind and sweet she was?"

Papa complained that although he and Wolferl gave recitals, no one paid them for their performances—a fa-miliar story. Wolferl had been invited to play at a famous conservatory of music. The students believed the diamond ring he wore on his little finger had magical powers and enabled him to play with incredible brilliance.

"So I took off my 'magic' ring and played the same pieces again," Wolferl wrote, "even better than before, and quelled their doubts. How Papa and I laughed afterward! But with or without the 'magic' ring, we took in not a single *lira*."

Even though they weren't earning anything, Papa or-dered new summer costumes for their public appearances. He described his dark red watered silk lined with sky-blue taffeta, and Wolferl's apple-green silk with silver buttons and a rose-colored taffeta lining. The description of their expensive new costumes irritated Mama. "I think we owe ourselves a little indulgence," she said, putting the letter away with the others. "A new coiffure, perhaps?"

Off we went to the friseur patronized by Salzburg's most fashionable ladies. Most girls I knew wore their hair carefully rolled and braided and drawn back, close to the head. But I wanted something grander, a coiffure fit for a baroness. I put myself entirely in the friseur's hands.

He claimed to have dressed the hair of the former archduchess Maria Antonia, who'd changed her name to Marie Antoinette when she married the dauphin of France. The friseur and his assistant spent three hours attaching a wire frame like a birdcage to the top of my head, then combing and fastening my hair over the frame to achieve the great height. To top it off, he pinned on a bouquet of silk ribbons, although I might have chosen some other decorative device, such as flowers or even a little animal made of papier-mâché.

"It's all the rage at Versailles," said the friseur as he stepped back to admire his work. "Some ladies prefer small sailing ships. I have seen one myself on the head of Madame la Dauphine."

Mama and I returned home, powdered and curled. That night I discovered one of the unspoken prices of beauty: I could not lie down. I had to sleep half sitting, my head propped on carefully arranged pillows.

But even with my elaborate new coiffure and the gasps of admiration from my two good friends, I was not satisfied. Now I needed to *do* something different. I decided to take singing lessons. They couldn't hurt, and they might increase my chances of accompanying Papa and Wolferl on a future journey. I proposed to study with the teacher who had prepared Magdalena Haydn for her stay in Venice. Mama wrote to Papa, who gave his approval, adding, "I am glad that Nannerl is working hard."

"As you deserve, *Liebling*," Mama said. "One cannot remain miserable forever. Especially at your age."

And so I began my lessons twice a week and practiced, practiced, practiced for hours in between, an hour of vocalizing alternating with an hour at the clavichord. I composed a few songs and sang them with my own accompaniment, and I sent a copy to Wolferl. "I am amazed to find how well you can compose," he wrote back. "In a word, the song is beautiful." He added another couple of sentences in the foul language he enjoyed using when he wrote to me, not to be quoted here. If he intended to shock me, he failed. I was used to his vulgar humor.

My days were filled with music, leaving little time for much else. But I did sometimes think about the handsome young baron who also loved music and wondered when I might hear from him again.

THE NEWS FROM our travelers in Italy was worrisome. Alarmed by reports of bandits infesting the roads between Naples and Rome, Papa arranged to make the trip as rapidly as possible in a *sedia,* a two-wheeled vehicle pulled by a pair of fast horses. There was an accident, the *sedia* overturned, and Papa received a deep gash in his leg. He wrote that he hadn't left his room for nine days, sitting with his foot propped on a chair. Reports of his suffering continued for more than a month.

Despite this misfortune, Wolfgang played for Pope Clement XIV. The Holy Father awarded him the Order of the Golden Spur, a handsome gold cross, and the Italian title of *Cavaliere*—Knight. Wolfgang started signing his letters in French, "Chevalier de Mozart." Then they made the long journey from Rome to Bologna, where Wolferl took the examination for admittance to the Accademia Filarmonica. No one under the age of twenty was accepted, but the members promised to change the rules if he passed the difficult test.

The examiners handed Wolferl a biblical text in Latin, "Seek ye first the kingdom of God," and instructed him to write an antiphon for soprano, alto, tenor, and bass. They shut him up alone in a little room while Papa was confined to the library so there was no way they could communicate. A half hour later Wolferl emerged with the finished piece, a complex blending of the four voices. Other candidates needed as much as three hours to complete the test. The examiners looked at what Wolferl had done and voted unanimously to admit him to the Accademia. He was only fourteen.

IN EARLY AUTUMN Mama and I received an invitation from Joachim von Schiedenhofen to visit him and his mother and sister, Luisa, at Triebenbach, their family castle near Lake Abtsee. I was thrilled, and so was Mama. Frau von Schiedenhofen offered to send a carriage for us, but Mama had her own idea. "We shall travel in the Pressburg carriage."

Papa had concluded that our handsome carriage, which had survived the arduous grand tour and a later trip to Vienna and Olmütz, would not do for the long journey through Italy and had it stored in a barn. Mama ordered it brought out to carry us to Triebenbach.

Was this the same Mama who so meekly bowed to Papa's every wish, and now decided that we would go off on a junket of our own? What would Papa say if he knew!

"We won't tell him," Mama said. "It's our secret."

We packed a small trunk with our best gowns, made an appointment with the friseur, and hired horses and a driver. Away we went on a sunny October day with a lunch of sausage and bread and a bottle of wine. We enjoyed our picnic in a field of white and yellow flowers, laughing like a pair of truant children.

Frau von Schiedenhofen greeted us warmly at the beautiful old castle and escorted us to our rooms while servants followed with our luggage. We tested the thick mattresses and examined every handsome object and wandered through the gardens. Mama dressed for the evening in her red satin gown, and I wore my embroidered ivory silk with the quilted petticoat. At the end of a fine meal Joachim rose and welcomed the guests—there were a dozen of us—adding, "We are honored to have with us today Fräulein Maria Anna Mozart, one of the finest musicians in the Empire!" He bowed in my direction. "Fräulein Mozart, would you be so kind as to favor us by playing something on our poor harpsichord?"

I was prepared for such a request, and acknowledging the polite applause of the other guests, I moved to the harpsichord at the end of the elegant salon. There was nothing "poor" about it—it was a beautiful instrument and well tuned. I began with a familiar Bach invention, moved on to a showier Scarlatti, and finished with one of the new pieces Wolferl had sent. But it seems I hadn't finished at all—the audience simply would not let me go. I knew that I played well, and I was glad I'd spent so many hours practicing.

Before that superb evening came to an end, Joachim asked me to accompany him while he sang. His voice was a strong, pleasant baritone, and, unlike Franz, he didn't need the influence of a stein of beer to perform. He suggested we rehearse a few duets to sing together the next day. He even talked of arranging some of Michael Haydn's melodies for the clavier. "You will remember, Nannerl, that we once danced to Herr Haydn's minuets at the Carnival ball?"

"I remember," I said. How could I forget!

Mama and I stayed at Triebenbach for five lovely days, walking by the lake during the sunny mornings, shooting air guns at painted targets in the long gallery on lazy afternoons, and passing the chilly evenings making music. Joachim paid me a great deal of attention. I hated to see our visit end.

"I do believe he has eyes for you," Mama said as we made our way back to Salzburg. The sunny weather had ended abruptly, and rain pelted the carriage, but I scarcely noticed. "He's the right age—just a few years older than you, Nannerl. He's very well situated. And he cuts a fine figure in his silk hose—did you notice?"

I surely *had* noticed! Just as I noticed the brown curls that reached his collar and the little smile that always seemed to play around his lips.

Naturally, then, having had such a fine excursion by Lake Abtsee and the excitement of a little flirtation with Joachim, I all but forgot about poor Franz, still patiently waiting for me to accept his love, calling upon me once a week as regularly as the cathedral bells called us to Mass. My feelings for Franz had faded and been blown away with last summer's flowers.

Instead, I allowed myself to daydream about what my life might be as the wife of Joachim with the long and impressive name. Papa would surely approve—Joachim was a member of the nobility! He admired my music. Was there a chance he might even encourage me to study in Italy? He'd complimented me several times on my singing as well as my keyboard technique. He would not object to music being my greatest love. Hadn't he said it was his as well?

One freezing day at the end of October I attended the funeral of Martha Hagenauer, the daughter closest to my age, who had been ill for some time. With me were Viktoria and Katherl, whom I now saw infrequently—Viktoria's devotion to her young brother and sister left her little time, and Katherl was serving as governess to the children of a wealthy family. Walking slowly back from the cemetery, we murmured kind things about dear Martha, whose betrothed had flung himself dramatically on her casket before it was lowered into the ground. Then Katherl asked about Franz.

"I don't love him," I admitted with a shrug. "It's as simple as that."

Katherl eyed me shrewdly. "Have you someone else?" she asked, lifting one eyebrow.

I shook my head, but my thoughts flew straight to Joachim, and I couldn't hide the blush in my cheeks.

"You do! I knew it!" Katherl exclaimed, so loudly that some of the mourners turned to frown at us. "Tell us who it is! No secrets, Nannerl! We know you've been away for several days."

But I was not ready to speak of Joachim. He had paid me flattering attention during my visit to his family's castle, and each day since then I hoped that a message might arrive from him, asking to see me. But two weeks had passed, and there'd been no message.

"I'll tell you about it another time," I promised. "Such a conversation is not proper with our friend Martha lying so freshly in her grave."

Reluctantly, they agreed. I had bought myself—and Joachim—a little time. Surely I would hear from him soon.

Chapter 13

ITALY

BOXES OF MUSIC and gifts that Papa and Wolferl had accumulated arrived every week, shipped over the mountains from Milan, a sign our travelers would soon be coming home. The boxes had to be carried up the stairs to our apartment, which was already beginning to feel too small again.

Wolferl's fingers ached so badly from composing hour after hour that he could hardly scribble more than a few words to us. He was working on his new opera, *Mitridate, Rè di Ponto*. It was a serious opera, he said, about a king who faked his own death in battle against the Romans to test the loyalty of his two sons. Both sons failed the test and fell in love with their father's betrothed.

Wolferl had written the choruses and recitatives while they traveled, but he'd left the arias until the principal singers arrived so he could suit his music to their voices. By early December the opera was ready to go into rehearsal, but the Italian tenor who was singing the title role complained about "barbarous German music" and demanded that his arias be rewritten. Wolferl did his best to satisfy him.

Mama dropped strong hints in her letters, asking Papa if it might be possible for us to join them in Italy before they returned to Salzburg. He responded in an icy postscript: "If you are so keen to travel to Italy despite the great costs and hardships, we invite you to the opera at Milan."

Clearly, Papa wasn't at all keen to have us. "I think it would not be wise for us to go after all." Mama sighed. "Unless, of course, your papa changes his mind."

Then, to make matters worse, Papa accused me of neglecting to send congratulations for his name day on November 13. "Indeed, it would not have killed Nannerl to write to me."

"But I *did* write!" I cried. "The letter must not have reached him! And neither he nor Wolferl sent me congratulations on my name day—they were too busy!"

Mama tried to soothe me. "*Liebchen,* put this out of your mind. Remember, we are here, and they are there."

In his next letter, Papa mentioned that my congratulations had arrived after all. But instead of apologizing for his harsh words, he tried to make it sound as though he'd only been joking. I knew he was not. And he said no more about our joining them in Milan. Evidently he hadn't changed his mind. I would have to swallow my disappointment and be satisfied with Papa's descriptions.

MITRIDATE, RÈ DI PONTO had its first performance on the night of December 26, 1770. Dressed in another new suit—this one scarlet, lined in pale blue satin and trimmed with gold braid—Wolferl played the harpsichord and directed sixty players and seven singers. It ran for three hours. The grumblings about German music were all forgotten. "*Viva il maestrino!*" the audience shouted. "Long live the little maestro!" Delighted music lovers gave Wolferl a title of their own: *Il Signor Cavaliere Filarmonico,* Sir Knight of the Philharmonic.

To celebrate Wolferl's success, Salzburgers living in Milan invited him and Papa for a fine dinner, serving Wolferl the food he loved the best: liver dumplings and sauerkraut. "A nice change from pheasant and capon," Papa wrote. Then he added, "How we wished that you and Nannerl could have had the pleasure of seeing the opera!"

Mama stuffed the letter in a drawer with the others and slammed it shut. "Is that not exactly what I tried to persuade him?" she huffed, adding, "'A nice change from pheasant and capon,' indeed! When was the last time you and I had to suffer so?"

———

SOON AFTER WOLFERL'S fifteenth birthday in January our travelers left Milan—not for home, as we'd expected, but for Venice where they lodged with another Salzburg family, the Widers. Frau Wider and her six daughters outdid themselves caring for them, washing their linen, mending their lace cuffs, cooking their favorite dishes, and generally spoiling them.

Wolferl gleefully described the sisters' attempt to seize him by the arms and legs and swing him back and forth, bumping his backside against the floor—apparently a Venetian tradition. "Somehow," Wolferl wrote, "I managed to escape."

Papa was upset by the goings-on. With young ladies behaving so boldly, he declared Venice "the most dangerous place in all Italy" and rushed to get Wolferl out of there before one of the Wider sisters succeeded in seducing him. They visited Verona and Padua and several other cities before struggling home through spring snowstorms, arriving on Holy Thursday, the twenty-eighth of March 1771. They'd been away for almost sixteen months.

Mama and I rushed into their arms, weeping for joy. But Papa walked with a limp, and Wolferl had dark circles under his eyes. Mama had bought a bottle of wine to celebrate the homecoming, and that night there was no sleep for anyone.

Wolferl could not stop staring at my new coiffure. "Like a ship setting out to sea," Wolferl said. "But how do you sleep?"

"Sitting up," I told him. "I've gotten used to it."

Friends came by to welcome them, and we stayed up late, listening to their stories. Wolferl showed off the Order of the Golden Spur awarded by the pope, and Papa endlessly repeated the story of the antiphon and Wolferl's acceptance into the Accademia Filarmonica. Even more dramatic was his description of Good Friday services at the Sistine Chapel: "As the altar candles were extinguished one by one, the choir sang the solemn *Miserere*—music never written down and one of Rome's best-guarded secrets. But Wolferl memorized all the parts and wrote down every note the minute we returned to our inn." Then Papa passed around the score of the "secret" music.

I had grown thoroughly weary of it and felt I could not smile at their stories even one more time. They seemed uninterested in *our* stories. Papa was more imperious than ever, issuing directives to Mama and me as though we were servants. If I hadn't been so happy to see Wolferl, I might have wished them gone again.

THEY'D SCARCELY UNPACKED before Papa began talking about another trip to Italy. Wolferl had been invited to compose a serenata for the wedding of Archduke Ferdinand, who had once caught my eye and smiled. The archduke was to marry Princess Maria Beatrice d'Este in October. Papa planned to leave for Milan in mid-August.

"A brief journey," Papa said. "We'll stay for several performances and return home at once."

This time I was determined not to be left behind. Papa
said the journey would be brief—how expensive could that
be? I started thinking of what gowns I would need. My
biggest worry was finding a capable friseur in Milan.

As usual when my brother was around, the mood was
brighter. Friends called nearly every day. Wolferl taught us
all to play *boccia,* a game of bowls played with wooden balls
that he'd learned in Rome. He'd brought decks of cards
with pictures of animals, fruits, flowers, and other things,
and introduced us to *Mercante in fiera*—"The Merchant at
the Fair"—a sort of gambling game played for small coins.
Wolferl always insisted on being the merchant, and he always managed to make it exciting.

He'd race up the stairs, shouting, "Come, Horseface, let's
make music!" And no matter what I was doing, I would
drop it and sit down at the clavichord.

We took turns—Wolferl would play a melodic line, cry,
"Now you!" and I'd improvise on it. Then he'd improvise
on my improvisation. "Next!" he'd command, and then it
was up to me to invent a melody. This was great fun, but
it was also much more than fun—it was our way of relat-
ing to each other, of once again becoming two halves of
the same whole. Papa didn't understand that or didn't
think it important, and he often put a stop to what

he considered foolery when Wolferl had so much work to do.

Wolferl was writing at top speed, composing two symphonies and another short opera in honor of the fiftieth anniversary of Archbishop Schrattenbach's ordination as a priest. This opera would be performed in January. "If I don't get it done now, the geese will bite me on the backside when we come back from Milan."

"When you say *we,* do you mean just you and Papa?" I asked. Papa had so far said nothing, and my doubts about being included were building like storm clouds over the Mönchsberg.

Wolferl drummed his fingers. "I don't really know, Nannerl. But here's a bit of advice from your old brother: Don't start asking him about it. Then the answer is sure to be no."

WOLFERL LOVED to tease me about the young men who escorted me, and he pretended to be more concerned about them than he was about *me.* "What a great flirt you've become, as well as a great beauty—and take it from me, a connoisseur of feminine attractiveness. All six of the adorably pretty Wider sisters together wouldn't hold a candle to you! You are breaking hearts, dear sister," he said, sternly wagging a finger. "Dozens of pocket handkerchiefs are soaking up buckets of tears being shed for you."

"Not true!" I protested, laughing it off. I had not become a "great flirt," as Wolferl claimed, although I was no longer the shy, tongue-tied girl of earlier years. As to being a "great beauty," I was well aware of men's admiring glances.

Franz von Mölk still came by, more out of habit, I thought, than love. I liked Franz, but I wished he'd find someone else. Joachim von Schiedenhofen was the only one who truly shared my passion for music. We had met two or three times to arrange Haydn's music for clavier, and at the end of these sessions I'd accompanied him while he sang. But so far he had not indicated any amorous interest, and that was a big disappointment. There were a few others who sought my company, but none interested me. Something seemed to be lacking in all of my prospects.

"You're waiting for the perfect man," Katherl commented, and she was close to the mark. "Let me tell you something, Nannerl. He doesn't exist!"

And she should know. Katherina Gilowsky, a year older than I, had set out with grim determination to catch a husband, with no results so far. She'd become something of a joke in our circle. Maybe it was the grimness that kept them away, for she was certainly attractive enough. I wondered if she might again turn her attention to Franz.

The Mölks were close friends of my parents. Their family included Franz's younger sister, Barbara, whom we all called Waberl but Wolferl called Babette. I knew Waberl rather well, since she was sometimes with our group when

I'd gone sledding with her brother. A lively girl with a pert, turned-up nose, she adored the French name bestowed on her by my worldly brother, and the two had become fast friends. Mama smiled benignly on the pair, but it got on Papa's nerves. I saw how he watched them and fretted when they disappeared after Waberl/Babette had entertained us by playing, more or less competently, a few pretty minuets. *Any* girl would have worried Papa. He did not want his genius son to be distracted.

Wolferl was fifteen but small for his age, and people — especially Papa—often treated him as though he were much younger. Papa blamed Fräulein von Mölk for enticing Wolferl into a relationship he was not ready for. I thought Papa was wrong. My brother had always hungered for the kisses lavished on him by powdered and perfumed noblewomen, but I was sure those were not the kinds of kisses he wanted now.

Viktoria and Katherl and I discussed the situation. Opinions were divided. Viktoria was not fond of Waberl. "She's much older than he is," she pointed out. "She's at least nineteen—four years older than Wolferl. And she puts on airs."

Katherl was more accepting. "Your brother is a charming fellow," she said thoughtfully. "And he's becoming quite famous. Is there a music lover left in Europe who hasn't heard of him? He may not be tall or even handsome—the pockmarks are unfortunate—but he'll always be able to have any girl he wants. Our little Waberl is just the first of many. Many!"

PAPA HADN'T definitely said Mama and I were *not* going to Italy, and so I clung to the hope that he intended to take us. I didn't dare to ask him myself—Wolferl had already discouraged me about that. Instead, I asked Mama, who agreed with Wolferl. "Don't speak of it to him," she warned. "You'll just irritate him."

Unable to bear it any longer, I ignored their advice. I knelt at Papa's feet and begged him to allow me to go. "Don't be childish, my dear Maria Anna," Papa said, using my formal name. He was frowning, impatient to have this unpleasant conversation at an end. His tone chilled my heart.

"But Papa," I pleaded, "ever since you came back at Easter, I've been asking in my nightly prayers that you'll see fit to take me with you. Mama, too." I still felt guilty about my earlier selfishness and disloyalty and was not about to again suggest leaving Mama at home.

Papa gave me a severe look. "If you wish to be invited to perform in Salzburg and elsewhere, you must remain here and attend to your practicing. What's more, it's time that you take on a few pupils and bring in a little income, instead of spending every spare kreuzer on your hair."

His words stung, and I must have looked as wounded as I felt, for his voice softened a little. "We must all put aside our individual wishes and make whatever sacrifices are necessary to further Wolferl's career. Remember, it is all for the good of the Family Mozart. Do you understand, Nannerl?"

I nodded, but I wondered exactly what Papa hoped to gain by our sacrifices. I knew he hoped for well-paid positions for Wolferl and himself, but I sensed he wanted more. Glory, perhaps? Whatever it was, I felt as though a heavy door had been slammed shut and locked. I knew I shouldn't blame Wolferl. It wasn't his fault. He knew nothing of the details of the journey that Papa was arranging. He wasn't permitted to worry about where they'd find their next meal or where they'd sleep each night. Wolferl's head was overflowing with music; Papa took care of everything else. Maybe I shouldn't blame Wolferl, but I did. Couldn't he *see*? Or didn't he care?

To console myself I bought a beautiful little yellow bird in a handsome bamboo cage, named him Herr Canary, and made up my mind to teach him to sing.

I WATCHED GLUMLY as Papa prepared for the journey. Wolferl managed to find me alone and asked if I would carry secret messages to Fräulein von Mölk, his "very favorite mademoiselle."

"I'll write in French," he said.

"Does Waberl read French?" I asked.

He frowned. "I don't know. I'll have to find out."

"Why don't you just send them to her yourself?" I asked, annoyed. "Why must I be your messenger?"

"Because Papa would not allow it, if he found out—you know that yourself, Nannerl," he said. "Papa doesn't want me to be distracted by thoughts of girls. You should have seen him when we were in Venice, and those silly Wider daughters were chasing me around. I received a stern lecture from him that lasted almost the whole way back to Salzburg. He told me he knew I had reached a very dangerous age, but I must exercise the utmost discipline and not allow myself even to think of—well, you know what. But I confess to you that I think of it all the time! Even when I'm in the company of the most proper and ladylike of girls! I have no intention of misbehaving—I just want to exchange a few tokens of affection with Babette. And for that I need your help, dear sister."

So, naturally, I said I would—it was my small way of defying Papa—and Wolferl gave me a little note sealed with wax. "*S'il vous plaît*—please—deliver this to Babette."

"Why do you call her Babette?" I asked, putting the note in my pocket. "Everyone calls her Waberl."

"Because it's French, and French is the language of love."

I rolled my eyes. "But you must promise to do something

for me, Wolferl," I said. "There's sure to be another journey after this one. Convince Papa to let me come with you."

"You've given me a hard assignment," he said doubtfully. "You know how Papa is. I haven't the slightest influence over him in even the smallest matter. I just do as he says."

Even though he was the chosen one, Wolferl was as much a prisoner of Papa's domination as I was.

Chapter 14

FACING THE FUTURE

MAMA AND I STOOD arm in arm in Getreidegasse, watching and waving as Papa and Wolferl drove away. The sun shone brightly—it was mid-August—and we dabbed the tears from our perspiring faces. The carriage rounded a corner and disappeared. "Try not to be so unhappy, *Liebchen,*" Mama said.

"I'm angry, Mama," I said. "I wanted so much to go!"

"Then try not to be so angry." She cupped my face in her hands. "It will spoil your beauty and make you look old."

Once again Mama and I arranged our lives around the mail, waiting for letters and hurrying to have our own ready in time for the twice-weekly post to Italy. It was a chore. I disliked writing letters and Mama also claimed not to enjoy it, but Papa insisted on a report of the smallest details of our daily lives. Everything they wrote to us about Italy sounded so much more interesting than anything happening in Salzburg.

The text for the serenata hadn't yet arrived from the librettist, and nothing could be done until it did—no choruses or recitatives written, no dances choreographed, no costumes stitched, no scenery painted. But "twenty thousand pounds of wax candles" (Papa liked to exaggerate) had arrived to illuminate the cathedral for the archduke's wedding.

The practical problems didn't bother Wolferl. He was more concerned that I remember to deliver his regards to his "favorite mademoiselle." He instructed me to tell the mademoiselle that he longed to be back in Salzburg, if only to receive once more such a present as he was given at her concert.

"She will know what I mean," he wrote. He signed it *Amadé*.

I knew what he meant, too—and I wondered at Fräulein von Mölk's generosity with her kisses. I sent her a note, and she responded with an invitation to visit. Dressed in my old striped afternoon dress, I went the next day to the Mölks' home near St. Sebastian's Church and sat with Waberl in the parlor. The maid brought coffee and pastries.

Nibbling a marzipan pastry, which I found a bit stale, I wickedly prolonged her wait for news of her devoted admirer. Instead, I passed on a nice piece of gossip from Papa's most recent letter. "Did you know," I asked, "that the empress was quite concerned that Archduke Ferdinand might not be pleased with his new bride? The princess is not at all beautiful, you know."

Waberl arched one plucked eyebrow. "And what have you heard?" she asked, leaning forward eagerly. It was obvious that Waberl painted her lips. I did, too, of course, although I took pains that it not seem obvious.

"I've heard he's entirely pleased, and they're very happy with each other. Papa says Princess Beatrice is friendly, agreeable, and virtuous, and everyone loves her, even the archduke."

"Fortunate woman," Waberl said, dabbing delicately at her too-red lips. "And has Wolfgang made any observations about the royal couple?"

"*Nein,*" I replied. I couldn't resist adding mischievously, "Has he told you about his proposal to Archduchess Maria Antonia long before she married the dauphin of France and changed her name to Marie Antoinette?"

"He has not!" she exclaimed, nearly dropping her spoon. "I beg you to tell me about it!"

I recounted the tale of our visit to the imperial family at Schönbrunn Palace years ago, when my brother and the archduchess were young children. He'd slipped and fallen, she'd helped him up, and he'd told her, "When we're grown up, I shall marry you!"

Waberl smiled sweetly. "He seems to have missed his opportunity."

"Or she missed hers," I said.

I decided to end her suspense and drew out the sealed letter. "Wolferl asked me to give you this message: 'Tell Fräulein von Mölk that I am longing to be back in Salzburg if only to receive once more such a present as I was given at her concert. *She will know what I mean.*'"

I pronounced the words with careful emphasis, and then I paused, helping myself to another pastry and allowing Waberl time to blush deeply. "I gather that you understand his meaning?" I asked, widening my eyes and pretending innocence.

"*Ja, ja,* I do. I understand," she said, gazing down at her lap.

When the visit ended, I rushed off to the Adlgasser house to tell Viktoria how Mademoiselle Babette had received the message. But Viktoria was in a foul mood, having just been in another argument with her stepmother. Little sister Anna wailed loudly, and little brother Josef scowled and stomped off.

"Never mind them." Viktoria sighed. "Tell me what happened."

I described the scene, down to the stale marzipan. "At least Waberl had the decency to blush."

"I've always felt she was a bit too free with her expressions of affection," Viktoria observed. "I have no proof of this, of course. It's just a feeling."

"Proof is never a necessity in such matters," I said in an attempt to lighten her mood. But she didn't smile. It was a relief to escape the unhappy Adlgasser household.

WOLFERL HAD TO WAIT eight days for the libretto to arrive in Milan, and he had only three and a half weeks to write all of the music, including sixteen choruses, several ballets and contredanses, and innumerable arias—an amazing achievement. In the end everything went well, and *Ascanio in Alba* was performed two days after the archduke's wedding.

A famous German musician, Johann Hasse, had been commissioned to write a more serious piece for the occasion. Hasse's work was applauded politely enough, but Wolferl's had received shouts of *"Bravissimo, maestro!"* from the bridal party and many others as well. It didn't hurt that the characters in *Ascanio* symbolized members of the imperial family: Ascanio, future king of Alba, represented the archduke; his bride, Silvia, represented Princess Beatrice; and Venus, Ascanio's mother, was of course Empress Maria Theresia.

Papa couldn't keep from gloating when he described the audience's reaction. Wolferl was more sympathetic: "One had to feel sorry for poor old Hasse when the audience threw flowers at the end of my little serenata." Papa added that courtiers and others constantly stopped them in the streets to offer congratulations.

If only Papa had not made it sound as though he had done us a great favor by leaving us at home, describing the insufferable heat and wretched entertainments we would have had to tolerate! And if only he had not issued the most irritating instructions for ordering the new clothes Mama told him we needed.

"Do not buy inferior materials, since to buy shoddy stuff is no economy," he wrote, as though Mama had no more common sense than a cabbage. "Wear your clothes from Vienna for everyday and save the new dresses for festivals and special occasions."

Mama seemed not to be offended by his advice, but it annoyed *me* no end. To put it out of mind, I turned my attention to teaching Herr Canary to sing. Without Wolferl, my only musical conversations were with my little yellow bird.

WOLFERL WAS PAID WELL for *Ascanio,* and the archduke gave him a watch set with diamonds. But still he and Papa didn't come home. "The opera has been performed several times," I remarked to Mama. "Why are they lingering?"

"Your father hopes that Archduke Ferdinand will offer a position to Wolferl," Mama explained, "and maybe to himself, too. If the conversation goes well, it could mean we'd all move to Milan. You wouldn't object to that, would you, Nannerl?"

Papa described his plan in his latest letter, written in a cipher, one letter of the alphabet substituting for another, to get his messages past the archbishop's censors and keep Schrattenbach from finding out he was looking for employment elsewhere. I deciphered the message and easily imagined the possibility of advancing my musical career in Milan.

WHILE PAPA and Wolferl waited for an audience with the archduke, Mama and I accepted a second invitation to Triebenbach from Joachim von Schiedenhofen and his mother. My hopes rose that something might yet come of this friendship.

Our five days in the country were a lot like our visit the year before: promenading by the lake, shooting air guns at targets, playing a few of my own compositions to entertain the other guests, which this time included a vivacious young lady named Anna Daubrawa von Daubrawaick and her aristocratic parents.

Later I accompanied Joachim while he sang. I sensed something had changed. He was courteous and friendly, but the easy intimacy between us was gone. He said no more about the two of us arranging more of Haydn's music for the clavier. When we did spend a few moments alone, all he wanted to talk about was my brother and his music, but not a word about mine. And when I happened upon Joachim and Fräulein Daubrawa and saw how he gazed into her eyes, I recognized that my hopes were in vain.

I was mostly silent, lost in thought, on the ride back to Salzburg. Mama reached over and took my hand. "You believe he's in love with her, don't you?" she asked. I nodded, unable to speak. Mama sighed. "Ach, *Liebling*, I'm afraid you're right." She pulled me close and let me weep on her breast as though I were a child again.

BY THE MIDDLE OF December, Papa and Wolferl were back in Salzburg, bringing some good news, some bad. Wolferl had received another commission, a new opera for Carnival in Milan the following year—a third trip to Italy—but Archduke Ferdinand had not offered Wolferl a permanent position. Then, just one day after they returned, before we'd even had time to celebrate their homecoming, Archbishop Schrattenbach dropped dead.

His death was a shock to everyone. We mourned, for Schrattenbach had been proud of Wolferl's feats and mostly supportive of the family travels. No one had any idea who would succeed him. Papa wondered what sort of arrangement he would make with the next man to hold the office. Weeks later Hieronymus Colloredo was elected prince-archbishop of Salzburg. Knowing the new archbishop's reputation for arrogance, Papa guessed that Colloredo would not be a great friend of the Mozarts, and he was more determined than ever to find paying positions somewhere else—*anywhere* else—for himself and Wolferl. Our future had never felt more uncertain.

In whatever way I was to make my life as a musician, a performer, a keyboard player, I understood my help would have to come from some other quarter. Not from the new archbishop. Not from Papa. My best hope now lay with my brother and his continuing success.

One afternoon when Mama and Wolferl had gone out, Papa and I were alone in the apartment. Papa was writing letters, and I sat by the window, whistling a little tune for Herr Canary. Papa laid aside his quill and pulled up a chair across from me. "The time has come to discuss your prospects, Nannerl," he said gravely.

There was no escaping. I continued to sit by the window, my hands clasped in my lap, my cheeks burning, while Papa outlined what my life was to be. I must begin earning income for the family, he said. Since I had done nothing to find a few pupils, he would endeavor to find them for me. I must practice more so that I might be invited to do occasional performances—nothing too difficult or demanding; he could arrange that as well. And we would all pray that I'd soon find a man willing to support me, and marry him.

I listened silently as Papa described the difficulties he foresaw if he had to provide not only for a wife but for an unmarried daughter as well. After all, he was no longer a young man, and he worried about how I would live.

"So, Nannerl," he inquired, "has no suitable young man come courting?"

I thought of Franz, who had once been in love with me but was now rumored to be courting another girl. I thought, painfully, of Joachim, who I'd hoped would fall in love with me but now had eyes for someone with a pretty, heart-shaped face and an unmusical name. I could have counted off a half dozen others who had danced with me, smiled at me, enjoyed bantering conversations with me, but hadn't asked to call on me.

"*Nein,* Papa," I said.

Papa gazed at me for an uncomfortably long time, as though he might discern why it was that his daughter had so far failed to find a proper mate. "Perhaps you have not yet made up your mind you want a husband. It's time you do, Nannerl."

"But I'm still young, Papa—only twenty! Surely there is yet time to make a musical career before I settle down to marriage."

"You must be realistic!" Papa rose from his chair and towered above me. "You will not be young forever. Do not continue to deceive yourself. The kind of career you think you want is not possible for you. You must accept that and proceed accordingly."

Papa returned to his letter writing. I sat perfectly still, nursing my pain, my mind ticking slowly, like a run-down clock. No one spoke. Herr Canary was silent. Then I heard Mama on the stairs. In a daze I rose and went out to help her with her parcels.

Chapter 15

THE TANZMEISTERHAUS

I LOVED HAVING WOLFERL at home. My brother was as necessary to me as my thumbs.

To honor my name day and my twenty-first birthday in July, Wolferl composed a sonata duet. The ink was scarcely dry before we were seated side by side at our new harpsichord, trying out his newest composition—one of his best, both witty and tender. Neither the Primo nor the Secondo part dominated, and this pleased me because I understood that he still saw us as equal players. And he wrote them so that our hands were constantly crossing, my left over his right, then his right over my left, fluidly interlacing. But I soon found I had trouble keeping up with the dazzling finger work. My fingers had grown stiff during the months Wolferl was gone. He didn't mention my clumsiness, except to say, "A little practice is all you need." My brother might tease me about almost anything, but he never said a critical word about my keyboard technique. I adored him for that.

Despite constant urging from Papa, I had lost the desire and the discipline to practice keyboard exercises for hours each day to keep up my skills, although I still loved to play. After a few months I had given up the singing lessons as well. *Why bother?* I thought. I was apparently going to be stuck in Salzburg for the rest of my life. With Schratten-bach dead, an unsympathetic man in the archbishop's Residenz, and no one actively promoting me, I saw little chance for a real career in music.

Instead of practicing, I read, did a little needlework, and walked the terrier we got to take the place of poor old Bimperl, who'd died. We named this new dog Bim-perl, too.

LATE IN OCTOBER of 1772 Wolferl and Papa left on their third journey to Italy to prepare another opera for Milan's Carnival season. I had no expectation that Mama and I would be included on this journey or even invited to attend. By now I knew Papa's arguments: It was too expensive, too difficult, too hot, or too cold. I didn't bother to try to counter these arguments. This time I was relieved to see Papa go, and Wolferl—the continuing reminder of my own lack of success—with him.

Over the summer Wolferl had lost his romantic interest

in Waberl von Mölk—Babette—and found a new "favorite mademoiselle." This one was Maria Theresia Barisani, a daughter of the court physician. Wolferl had scarcely arrived in Milan when he wrote, begging me to visit "a certain young lady" to give her his compliments.

The Barisanis lived in a large house on the grounds of the palace belonging to the Lodrons, one of Salzburg's most prominent families. I bowed my head against the chill winds sweeping down the Salzach and hurried across the bridge to the New Town. Theresia greeted me with enthusiastic kisses. I managed to persuade the girl to cease her giggling and simpering long enough for me to deliver Wolferl's message. *What could he have found attractive in this child?* I wondered, when at last I could free myself to rush out into the cold again.

DURING THIS ABSENCE my ever-playful brother went to the trouble of sending me one of his zaniest letters. He'd written it around midnight, after he'd stopped composing for the day. Every other line was upside down, so that I had to keep turning the letter, first this way then that, to get the sense of it. There wasn't much sense to it, even rightside up. He ended it, "Farewell, my little lung. I kiss you, my liver, and remain as always, my stomach, your unworthy frater/brother, Wolfgang."

A few weeks later he sent another, the words so jumbled that I copied them out in columns to decipher the message. This was followed by a letter entirely in Italian, in which Wolferl was now fluent, and I had to puzzle it out however I could. Still another was made up of a single long, complicated sentence. He signed another, *Oidda, Gnagflow Trazom*—"Addio, Wolfgang Mozart," spelled backward. These wildly absurd letters must have been a relief from the pressure under which he worked.

His new dramatic opera, *Lucio Silla,* based on the story of a Roman dictator in love with the daughter of his archenemy, had its first performance the day after Christmas. Archduke Ferdinand came late and, since they couldn't start without him, kept the audience waiting in a stuffy opera house for several hours. With its three ballets the whole thing lasted more than six hours. Still, it went off splendidly: the prima donna was spectacular, the famous castrato sang brilliantly, and at the end people leaped up and shouted *"Viva maestrino!"* and women blew kisses.

WE EXPECTED PAPA and Wolferl to come home as soon as the opera had been performed, but Papa suddenly began to complain of an attack of rheumatism, which kept him from traveling. In letter after letter he described his suffering; he couldn't use his right arm and was almost completely crippled (but he didn't explain how he could still write such long letters). At the end he added a note in the family cipher telling Mama not to worry, he was perfectly fine. It was all a ruse to keep Archbishop Colloredo from learning that Papa was still trying to get appointments for himself and Wolferl in Milan or Florence.

But all that deception came to nothing. There were no positions available. Papa and Wolferl arrived home on the thirteenth of March 1773, exactly one day before the anniversary of Colloredo's election as prince-archbishop. It would have gone badly indeed for Papa if he had not returned in time for the celebration.

At seventeen Wolferl could no longer be called a *Wunderkind,* and hardly anyone still spoke of him as a prodigy, but he was certainly a virtuoso—and a restless one. He continually asked Papa when they might make another journey. Papa, also restless, agreed to make a trip to Vienna to petition Empress Maria Theresia for a post for Wolferl. Mama and I were again told to stay at home. Mama pleaded that we deserved to go; and she didn't give up, even after Papa and Wolferl left Salzburg in July.

She wrote to Papa, "It would be minimally expensive because we have received invitations from two different sets of friends, both eager to have us enjoy their hospitality."

One of the invitations had come from Dr. Franz Anton Mesmer, owner of the glass harmonica. I would have loved the chance to play it. But Papa used the fact that we had *two* invitations as a reason *not* to allow us to come. "Accepting the invitation of one will surely put the other out of sorts."

Now I understood perfectly: My father *enjoyed* traveling without Mama and me. We would have interfered with his ability to live like the aristocrat he wanted to be. Couldn't she see that? If she did, it must have hurt too much to talk about it.

ON PAPA'S ORDERS I accepted two young girls as pupils. The more talented one—this was not saying much—was Mademoiselle Zezi, the sweet-faced daughter of a grocer who kept a shop nearby on Getreidegasse. The other, Antonia Weiser, was taking lessons only because her wealthy merchant father insisted. She seemed so lacking in both the most basic musical talent and the most basic interest that I was reluctant to accept the fees her father paid.

By the end of September, Papa and Wolferl were back from Vienna, having failed again in their quest to secure a position for Wolferl at the imperial court. The explanation was always the same: There were no positions available, and plenty of older, more experienced musicians were ready to move into any vacancy that might open up. Papa seemed resigned to staying in Salzburg.

At last the new archbishop granted my brother a salary—a very small one—in recognition of his title as Konzertmeister, and Papa decided we could afford to move to larger quarters. He arranged to rent a large apartment in the Tanzmeisterhaus, the Dancing-Master's House, in the new part of town across the river from Getreidegasse.

I loved the Tanzmeisterhaus. Our eight rooms on the

first floor above the ground floor included an elegant salon with tall windows overlooking a pretty square, Hannibalplatz. I had a large room all to myself with a nice bed, a clothes chest with almost enough space for my dresses and hats, and a little sofa upholstered in red velvet. It was my idea to use the salon for our Sunday afternoon target-shooting contests, a favorite Salzburg pastime. Mama now had space for a large cage in which to keep several kinds of finches and Herr Canary. In the back of the house was a courtyard garden, which Wolferl declared ideal for playing *boccía*. Even Bimperl had a little patch there to call her own.

The Tanzmeisterhaus stood across from Holy Trinity Church with its two graceful towers. The large wings of the church housed the Collegium Virgilianum, the Knights' Academy, where the sons of the wealthy nobility were sent to be educated. The apartment was also near the grand palace of the high-ranking Lodron family—"Count Potbelly," as we called Ernst von Lodron, and his wife, who had established herself as Archbishop Colloredo's most influential hostess. I couldn't bear the countess; I found her haughty and not at all to be trusted, and her four daughters were spoiled brats. But with such neighbors we had clearly risen in the world.

Wolferl continued to compose at a dizzying pace. In fifteen months following his last trip to Vienna he completed—among other things—several symphonies and concertos, assorted church music for the archbishop, a sonata, and a serenata. And he'd made a good start on another opera, *La finta giardiniera,* "The Pretend Garden-Girl."

"This is the silliest libretto yet," Wolferl told me. "The most important event happens a year before the action begins—the count stabs his beloved in a fit of passion. He thinks she's dead, but she's not. She disguises herself as a gardener and goes looking for him. From then on, everything is complete madness. But it ends happily."

"He stabs her and it ends happily? How can it?" I asked doubtfully.

"Because I'm writing the music," he said, laughing, and pinched my cheek.

In the midst of his frenzied composing he managed to find a new ladylove. This particular *Jungfrau* happened to be Fräulein Antonia Weiser, the wealthy merchant's lazy daughter to whom I'd had the dubious honor of giving lessons. Wolferl swore me to secrecy—Papa must not know. How he could handle even a mild love affair, given that Papa was hanging over him night and day, I could not imagine. Somehow he did.

Wolferl was happiest when he was composing. It was as if he were in a trance, literally seeing and hearing nothing but the music in his head. But he had an uncanny ability to shift from being deeply engrossed in his work to being completely zany. Unpredictable as quicksilver, one minute he was joking, punning, warbling scandalous songs, and arranging a secret rendezvous with Fräulein Weiser. Then like a wizard with the ability to change shape, in the next instant he was transformed into a serious, disciplined composer again.

Papa was barely able to tolerate those lightning-quick shifts and gave him no respite. "You must work harder, Wolferl. It's important that you have many different types of music to show any potential employers."

I did understand Papa's worries: How was my father going to earn a living, provide for a family, and secure Wolfgang's future? All of us were called upon to make sacrifices, he reminded us, and in general I agreed. But it seemed to me that Mama and I were making the biggest sacrifices. I felt abandoned by Papa. I knew that I had only myself to blame for my stiffening fingers and my vanishing virtuosity. But what need did I have to practice, when it seemed unlikely I would ever again be given a chance to perform before an important audience?

My social life in Salzburg was lackluster. No young men came to call on me. I saw Viktoria and Katherl when I could and listened to their sometimes tiresome chatter with only half an ear. Viktoria was miserable—she'd come to despise her stepmother and feuded with her endlessly. Katherl had still not managed to snare a husband and was extremely jealous of our friend Liserl Haffner, who had recently become engaged to marry.

"She isn't even such a beauty," Katherl complained petulantly.

"But she's rich," Viktoria pointed out.

"Money makes up for lack of beauty," I said. "We all know that."

PAPA, MEANWHILE, was making plans for a journey to Munich at Carnival for the performance of Wolferl's new comic opera, *La finta giardiniera*—"The Pretend Garden-Girl"—the one beginning with a stabbing. This time, plans could possibly include me—or possibly not. I was desperate to go. I hadn't been to a city since our journey to Vienna five years earlier. I hadn't even been out of Salzburg since Mama and I made our two visits to the Schiedenhofen country estate.

"I'll go mad here if I don't soon have a chance to travel," I told Wolferl.

"I feel exactly as you do, Nannerl," Wolferl said. "I used to love Salzburg, but now I can't wait to get away from it. One could suffocate here! With luck we'll both have a chance to leave."

It was not so simple. The problem, Papa explained, was that if both Mama and I went along to Munich and all four Mozarts were absent from Salzburg, then Archbishop Colloredo might conclude—correctly—that the family had gone to search for a new situation. And that was the wrong message to send the archbishop.

Papa decided Mama must stay at home to keep up appearances. This created a different problem: Without

Mama, it would be difficult, perhaps impossible, to arrange proper accommodations for me. Finally Papa agreed that I might join him and Wolferl in Munich if respectable lodgings could be found and if an inexpensive way could be arranged for me to travel. If, *if*, IF!

This time I didn't shed a single tear when Papa and Wolferl left. This time I resolved that somehow I, too, would go to Munich.

Part 3

WOLFGANG
1775

Chapter 16

MUNICH

FOR WEEKS ALL I thought about was Munich. There was sure to be lots of music in addition to Wolferl's opera, and I knew my brother and I would find plenty to entertain us, if the practical problems could be solved.

Mama got in touch with a friend, Josef Gschwendner, who invited me to travel in his chaise with another family friend, Frau Robinig, and her daughter. All planned to attend the performance of my brother's opera. Papa would be pleased—it would cost us absolutely nothing. But Herr Gschwendner was uncertain when he would leave Salzburg, it was uncertain when Wolferl's opera would have its first performance, and all of this uncertainty added up to having everything undecided until the last moment.

Papa wrote from Munich on the ninth of December

and again five days later, saying no suitable accommoda-
tion had yet been found for me. On post days my mood
swung up and down, depending on Papa's latest letter.
Mama, always philosophical and resigned, tried to convince me everything would work out. But Mama was not
twenty-three and eager to enjoy something more than
dreary old Salzburg had to offer.

At last Papa secured a room with a respectable young
widow who had even offered to provide a clavichord so
I could practice for any performances I might be invited
to give.

"Frau von Durst is very quiet and retiring," Papa wrote,
"and does not care for the society of philanderers."

"Listen to this," I told Katherl and Viktoria, waving
Papa's letter. "Frau von Durst fears I might attract the
wrong sort of male visitors!"

"You should be flattered, Nannerl," Viktoria said. "She
must imagine you're a seductress of the most dangerous
sort."

"A femme fatale," Katherl added with a sly wink.

And that set us all laughing—even Viktoria.

Each post day brought fresh instructions from Papa and
a long list of music he wanted me to pack. Also, would I
remember to bring him a supply of Spanish snuff from a
particular snuffbox? And some sort of costume for me to
wear to the Carnival balls?

He lectured at tedious length about how silly it was of

me not to be able to do my own hair or make up my own face without assistance. The only person who could comb my hair as it should be—aside from the friseur—was Viktoria, and Mama always helped with cosmetics. Too bad I couldn't take them with me to Munich! My solution was to instruct the friseur to create a coiffure that would survive the journey. I would somehow have to manage the cosmetics myself.

A FEW DAYS BEFORE I was to leave, I received a cryptic note from Wolferl. "Don't forget to keep your promise to pay the call we both know of. I beg you to convey my greetings there, in the most tender fashion."

I knew what he meant. And so, with everything else I had to do to get ready for my journey, I hurried off to call on my brother's latest ladylove. Fräulein Weiser had quickly lost favor, and Mademoiselle Zezi, another of my clavier pupils, now held his heart in the grasp of her clumsy fingers.

That afternoon I seated myself in the grocer's parlor. Mademoiselle Zezi smiled charmingly when I conveyed my brother's messages. Then, to make conversation, I described my plans for the journey. "I must bring a costume to wear to the fancy dress balls, and I haven't the least idea what to take," I told her. "Do you suppose a peasant dress would do?"

"I have just the thing for you!" cried Mademoiselle Zezi,

who was far more skilled with the needle than with the keyboard and had sewn several clever costumes for herself. Her favorite, made for last year's Carnival, was the costume of an Amazon, a female warrior of Greek mythology, but her father had felt it was too startling for staid Salzburg and forbade her to wear it. "It would surely create quite a stir in Munich," she said, and insisted I try it on.

The simple gown of white fabric fell in soft folds, and a pasteboard shield and wooden spear completed the theme. "How glamorous you are, Fräulein Mozart!" Mademoiselle Zezi sighed. "How elegant!"

"Papa may not approve," I murmured, turning this way and that in front of the looking glass and admiring the effect. The costume made me look taller and emphasized my bosom.

As I prepared to leave with her costume, Mademoiselle Zezi suddenly kissed her fingertips and placed them lightly on my lips. "Give this to Wolferl for me," she whispered. Then she turned and ran back into the grocer's house, and I hurried home carrying the makings of a warrior.

On the day before our departure I took my felt boots to Herr Gschwendner's house to warm them by his stove, per Papa's instructions, and arranged to have a friend keep watch over my keyboard pupils. Mama promised to look after Herr Canary.

The only problem now was my baggage. Papa had said that I must pack everything in one box, but that was hardly possible with everything he'd wanted me to bring, and all the dresses and caps and so on that I needed. With Mama's help I wrapped the Amazon's shield and spear in canvas and buried the bundle in the straw spread on the floor of the carriage for warmth.

I left Salzburg in Herr Gschwendner's open chaise, swaddled from head to foot in furs with a woolen scarf over my face, a fur rug spread on my lap, and my feet in foot bags of wolf's fur over the felt boots. I could scarcely move. Despite the extreme cold, I felt quite comfortable. No longer could Papa use the argument, as he had in the past, that I would not be able to stand the cold.

WE ARRIVED IN MUNICH the next day, and Herr Gschwendner delivered me to the widow's home. She was a young woman, small and dark haired, dressed in stark black. She showed me to a little room with a narrow bed that left just enough space for the clavier. I much preferred the main parlor overlooking the lively market square. Frau von Durst's little yapping dog perched on a large cushion by the window. At last, I was back in a big city!

Within hours I was drinking coffee with Wolferl and catching up on the gossip. My brother, that *Spitzbube*—that rogue—was most interested in my report on Mademoiselle Zezi. "Tell me every little thing she said during your visit," he ordered. "Describe how she breathed, whether her corset was drawn too tight, everything!" I answered his questions and passed on the greeting from Mademoiselle Zezi, exactly as she'd delivered it to me, kissing my fingertips and placing them on Wolferl's lips. He pretended to swoon.

No matter what Papa thought, my first stop in Munich had to be the salon of the best friseur I could find. Forced to choose between preserving my neck and ears from freezing or preserving the hairstyle created for the journey, I had chosen warmth, and my coiffure was smashed nearly flat and somewhat lopsided. The damage must be repaired.

Frau von Durst looked down her prim widow's nose at such an indulgence, but I succeeded in convincing her that she, too, might enjoy a little of the friseur's artistry. I'm sure she feared I was leading her down the path to ruin, inviting the company of philanderers, but in the end she seemed pleased with the results. And we began to talk together more easily.

LA FINTA GIARDINIERA was performed a week later. As Wolferl told me earlier, the plot seemed silly and the characters quite mad, but the music was sublime, Wolferl's lovely arias wringing emotion from everyone in the audience until we were spent. Wolferl claimed Germans were not so energetic as Italians in showing their approval, but I saw it differently. After the first tenor aria there was a terrific noise, hands clapping and cries of *"Viva Maestro!"*

ringing in the crowded theater, and that's how it continued. The arias sung by Violante, disguised as a garden-girl,
were so beautiful they broke our hearts. After the final
chorus we were all on our feet. The applause rolled on and
on as my brother took bow after bow, and the elector and
electress were calling out, "Bravo Mozart!"

I had a lump in my throat. Papa tried, unsuccessfully, to
look on with a neutral expression, but his face glowed with
pleasure. Afterward my brother showed himself an accomplished hand kisser, not missing the elector and the
electress and whatever royalty happened to stick their
paws anywhere near his lips.

"They'd be fools not to hire him," Papa said.

A whole month flew by, and I adored every minute of
it: balls, concerts, receptions. I made my dramatic appear-
ance at the fancy dress ball carrying the Amazon's shield
and spear. Papa's eyes started from his head and he gasped
when he first saw me, but people were very complimentary, calling me "a sensation." I'd even managed the cosmetics myself.

The widow von Furst escorted me to Mass every morning at a different church, no matter how weary I was from
the night before. Later she took to visiting coffeehouses
with her friends in order to let her new coiffure be seen
and admired. I often accompanied her. Young men noticed me and paid attention, although none seriously.

But we were in for several disappointments. Even after

all Papa's fussing, the arrangements for the clavier at the widow's home, and my efforts to sharpen my skills, I received no invitations to perform. Not one. For all the success of his opera, neither did Wolferl. Worst of all, Papa was told there were no positions available for one so young as my brother.

"Never mind that he has the talent of a man twice his age!" Papa cried out in frustration.

I dreaded the idea of going back to dreary Salzburg. Wolferl felt the same. "At least in Munich I can breathe freely," he told me. "Not like in Salzburg." He clutched his throat and rolled his eyes, as though he were being choked.

WE LEFT FOR HOME on the sixth of March 1775. Papa rode in silent dejection throughout the journey. Wolferl's mood was not much better. When we stopped for the night in Wasserburg, Papa was so exhausted that after a little supper he trudged upstairs to bed. Wolferl and I stayed on in the parlor of the inn, drinking mulled wine. A late winter storm howled outside, and a few shivering travelers arrived, stamping snow from their boots. Around midnight the innkeeper banked the fires, gave us each a candle stub, and retired.

We talked about many things that night, mostly about my brother's growing desire for independence and his yearning to live on his own. "Papa refuses to allow it,"

Wolferl said. "He reminds me almost daily that I don't have a practical bone in my body, that I haven't the slightest notion of how to pack, how to travel on my own, how to find accommodations." He lifted his hands and let them fall helplessly.

"But *can* you?" I asked, troubled, for I hadn't those skills myself. I was used to someone taking care of me. That's what men did, I thought.

"I don't know," he said. "I've never tried."

Somehow Mama had learned. When Papa was away, things ran smoothly in the household and Mama took care of business matters with no difficulty. I could see that his tedious instructions irritated her, as though she were incapable of handling even the smallest detail without his advice. But what about Wolferl? How does a man learn to do those things if they're always done for him?

The log in the fireplace had turned to glowing embers and then to ash. The candles guttered in the candlesticks. The pitcher of mulled wine was empty. "We should get some sleep," I said. "The coach leaves early in the morning."

But neither of us moved to go. There was something about being away from home in a place where we had no ties that loosened our tongues.

"I can't stand the idea of spending any more time in Salzburg," my brother grumbled. "Archbishop Colloredo doesn't care for my compositions. He hates my symphonies.

He can't deny that I'm a superb performer, so he'll want to keep me around, but on a short leash. I'll be compelled to write only the kind of music Colloredo wants. The one thing that pleases him is my church music. Am I to spend the rest of my life writing masses?"

"Still," I reasoned with Wolferl, who seemed close to tears, "it's an income."

"I see none of that income!" he exploded. "Papa claps hands on everything I earn. I haven't a kreuzer of my own."

I was too shocked to answer. I knew nothing of this— we'd never discussed it. We sat silently for a while. The room had turned cold, and I shivered. My eyelids were growing heavy.

"And what about you, Nannerl?" Wolferl asked at last. "No serious sweetheart? No wedding in the offing? I shall never become Uncle Johann Chrysostom Wolfgang Amadé if you don't get something started."

His tone was gently teasing, but his words were true, and they stung. I was twenty-three. With the exceptions of Katherl Gilowsky, who was becoming the butt of jokes for her strenuous efforts to snare a husband, and Viktoria, enslaved to her stepmother, most of my acquaintances were marrying, becoming parents. I was no closer to that than I had ever been.

"*Nein,*" I said. I wiped away tears with the back of my hand. "I haven't really tried. My first love has always been music. It still is. But that love has spurned me. I'm not like you."

"Nannerl," he said, leaning forward intently, "you will always have that love."

"It's not enough to live on." I started to leave, but then I sat back in my chair and asked quietly, "Did you know that while you were in Italy, I was much attracted to Joachim von Schiedenhofen? I thought he had feelings for me. We had music in common. I played for him. We even composed a little together. That's what makes it so hard! But . . ." I trailed off, unwilling to continue.

Wolferl sat up, his attention fully focused on me. "But what?" he asked. "What happened?"

I shrugged and turned away. "He found someone else, I think. Anna von Daubrawaick."

"Huh!" Wolferl snorted. "Her family's filthy rich, that's why. What a bloody fool! I should challenge him to a duel. Teach him a lesson."

I smiled. My brother, furious and ready to fight on my account! "Too bad life isn't like a comic opera with everything turning out right in the end, even when it begins with a stabbing." I rose and picked up one flickering candle, leaving the other for Wolferl. My brother's face was in shadow. I reached out and touched his cheek. "I shall always love you best," I murmured. My voice and the hand that held the candlestick were unsteady.

"And I, you, Nannerl."

I turned to climb the stairs to my bed. *"Gute Nacht,"* I said. "Good night."

"Schläf gut," he called after me. "Sleep well."

I left Wolferl sitting alone in the parlor of the inn, staring at the dead fire.

Chapter 17

Mama's Journey

After Munich, Papa resumed his chores as vice-Kapellmeister, attempting to please the tyrannical archbishop and inspire the lazy choirboys and resenting all of it. Wolfgang—he no longer wanted to be called Wolferl—despised Salzburg and the suffocating damper it put on his creativity. The Salzburg *Fräuleins* who were throwing themselves at him didn't seem to make up for it. There was no longer a theater in our town and no company to perform an opera if Wolfgang wrote one. He hated being obliged to dress in the archbishop's livery when he played the violin in the court orchestra. Everything about his life as a musician in Salzburg exasperated him.

"I feel as though I'm half asleep here," he muttered.

At Papa's insistence I began giving clavier lessons to the

Lodron girls, bratty daughters of Count Potbelly and his haughty wife. "You will benefit if you accustom yourself to teaching another person very thoroughly and patiently," Papa lectured when I balked at taking these new pupils. But the Lodron Ladies, as I called them, would have tested the patience of a saint.

Louise was fourteen when she plopped herself down at the clavier; her sister, Pepperl, was ten, Tonerl nearly eight, and Maria Anna not quite six. A fifth daughter, Maria Theresia, was only three and too young for lessons. I suspect Louise would have preferred to have my adorable brother sitting next to her at the clavier. She could sigh all she wished, but Wolfgang found excuses to leave the Lodron Ladies entirely in my hands.

DESPITE THE BLEAKNESS of the musical scene at court—or maybe because of it—the Tanzmeisterhaus became a center of socializing and music making. Nearly every day people came to call. Nearly every Sunday we held a concert in our salon. Our target-shooting club brought their air guns, and when we tired of shooting, we played cards. At the end of the afternoon Mama brought out her pretty china cups and served coffee accompanied by a hazelnut torte, her specialty.

In the summer of 1776 our very rich friend Liserl Haffner was married. Her brother commissioned Wolfgang to compose a serenade, a lovely piece for strings and wind instruments, and Wolfgang himself played the violin solos when it was performed on the eve of her wedding.

A few weeks later Wolfgang arranged a Sunday concert in our courtyard in honor of my name day, July 26, and my twenty-fifth birthday four days later. He'd composed a divertimento called the "Nannerl Septet," scored for oboe, horns, and strings, and invited all our friends, including Joachim von Schiedenhofen. "Better than fighting a duel," Wolfgang suggested. "And I've heard nothing of an engagement. You might still have a chance."

Joachim called on me with his congratulations on the name day itself, a Friday, as he made the rounds of the Annas he knew, and there were a good many—including, I supposed, pretty Anna von Daubrawaick. "Shall I play something for you?" I asked.

"Another time, perhaps, Fräulein Mozart," he said, putting me off with his use of my formal name.

At that moment Wolfgang entered, appraised the scene, and backed out again—but too late. Joachim seized him by the arm and walked out with him, making excuses for not being able to attend our Sunday concert.

"What an oaf!" Wolfgang said later. "Should I run him off the next time he comes by? The duel is still a possibility."

I shook my head. I tried not to care.

———

AUTUMN CAME, and Josefa Duschek, the brilliant soprano from Prague, asked Wolfgang to write an operatic piece for her. "What a pleasure," Wolfgang said, "to work with a singer who knows something of a world bigger than Salzburg and to show her that I truly compose operatic music."

Then winter began, and Carnival season was upon us. Balls often went on until dawn. I attended as many as possible, although I found them less exciting now than I once had. Masquerade balls were the most popular, and I did enjoy the costumes that were often imaginative and sometimes utterly hilarious. One night Papa dressed as a porter and Wolfgang as a friseur's assistant, carrying a couple of perukes and a box of wig powder that he dispensed liberally. I wore my Amazon costume again, brandishing my sword and shield, and frankly enjoyed the admiring looks it attracted. Mama, gotten up as a Tyrolean maidservant, made us all laugh. We all overindulged in the sweets and pastries that would soon be forbidden from Ash Wednesday until Easter.

Joachim von Schiedenhofen was there with Anna on his arm—the first I had seen them together since we were guests at his country estate. Franz von Mölk, my only suitor thus far, had completely disappeared from the picture. Katherl heard the rumor that he wished to marry Josefa Barisani, but Archbishop Colloredo refused to give his permission.

"No one quite knows why," Katherl said. "My father thinks it's because of Colloredo's quarrels with Dr. Barisani, his personal physician."

And so I danced with this young man and that older one and several of indeterminate age, smiled at them all, and waited for my *real* life to begin—whatever it was.

THE TANZMEISTERHAUS—the Dancing-Master's House— might well have been known as the House of Discontent. Papa continued to search secretly for a better position. He wrote to Archbishop Colloredo, asking permission to travel again, and received a blunt reply: "Leopold and Wolfgang Mozart are free to travel as much as they like. Effective immediately, they are no longer in our employ." They had both been dismissed.

Stunned by the archbishop's harsh response, we sat glumly at the table and contemplated this completely unexpected turn. Then Papa slapped his hands on the table and announced wearily, "I shall crawl on my hands and knees, if necessary, and plead with the archbishop for reinstatement. If he agrees, I shall resume my duties at the Residenz. Wolfgang will go off in search of a suitable position." I will never forget his next words: "Anna Maria, you will travel with our son. Nannerl, you will stay here and keep house for me."

I gaped at Papa. Mama, travel with Wolfgang? I, stay home and keep house? Was he joking? I didn't know the least thing about keeping house! Mama and our house-maid, Tresel, always took care of everything. Papa was in for a rude shock. *Why must I be left behind again?* A little pulse began to throb in my temple.

Everyone was talking at once. "You want *me* to go?" Mama gasped, seeming as stunned as I was.

"You are not going, Papa?" Wolfgang asked in shocked surprise.

"Surely I could be of more use—," I began.

"Silence!" Papa thundered, and we stopped in mid-sentence. "There is nothing more to discuss. We shall begin preparations immediately. Mama and Wolfgang will leave within the month."

I watched in disbelief as Papa made the decisions and briskly set the plans in motion. Mama and Wolfgang would visit Munich, Mannheim, and Paris. "In one of these three great cities of music," Papa told Wolfgang, "you will surely be able to find a position that pays you a living."

Papa and Mama stayed up late every night, working out the details. Wolfgang ran around grinning from ear to ear. He was always ready to get away from Salzburg, the destination unimportant. I brooded and sulked. I certainly didn't want to stay at home again, not after tasting the pleasures of my trip to Munich. And I could not think how Papa and I would manage to get along for such a long period. There had been constant friction between us, and I imagined it would only grow worse.

"Why can't I go with them?" I asked as calmly, as reasonably, as I could.

"Because you have pupils here, and your income is needed. Sending Wolfgang abroad has put me deeply into debt," Papa explained with increasing exasperation. "And because it is your duty, Nannerl!" he shouted at last.

The strain proved too much. A week before Wolfgang and Mama were to leave, Papa fell ill and could scarcely rise from his bed. I was wracked with headaches. Mama complained of tiredness. Only Wolfgang felt fine.

Papa and Wolfgang packed their baggage into the chaise that had replaced our old Pressburg carriage. At six o'clock in the morning on the twenty-third of September 1777, we once again said our tearful farewells—but this time everything was different. Mama and I bid each other *Auf Wiedersehen*. Papa and I watched from the window above Hannibalplatz as the chaise rolled toward the city gates. Papa stayed by the window, sending his blessing after his wife and son. I retreated to my bedroom.

Overcome by the most dreadful headache and roiling stomach, I retched and vomited. I called Tresel, the housemaid, to close the shutters, and crawled into bed with a cold cloth on my head. Bimperl curled up beside me. When Papa came at one o'clock to wake me for lunch,

I could not swallow a single bite. Every time I thought of Mama and Wolfgang, on their merry way to new opportunities in which I would have no part, my head throbbed again, my stomach churned, and the tears poured down my face. Even our pet birds seemed to suffer—Herr Canary could no longer bring himself to sing, and Mama's finches fell silent and torpid without her encouraging smile.

I HAD NEVER paid much attention to Tresel—she was Mama's responsibility. Tresel was a countrywoman from the Tyrol, and had never gotten used to city ways. She spent most of her time in the kitchen, spinning wool into yarn she then knit into misshapen stockings for her younger brothers. Now I discovered that the woman left the kitchen a mess and didn't always tell the truth about why this had been done incorrectly or that had been neglected. I scolded her and made her cry, and then I felt sorry and came close to apologizing, until I realized *she* was the one at fault, not I.

"Frau Mozart doesn't do it that way," she said, frowning darkly, arms crossed over her large bosom, when I asked why the butter had not been put in the cupboard.

"Frau Mozart is not here," I reminded her sternly. Immediately she began to weep again.

"*Ja, ja,* I know," she said, wiping her face with her apron, which I noticed was none too clean, "and that's what makes me so sad."

The sight of fat tears rolling down her red cheeks made *me* burst into tears. We fell into each other's arms and wept together—she noisily, I quietly, both of us missing Mama. After that, we got along somewhat better; Tresel tried harder to please me, and I tried harder not to scold. But it was still up to me to keep things tidied up, to see to the ironing because she was likely to scorch everything, and to the mending, which I disliked. It did nothing for my mood when Papa referred to me—jokingly, I supposed—as his housekeeper.

PAPA WAS CONFIDENT that Wolfgang would quickly secure a position and our family would be reunited. We'd move to a city where everything would go well for us. I would have real musical opportunities. I could marry or not, as I chose, and Wolfgang would be able to support us. Meanwhile, he must earn enough with private and public concerts to cover living expenses without dipping too deeply into funds Papa had borrowed from Herr Hagenauer and several others. And he'd have to arrange those concerts himself; Papa had always done that, but now Wolfgang was on his own.

Soon the first cheerful letters arrived from Munich. Wolfgang and Mama seemed to be enjoying themselves, dining with friends and attending the theater; only occasionally was Wolfgang giving concerts. He sounded delighted to be out from under the archbishop's thumb. And maybe Papa's, too.

For his part, Papa dispensed endless advice about whom Wolfgang should meet and how he should go about impressing Elector Maximilian. But when Wolfgang finally managed to meet the elector face-to-face, Maximilian told him firmly, "My dear boy, I have no vacancy." It was the same disappointing story, and in this case we believed it was true.

The Munich letters continued to be merry. "He's having a fine time, but he hasn't earned a single kreuzer," Papa fumed. "They must move on."

BY MID-OCTOBER they were in Augsburg, where they visited Papa's brother and his family. I remembered well the impudent little girl from our visit at the start of our grand tour, when Wolfgang was seven and the daughter, whom he called the *Bäsle*—Little Cousin—was a boisterous four-year-old. Papa read Wolfgang's letter silently and passed it to me.

"I declare that the *Bäsle* is beautiful, intelligent, charming, and talented," Wolfgang had written. "We two get on extremely well, for like me she is a bit of a scamp."

It was clear the two were together all the time, and I had a pretty good idea of what those two scamps were up to.

My brother was twenty-one, and I could scarcely fault him for his interest in members of the opposite sex. However, I did think his little flirtations with the mademoiselles in Salzburg were as far as matters should go at this point. I wondered how Mama was dealing with his infatuation with the charming *Bäsle*. Mama's brief message at the end of Wolfgang's letter didn't mention a word about this paragon of beauty, intelligence, and talent.

I passed the letter back to Papa. "After all I've told him about keeping himself clean and pure," he said with a grimace, "I'm afraid this *Bäsle* is leading him astray."

Fortunately, Wolfgang and Mama were soon on their way to Mannheim, and Papa breathed a little easier. But Wolfgang had earned next to nothing in Augsburg, not nearly enough to cover expenses, and the drain on his purse must have been heavy indeed.

Chapter 18

THE WEBERS

WITH HALF THE FAMILY gone, we the orphaned half struggled to get along. I resented Papa's expectation that I would take Mama's place and become the efficient mistress of the household. I hated being treated as though I had no common sense, the way he often treated Mama. We argued about every little thing—the cut of meat I bought from the butcher, my occasional escapes to a café with Katherl or Viktoria, the money I sometimes spent on my coiffure. The one thing that brought us some agreement was music.

We fell into a routine. Every evening we played, just the two of us—Papa with his violin, I at the clavier, often trying out new compositions that Wolfgang sent. We found ourselves working together harmoniously, discussing the andantes and the prestos, debating which instrument should take the lead in a certain section. Our bond of music helped to ease Papa's dissatisfaction and my resentment.

I began to practice again for several hours each day, my fingers regained their agility, and Papa's interest in my musical education reawakened after all these years. He discovered that my skills were uneven: I excelled at playing the sonatas and concertos I'd had ample time to practice, but I was not so good at sight-reading or playing in some of the most difficult keys. Papa helped me improve.

"You are as accomplished as any Kapellmeister," he told me at the end of an exhausting session. It was the highest praise he'd given me since my days as a *Wunderkind,* and I basked in his approval. I was sure to find opportunities to play wherever we lived.

During the day while Papa was out of the house, I played for myself. This was a lonely time in my life as I waited for the next chapter to begin, and I expressed my longing the only way I knew how: through music. Eyes closed, I re-created some of the performances I'd shared with my brother. Sometimes when I opened them, I discovered Tresel in the doorway, a half-peeled potato in her hands, her face bathed in tears.

Six days of the week Papa and I worked hard, and on Sundays we tried to enjoy ourselves. After Mass at Dom St. Rupert—Papa had official duties—we arranged a concert at the Tanzmeisterhaus, just as we had when Mama was there, with the Adlgassers and the Schachtners and whoever else came around. After lunch the members of our shooting club arrived. The club included Katherl Gilowsky and Abbé Josef Bullinger, a Jesuit priest who was tutor to Count Leopold von Arco, one of Papa's pupils. Bullinger often brought along young Leopold. In a member's absence, another could shoot for him—Papa shot for Wolfgang; I took Mama's place.

Each week a different member supplied a painted target ordered from a local artist. A great deal of thought went into these targets. When Wolfgang's turn came, my naughty brother sent instructions for a vulgar illustration and a rude motto. Katherl was also a favorite subject of these paintings. She was twenty-seven and, as everyone knew, eager to marry. I once ordered a target showing her clutching the wax figure of a man with two pilgrimage churches in the background.

"At least I'm honest about it," Katherl said airily, pretending not to mind my joke at her expense. "Which is more than I can say for you, Nannerl."

"I'm not desperate," I retorted, ignoring the sting of regret I felt whenever I thought of Joachim. He had recently announced his intended marriage to Anna, who was now seen everywhere with him. One could not attend a concert without witnessing their glowing faces.

Joachim had told me about it himself when he came

to call on Papa. "My best wishes to you," I said, forcing a smile and thinking, *I would have made you a better match. What does she know about music?*

"It's obviously a marriage of money and rank and has very little to do with love," Papa said after Joachim had gone. "But the young lady is quite pretty," he added. I had never told Papa of my interest in Joachim, but he may have guessed how I felt.

LETTERS BEGAN TO arrive from Mannheim, a city boasting one of the finest orchestras in all of Europe. How I wished that Wolfgang would find a position there! Since Joachim's engagement, I longed more than ever to be away from Salzburg.

But Mannheim had nothing for my brother. When Papa realized no opportunities existed there, he was extremely agitated. He often spent half a day writing to Wolfgang, pen racing furiously across page after page—ordering, demanding, threatening. Wolfgang must waste no more time and money. It was a great sacrifice to send him on this journey, and Wolfgang could not afford to fritter away what little money he had. "You must move on to Paris, where opportunities are certain to be better," Papa instructed.

It took six to eight days for a letter to travel from here to there, another six to eight for a reply. While Papa waited for Wolfgang's answer, he stormed angrily through our rooms or sat in silence. I stayed away to avoid his wretched moods.

When the answers did come, they were not reassuring. Sometimes his letters were full of jokes and puns, or endless alphabetical lists of people to whom he was sending greetings. Only rarely was there the detailed accounting of expenses that Papa demanded.

"Traveling is a serious occupation, and not a single day must be wasted," Papa wrote in exasperation.

Papa and Wolfgang seemed locked in a struggle, Papa determined to control and dictate, Wolfgang determined to be his own man. They argued about everything: where to stay, how long to stay there, when to go to Paris, and with whom. Arrangements were made, then changed, and changed again. When he ran short of money, Wolfgang proposed selling the chaise. This sent Papa into an apoplectic rage.

Poor Mama simply wanted to come home. She complained of the cold room where she spent long, lonely days while Wolfgang was out and about. She was homesick. Yet, much as she longed for all she had in Salzburg, she dreaded the idea of making such a journey in the middle of winter, which was fast closing in.

Papa's letters scolded them both. "Your mother doesn't heed my advice," he said to me, "no matter how carefully I

lay it out for her, and your brother seems incapable of attending to his affairs. I'm afraid his head is always full of
music and not much else."

"Mama is quite capable," I reminded him. "She has
always handled things well when you and Wolferl were
traveling."

"Of course she did! She was at home where everything
was familiar!"

It was useless to argue with Papa. Besides, he was mostly
right about Wolfgang. His head was certainly full of music,
but also of women. He was so easily distracted—and this
worried me, because my future depended on him.

WHILE WE WORRIED about Mama and Wolfgang, my
dear friend Viktoria suffered a great tragedy. Her father,
the only organist at Dom St. Rupert since Wolfgang's departure, had a seizure while he was playing for vespers. I
was sitting in the congregation with Katherl; we were distressed to hear random dissonances issuing from the great
organ.

"Is he drunk?" Katherl whispered as the chaotic sounds
continued. At last the organ fell silent, the ailing man was
carried out of the cathedral, and the service went on as
though nothing had happened.

Later, as I hurried home, I met a weeping Viktoria,
rushing to the chemist's shop. The doctor had sent her to

fetch a bottle of spirit of hartshorn to hold under her father's nose to revive him. "He's very ill," she sobbed. "I fear that he's beyond help." Viktoria was right. Adlgasser died the next day.

Muffled in our fur cloaks on that cold Christmas Eve, we gathered in the churchyard behind St. Sebastian's to say farewell to our old friend. Viktoria, pale as death herself, huddled with her arms around little Anna and Josef, now a tall seventeen-year-old, all of them shivering and sobbing and crying out for their father. The new widow, Anna Fesemayr Adlgasser, stood silently apart. It was a heart-wrenching scene.

"What will happen to them now?" I asked Papa when we'd returned to the Tanzmeisterhaus and warmed ourselves with a bowl of steaming veal soup. I was thinking particularly of Viktoria. "How will they live?"

"They've lost his salary, of course," Papa said, spooning up noodles. "Anna still draws a court singer's salary, but it's not enough to support her and her stepchildren. The archbishop will allot them a pittance, barely enough to survive, and only for one year. Viktoria will undoubtedly have to go into domestic service."

"If she's able," I said, and reached for a handkerchief. "Did you notice her pallor? She's not been feeling well for some time. Dr. Barisani prescribed a tonic for her, but it hasn't seemed to help."

We stared morosely into our soup bowls, thinking our

separate thoughts. *What would I do if Papa were to die, and I had no way to support myself?*

Christmas at the Tanzmeisterhaus was a melancholy affair.

THE SUDDEN DEMISE of Anton Cajetan Adlgasser was not the only death to affect the Mozart family. Days later Elector Maximilian of Munich succumbed to smallpox. Karl Theodor, elector of the Palatinate, which included Mannheim, was named his successor. The Mannheim court also went into mourning, and both cities came to a complete standstill. There was now no possibility for Wolfgang to give any concerts or to earn a single gulden.

A couple of weeks later Wolfgang's fortunes improved. He secured an invitation to play the organ for Karoline, princess of Orange, the same princess who had been so kind to us when both Wolferl and I fell ill in Holland. This was good news—he would be well paid. But he did not travel alone to the town of Kirchheimbolanden for the concert. He was accompanied by an impoverished court musician named Fridolin Weber and his daughter, Aloysia. "A gifted singer," he wrote.

"Have you heard of these people?" I asked Papa.

"I have not," Papa said. "It does seem that Wolfgang is performing and earning money, although Mama is left alone while he goes off with his new friends."

In his next letter Wolfgang described in detail the organ

in Kirchheimbolanden, the music he'd played, the manner in which Princess Karoline received him after all these years, and the amount he'd been paid. It was a good sum until he'd handed a big share over to the Webers. I sensed trouble brewing when he went on and on about the wonders of seventeen-year-old Aloysia's lovely, pure voice and how admirably she accompanied herself on the clavier.

Then he announced his decision *not* to go to Paris after all.

The reason he gave was so ridiculous that I could not believe he had the audacity to offer it: The two men with whom he had arranged the journey to Paris, musician-friends of whom he had spoken highly in the past, were now deemed unsuitable. One of them was not religious enough, and the other was a person without moral standards. The idea of traveling in the company of these men whose principles were so different from his own was unthinkable!

Then, after praising the Weber family and especially the talented Aloysia, Wolfgang laid out his new plan. "I have become so fond of this family that my dearest wish is to make them happy," Wolfgang wrote. "Instead of going to Paris, I've made up my mind to go to Italy with the Webers to launch Aloysia in a singing career. Herr Weber and two of his daughters will have the honor of visiting you in Salzburg on our way."

I threw down the letter, unable to stomach another line. Had my brother gone completely mad? He was obviously in love with this Fräulein Weber. But had love made him lose all reason and common sense? I retrieved the letter and plowed on. "The thought of helping this family delights my very soul."

To the devil with his soul! How dare he go to all this effort to launch *her* career when he'd done absolutely nothing to help mine!

Papa's roar like a wounded beast echoed from one end of the Tanzmeisterhaus to the other. For two days he didn't eat or sleep, complained of heart palpitations, and paced from room to room, sometimes utterly silent, sometimes ranting at the top of his voice. "She has bewitched him! She and her father—the whole lot of them—wield some unholy power over him!"

Bimperl came to hide under my bed, and Tresel refused to leave the kitchen while my father was in such a state. And I—I could do nothing but cry. How could Wolfgang cast aside all our plans and sacrifices so easily, and for utter strangers? There was virtually no chance that he could start this young girl's singing career. No one would take her seriously. We had already seen that no opportunities existed for him in Italy. How did he intend to support the Weber family when he was unable to support himself?

Soon Papa was scribbling another of his long letters. This one went on for several pages. I managed to see it before he had sealed it.

"Nannerl has wept her full share during these last two

days," he wrote. Didn't Wolfgang see that he was leading our family to ruin? Papa had devoted his life to my brother's career, and, as he reminded me every time I wanted to spend a kreuzer on myself at the friseur or in a café, had gone deeply into debt to finance this tour that seemed to be leading nowhere. Of course I wept!

The reply, when it came, did nothing to soothe my feelings. Quite the opposite. Wolfgang had the effrontery to chide me for weeping over his new circumstances. "If you continue to shed tears over every silly little thing, I'm never coming home again," he snapped, and that made me weep all the harder. Did he understand *nothing*?

I was hurt that my brother seemed to have turned away from us so easily. If Papa were to die suddenly, as poor Adlgasser had, Wolfgang could not be counted on to support Mama and me. While he dreamed of introducing the incomparable Fräulein Weber to all of Europe, his poor sister faced a future of domestic servitude and probable penury.

Papa and I could no longer enjoy a night at the theater, nor could we afford the pleasure of the Carnival balls. The quarterly rent was due on our apartment. There was no way to repay Papa's debts, taken on Wolfgang's behalf, which amounted to more than two years of his salary. Yet despite these worries, Papa was determined to keep up a good front, not only to the friends who came to the Tanzmeisterhaus for concerts and shooting contests but also to the archbishop and people like the Lodrons and the Arcos. Papa pretended that all was going splendidly for Wolfgang, who was much in demand in the cities he visited, and that an appointment in one of the cities was imminent.

But Papa was honest with his good friend Abbé Bullinger. "I'm forced to do it," he confided. "I must, in order to make the archbishop understand the mistake he's made in letting Wolfgang leave. Then, if Wolfgang's efforts to find a position elsewhere are unsuccessful, my son can come back to Salzburg and be assured of one here. His good fortune and success will be our sweetest revenge against those who would see us ridiculed."

Papa continued to do his best to pry Wolfgang loose from the enchantment of the Weber family, and especially of Aloysia, to whom I was sure he had lost both his heart and his head and possibly his virginity. But my father seemed to be getting nowhere.

"Off with you to Paris!" he commanded. It remained to be seen if his order would be obeyed.

Chapter 19

OFF TO PARIS

PAPA'S LETTER crossed Mama's in the post. Hers, written in secret while Wolfgang was dining with friends, was enough to break my heart: "Our son prefers other people to me." Nevertheless, she prepared to go with him to Paris.

Papa lectured Wolfgang on what he must do in Paris (avoid women), and what he must not do (become involved with women), laying on him a heavy burden of guilt and responsibility. I could only imagine how my brother would react to Papa's admonitions. We were both adults—Wolfgang was twenty-two, and I was twenty-six—and we revered our parents, but each of us longed for a degree of independence Papa was unwilling to allow. Wolfgang had the advantage of being far away. But how does one free oneself, if one is a female under the constantly watchful eye of an autocratic father?

A week earlier I had suffered from a heavy chest cold. I soon felt well enough to go out, but Papa forbade me to leave the house, as though I were a child, and turned away friends who came to call on me. I resented his authority, but I did not have the strength to challenge it.

Later, when I was finally allowed to go out, I met Katherl for a walk. "I wonder if any man will ever be able to get past your father to court you," she mused. "It won't be easy. Nor would it be an easy matter to have Leopold Mozart for a father-in-law."

"I haven't met a man in ages who even wanted to try," I said ruefully and thought of Franz von Mölk. He'd probably not had any notion of what he was up against.

Wolfgang's reply to Papa's angry letter was full of ideas for making things right again. He agreed to give up his fantasy of a journey to Italy with Aloysia Weber and began preparations for Paris, even ordering a black suit, which he thought more appropriate than his braid-trimmed German clothes. To show my support for this sensible decision to move on, I sent him fifty gulden, money I had set aside for my own future.

In the middle of March Wolfgang gave a farewell concert for his Mannheim friends at which his dear Aloysia sang and they both played his compositions. He tore himself away from the Weber family, and he and Mama began the long, slow journey to Paris.

———

I SORELY MISSED Wolfgang, as I always did when he was absent. I also missed Mama, whose calm, cheerful presence in our household was as quiet and steady as a beating heart. Our letters had become more intimate, exchanging what Mama called "women's chat" about fashions and such. She promised to bring me a new cap from Germany that she said was much prettier than those worn in Salzburg.

Now I had to endure Papa's dour presence, his frustration and distress, his constant worries about the future and about the present, too. When the tailor's bill arrived for Wolfgang's black suit, he had no way to pay for it. The rent was again due, and Tresel had not received her wages for some time and was asking for them. All of this weighed on him, and therefore affected my health as well, bringing on headaches, stomach problems, and weakness in my limbs.

My only solace was my music. For hours each day I withdrew to that place within myself where doubts and fears gave way to a fusion of harmony, melody, and rhythm. Music was everything—but it still wasn't enough.

DESPITE HIS WORRIES, Papa remained confident that Wolfgang would soon make his way in Paris. There were many opportunities for musicians in that marvelous city, but there were also many musicians eager to exploit the possibilities. Competition was keen. Fortunately, Wolfgang had our old friend Baron Grimm to help him.

The first challenge Mama and Wolfgang faced was to find living quarters. The rooms they procured were so dark, Mama wrote, that both day and night looked the same when she peered out at the dismal courtyard. Wolfgang quickly made social contacts and was invited out to dine nearly every day, but those invitations never included Mama. She had to order food from a cookshop. "One would think the French would learn to cook," she complained. "I can barely choke down what they send me."

Soon Wolfgang had launched a number of projects: choruses for Holy Week services, a *sinfonia concertante,* several sonatas, and a concerto. He'd found a few pupils.

But still Papa fretted. "If only he can earn enough to cover his expenses! If he's forced to borrow more, it may get back to Salzburg that I'm still supporting him, and that will do great harm to our family honor."

I, too, fretted, but less about family honor than who would support me if I failed to marry. Then Johann Josef Adam arrived in Salzburg. Herr Adam was valet to young Count Leopold von Arco and was introduced to me by the count's tutor, our dear Abbé Bullinger. He was tall and blond and of excellent bearing, danced exceptionally well, and seemed to have a pleasant disposition. But he appeared rather dull-witted and preferred riding and hunting to any sort of music. "As a matter of fact, my dear Fräulein Mozart," he said the third time he came to call on me, "I can barely tolerate to sit through a concert. My buttocks won't stand for it!" He laughed heartily at his own humor. I got rid of Herr Adam as soon as I decently could.

Katherl was surprised that I had rebuffed him so quickly. "You should have more patience," she advised. "Johann Adam has many good qualities. You could have won him over, and I'll wager he would have learned to enjoy music for your sake."

I brushed off her suggestion. "I can't imagine having to *win over* a person to enjoy music. It's not quite the same as persuading someone to eat oysters. One is either born loving music, or one is not."

Katherl nodded as though she agreed, but I could guess what she was thinking. "Go ahead," I said. "If you think he's worth your efforts, I'll ask Abbé Bullinger to arrange a proper introduction."

"Oh, would you?" she cried.

I did, and soon Herr Adam had begun to call on her. Naturally, I never saw them at any musical events, and I hoped for her sake all would go well. Katherl felt that a pilgrimage to the church at Maria Plain might help. She convinced me to make the pilgrimage with her, and we asked Viktoria to join us.

On a bright June day the three of us set off toward the village of Bergheim, an hour distant. Katherl and I realized that Viktoria was walking more slowly, and we adjusted our pace, pausing at several little chapels to recite the rosary and stopping for lunch at a rustic country house. Viktoria, who'd always been plump, was now so thin and gaunt that her fetching dimples had disappeared. Her pallor was unmistakable, and I thought she seemed very tired.

"What are you going to petition Our Lady for?" Katherl asked, oblivious to Viktoria's distress. "The Virgin is probably sick of my prayers for a husband. Maybe this time will do the trick. Surely all the times I've climbed this hill to her shrine ought to have convinced her I'm serious about finding a husband. Johann Adam is a good prospect."

"Even if he dislikes music?" I teased, but when she looked embarrassed, I relented. "I'm petitioning for success for Wolfgang, that he'll make his fortune in Paris," I answered more seriously. "Then Papa and I will go to join him at Versailles, if he accepts the position there. Queen Marie Antoinette is an old friend, you know—we made her acquaintance at Schönbrunn when she was just a little archduchess. She and Wolfgang hit it off famously." This was an exaggeration, and so was the notion that Wolfgang had actually been offered a position by the queen, but neither was so far from the truth as to be an outright lie.

Katherl said, "The gossip is that since your friend Marie Antoinette became queen of France she's treated money as though it's her duty to get rid of as much of it as possible. I've heard she spends more on her shoes than Archbishop Colloredo does on his entire court."

"Then maybe she'll lavish some of it on her musicians

as well," I countered. "And since the queen has just announced she's expecting her first child, there are sure to be all sorts of commissions for music to celebrate the birth."

Katherl looked at me and sniffed. "You'd be better advised to pray for a husband for yourself," she said, tossing her blond curls. "Don't depend on that scamp of a brother to take care of you."

I ought to have been offended, but I knew she was right.

"And you, Viktoria?" Katherl asked, turning to our friend. "What are you praying for?"

"I shall ask the Blessed Virgin for help for my brother and sister. Poor Josef has gone nearly mad with grief since our father's death, and little Anna is very frail. I worry about them both, and our stepmother is no help at all."

"You're too good-hearted, Viktoria," Katherl said firmly, reaching for a handful of ripe cherries from a bowl. "You should be asking the Virgin to send you good health and a situation with a good family, or—best of all—an adoring and adorable husband."

Viktoria barely managed a smile.

We finished our lunch, and when Viktoria claimed she was well rested, we set off again for Maria Plain. The last part of the pilgrimage was the climb to the twin-towered church on a hilltop. The sun blazed down on us, and we arrived breathless and perspiring. We turned to look out over Salzburg, the Salzach River winding through its heart, and picked out the steeples of Dom St. Rupert and

St. Stephen's, the forbidding fortress on the Mönchsberg, and the white-capped Alps looming in the distance.

Suddenly Viktoria slumped to the ground in a graceless heap. We half carried her into the church, where it was cool. Once she'd come around, she insisted she was all right and managed to kneel before the miraculous image and to murmur her petitions to the Virgin. I prayed for Wolfgang and Mama, for Papa, and for myself, adding Viktoria and the Adlgasser children as well as Katherl to my list of those in need of divine intervention.

When our devotions were finished, we began the slow descent on the path that would eventually take us back to Salzburg, Viktoria clinging weakly to our arms.

THINGS SEEMED TO BE going better for the Family Mozart. We hadn't much idea what was happening in Paris, but it did look as though Countess Lodron might persuade the archbishop to lure Wolfgang back to Salzburg as court organist, offering him a decent salary and leave to travel. And that was encouraging.

Then on the twelfth of July, everything changed as drastically as though the sun had suddenly fallen from the sky. The postman brought a letter from my brother. Papa was at his writing table, sending congratulations to Mama on her name day in two weeks and describing his diplomatic negotiations with the archbishop by way of Countess Lodron. I always waited for Papa to read their letters before he passed them over to me, but his cry made me rush to his side. His eyes streamed with tears. He handed me Wolfgang's letter without a word and buried his face in his hands.

"I have very sad and distressing news to deliver," Wolfgang had written in a shaky hand. "My dear mother has fallen ill. She was bled and seemed to recover, but soon she complained of chills and fever and a headache. No matter what we tried, her condition worsened. She could neither speak nor hear. The doctor sent by Baron Grimm gives me some hope, although I confess that I haven't much. I have resigned myself to God's will and pray you both will do the same."

I sank to the floor, stricken with fear and disbelief. *This can't be!* When I was calmer, I read on, thinking I would find some explanation.

Unbelievably, the letter then shifted abruptly from Mama's illness and God's will to a description of a new composition, Wolfgang's continuing dislike of Paris and of all things French, his decision not to accept a position at Versailles even if it were offered, and of some new project he had conceived but of which it was too soon to speak. How could he write about such matters when Mama lay dying? I sensed the presence of Aloysia Weber at the center of this new project.

Papa pulled himself together somehow and immediately resumed writing the half-finished letter on his table. He had a hundred questions about Mama's illness, and he demanded answers.

The shooting club was to meet at our house that day, and it was too late to call it off. The members arrived, Katherl and all the rest, including Abbé Bullinger, to find us in a deeply distressed state. Papa explained the letter we'd received only a couple of hours earlier. Our friends expressed their loving concern, and most of them left quickly. My head had begun to throb. Katherl sat by my side and brought me cold cloths, but in the end I sent her away.

Only Abbé Bullinger remained. By then Papa had come to the worst possible conclusion. I heard them talking in low voices. Painfully, I rose from my bed and stood in the doorway listening.

"I am convinced my dear wife has already died," I heard Papa say miserably.

"I am inclined to think the same," Abbé Bullinger murmured.

After a long silence, Papa spoke again, his voice anguished. "I believe my dear wife is dead, and that she was dead when Wolfgang wrote this letter. And I have a strong feeling Wolfgang wrote you the truth at the very same time, and asked you to come here to console me and break the truth to me as gently as you can."

Abbé Bullinger sighed. "*Ja,* my good friend, everything you say is true. Your good Anna Maria is dead."

I turned away without speaking and flung myself on my bed, overwhelmed by our loss. Sometime later Papa came to sit by my side and gently stroked my hand. "It is God's will, Nannerl," he murmured. "We must accept that."

But I did not want to believe God could be so cruel.

Chapter 20

MOURNING

I HAVE ONLY a pale memory of the days following the news of Mama's death. It seemed very unreal. I had not seen my mother in her final illness, been present when the doctor was summoned, or heard her murmur her confession to the priest as he anointed her with oil and prayed for her salvation. I hadn't seen the black angels or heard the beating of their terrible shining wings. I hadn't watched the nurse close Mama's eyes for the last time. I hadn't seen her dressed in her favorite violet silk and laid out in her coffin or witnessed the coffin being lowered into the ground and the dirt shoveled over it. Now her bones lay in a faraway city, and I might never visit her grave. I awoke each morning filled with disbelief that I would never see my mother again. Never again would she smooth my hands with her scented creams, telling me, "Such talent in those fingers!"

Friends came to whisper their condolences. Acquaintances and even people I scarcely knew stopped by to leave their black-bordered calling cards; Mama had many friends. Among those who called on us was Armand d'Ippold, a captain in the imperial army and the director of the Collegium Virgilianum, the Knights' Academy, across the street from the Tanzmeisterhaus. We had met on a few previous occasions; now he spoke warmly of his admiration for Fräu Mozart, and I accepted his expression of sympathy.

During that dark period I was especially glad for the company of Viktoria, who had lost her dear father only months earlier. Abbé Bullinger came every day to sit silently with Papa and me as we grappled with our loss.

Tresel urged us to eat. "You are sure to meet again in heaven," she said, her eyes red from weeping. "Now, *bitte schön*—please—do have a little soup."

GRADUALLY WE PICKED up the frayed threads of our daily lives. I attended Mass every morning, practiced on the clavier, took Bimperl for long, solitary walks, and only occasionally went out for coffee with friends.

Katherl Gilowsky's situation as governess to the youngest Lodron girls kept her so busy she was seldom able to visit. But one day she arrived unexpectedly, explaining that her petition to the Virgin at Maria Plain had not brought about the desired result.

"Johann dropped me," she said, weeping quietly and muffling her sobs with a handkerchief. "He was so attentive, so loving, and then suddenly it was over! And I would have done anything to please him! Anything!"

I looked at her sternly. "I hope you don't mean what I'm afraid you mean, Katherl. Did you allow him to seduce you?"

She shook her head. "*Nein,* I didn't." She peeped over her crumpled handkerchief. "But almost."

"*Tch tch,*" I clucked and shook my head. "But why did he end it?" I asked.

"He told me he wanted a woman who enjoyed riding, and I'm afraid of horses."

I resisted the urge to say, *But couldn't you have learned to like them?* Instead I embraced her and held her while she cried. *Everyone loses someone,* I thought, aching for Mama, and wept with my friend.

PAPA THREW HIMSELF into writing letters to Wolfgang with two ends in mind: One was to extract every last detail of Mama's illness and death; the second was to hasten my brother's return home. Early letters from Wolfgang discussed almost everything *except* Mama's death. There was too much about the Weber family, Wolfgang's plans for the future, social engagements he'd enjoyed, and a great deal about music, but *not a single mention of our mother.* It was almost as though she had never existed. Perhaps he couldn't bear to think of what had happened. Perhaps he felt guilty about his neglect of her.

Finally he did answer Papa's most persistent questions. Mama had refused to consult French doctors, whom she didn't trust. The elderly German physician who finally came to tend her was utterly incompetent. "This doctor refused to allow her even a sip of water!" my brother complained.

Papa had begun to blame Wolfgang for Mama's death, faulting him for stubbornly persevering with plans that required Mama to delay her return. "If your mother had come straight home from Mannheim, if she had not gone with you to Paris, she would not have died," Papa insisted.

But Wolfgang argued her death was preordained by God. Her time had come, and whether she was in Paris with Wolfgang or in Salzburg with Papa and me, she would have died no matter what anyone could have done.

Their arguments confused me. I slid from one side to the other: Was it Wolfgang's fault or God's will? I didn't know, and in the end what did it matter? My mother was dead.

But Papa would not let him wriggle free. "You very seldom have followed my advice," Papa wrote angrily. He called Wolfgang's trip to Kirchheimbolanden with the Webers "stupid," and argued he would have done better to go to Mainz, where opportunities were much better. The blaming and the scolding continued.

I saw as clearly as Papa did that Wolfgang had lost his head over this Weber girl with a pretty face and a lovely voice but no experience. After all our sacrifices, my brother was ready to forget his family and to throw all his efforts into establishing this little dove he'd fallen in love with. For that, I, too, blamed him. But I could not, in my heart, hold him responsible for our mother's death.

GRAY AUTUMN SKIES settled over Salzburg. One day as I was out walking Miss Bimperl, my head lowered and dark thoughts absorbing my attention, I glanced up and saw Captain d'Ippold of the boys' school striding briskly toward me. "*Guten Tag,* Fräulein Mozart," he greeted me.

I returned his greeting—"Good day, Captain"—expecting to continue on my way uninterrupted. But the captain fell into step with me. "May I walk with you a little?" he asked.

His manner was pleasant, and I really didn't mind. He asked a number of questions about Wolfgang, which I answered carefully. He seemed to be under the impression that my brother had accepted a position at Versailles in the court of Louis XVI and Marie Antoinette.

"Far more likely he will settle here in Salzburg," I explained. "We expect him to return shortly." And then— what prompted this, I don't know, but it may have been the kindness in his earnest blue eyes—I added, "Perhaps when he arrives home you would do us the honor of lunching with us."

"I should be delighted, Fräulein," he said, raised his hat and bowed, and strode off toward the Virgilianum.

Bimperl strained at her leash, wanting to follow the captain, but I marched her in the opposite direction, toward the Dwarfs' Garden.

A MONTH PASSED with no word from Wolfgang, driving Papa to distraction. But when letters did begin to arrive, always out of phase with Papa's, his frustration deepened. Wolfgang was eager to leave Paris, a city he now declared that he hated, along with everything French. "These stupid Frenchmen seem to think I'm still seven years old, my age when they first saw me," he wrote.

He was disgusted with his host, Baron Grimm, who had been so unfailingly kind and helpful. He disliked the quarters furnished him at no cost by the baron's mistress, Madame d'Épinay, who also graciously fed my brother many of his meals. "But no more than fourteen times in the two months I've been here," Wolfgang protested. "And anyway they would have lunched whether I was at their table or not." I thought him ungrateful and rude.

And there was more. Colloredo had offered to take Wolfgang on again as Konzertmeister and organist, but my brother was adamant about what he would and would

not do as a member of the court. "Under no circumstances," Wolfgang declared, "will I agree to be a fiddler."
This, after Papa's efforts, and the Countess Lodron's, on
his behalf! A few lines further on he proposed to buy a
cabriolet, a small two-wheeled carriage. It was an expense
he could ill afford. And he was determined to take the
long way home, stopping off in Mannheim to pay a visit to
those dear friends, the Weber family.

"It's all about that Weber girl!" Papa exclaimed. "I'm
sure he's determined to marry her, no matter how foolish
his schemes may be."

There would be no purchase of a cabriolet, Papa wrote,
not when Wolfgang continued to borrow money and debts
continued to mount. And there would be no roundabout
visit to Mannheim.

AT THE END OF September 1778, Wolfgang left Paris
bound for Strasbourg. But after several days had passed
with no further word, our worry deepened. Whenever
Abbé Bullinger appeared at our door, our imaginations
leaped to awful conclusions. We fretted over reports we'd
received of robberies on the road to Munich. We would
not stop worrying until Wolfgang was safely back in Salzburg.

Eventually we received letters describing concerts he'd
given at which he'd taken in virtually no money, spent too
much on rooms and meals, but received enthusiastic cries

of *Bravissimo!* These reports enraged Papa, who fired off letter after letter, begging, pleading, cajoling, *demanding* that Wolfgang listen to him, obey him, and return to Salzburg at once. "People praise him, and that's always enough for him!" Papa thundered. He flung the letter across the room. It was at least an hour before he was calm enough to sit down, plunge quill into inkwell, and pour out another torrent of words.

The next morning as I knelt in the chapel of the Mirabell Palace, my eyes on the altar and Wolfgang on my mind, Katherl slipped in beside me. When Mass ended and we were walking out together, I whispered, "Are you in a hurry? I need to talk to you in strictest confidence."

"I have a little time," she said. "Let's walk through the cemetery. We can talk all we want there without being overheard."

An icy mist clung to our faces as we wandered among the gravestones. "Now tell me," Katherl said, "what is it?"

"Wolfgang," I said. "I'm furious at him."

Katherl laughed. "Ah, that *Spitzbube!* What is that rogue up to now?"

It surprised both of us when I burst into tears. "We make every sacrifice for his sake, and he's throwing it all away! He finally has the freedom he wants, but it's ruining him. It's ruining all of us!"

Katherl listened soberly as I described a long list of Wolfgang's misdoings, from his romantic attachment to

Aloysia Weber to his irresponsibility with money. "Papa pretends to the shooting club and our friends and especially the archbishop and the Lodrons that everything is fine—that Wolfgang is in demand all over Europe and earning lots of money, and that he's about to accept a position in some foreign city. But none of it is true; he's plunging Papa more deeply in debt than ever, and still he doesn't come home!"

"You know something, Nannerl? I love Wolferl—sorry, but I'm not going to call him by an adult name, because he's a twenty-two-year-old child! Your brother may be the most brilliant composer and the greatest virtuoso in all of Europe—perhaps the most charming young man I've ever met; women fall all over themselves to be with him—but he is a spoiled brat, and he thinks only of himself! Believe me, Nannerl, you'll never be able to count on him to take care of you, or to help you make the career in music you've wanted for as long as I've known you. The best advice I can give you is to find a good man and marry him—if you're lucky, he'll want you to have the life in music you deserve."

I gasped. Her honesty shook me to the depths of my soul. But I understood that she spoke the truth. I bowed my head. "You're right," I said.

DEFYING PAPA'S WISHES once more, Wolfgang made a detour to Mannheim after all. But there he discovered that the Webers' fortunes had suddenly changed for the better. Aloysia and her father had both received appointments to positions in Munich in the newly formed court of Elector Karl. The family had already left Mannheim, and Wolfgang seemed determined to follow them.

He continued to send letters from here and there, everywhere except where he was supposed to be. We expected him home for his name day on October 31, or certainly for Papa's on the fifteenth of November. When both days came and went, Papa felt sure Wolfgang would be with us for Christmas, and when Christmas passed, New Year's became the next goal, and then Twelfth Night. There was still no Wolfgang.

Papa fumed and ranted, nearly tearing holes in the paper with his furious pen:

> I have told you over and over that our interests and my prospects demand that you must return to Salzburg at once. I am heartily sick of composing these letters and during the past year and three months have almost written myself blind. But to what end? I command you to leave at once, for your conduct is shameful. Am I to take the mail coach and fetch you myself?

Every letter from Wolfgang began "Dearest, best beloved father," and every letter ended "I kiss your hands a thousand times and am ever your most obedient son, W. A. Mozart." I knew that Papa loved Wolfgang boundlessly, but he also demanded boundless obedience. Wolfgang, for his part, adored Papa but went on to do exactly as he pleased—scarcely a "most obedient son." The two were at swords' points.

Then on the twenty-ninth of December, Wolfgang wrote from Munich, "Today I can only weep. I really cannot write—my heart is too full of tears. I hope you will write to me soon and comfort me." Something must have happened, but what?

Much later we learned the cause of the tears: When Wolfgang arrived in Munich, his beloved Aloysia coldly rejected him. Wolfgang's heart was broken.

Ah, Wolfgang! I thought when I heard the explanation. *All this weeping for a girl who probably didn't love you in the first place! And where are the tears for Mama? Do you still think only of yourself, just as Katherl said?* I felt ashamed of him.

"*Humph!*" Papa snorted. "I could have predicted this from the beginning."

NEARLY EVERY TIME I took Bimperl out for her morning walk, I could count on Armand d'Ippold to appear. The captain had pocketed some small treats for the dog and asked leave to give them to her. Bimperl became his devoted friend.

I looked forward to these morning greetings, which

later turned into a short stroll. I found the captain's looks appealing. He was tall and lean, his dark hair streaked with silver. He was clearly much older than I, but I was attracted to his gentle, courtly manner. I knew that he loved music, because I'd seen him at many of the Salzburg concerts, and I attended nearly all of them.

I made up my mind to ask Katherl what she knew about him. If there was an available male in the city of Salzburg she hadn't fully investigated, I would have been surprised. When Katherl next came for a shooting party, I got her alone in my room and put the question to her, knowing she would be painfully honest: "What can you tell me about Captain Armand d'Ippold?"

"So the handsome captain has caught your eye! And am I to gather that you've caught his as well?"

"Possibly," I admitted.

"Well, you have admirable taste, Nannerl. I've always thought so. If the captain had ever glanced in my direction I would have done everything possible to keep him looking! He's a widower, I believe. No children that I know of. He's had a commendable military career, working his way up from the bottom as there's neither wealth nor a noble bloodline in his background. But my dear Nannerl, he's nearly fifty, if I'm not mistaken, and you're twenty-seven. Too old for you, don't you think?"

"I don't think anything," I said and tried to change the

subject. "Now come, Katherl, I must set out the refreshments. The shooters will be here soon."

She laid her hand on my arm. "Remember what I told
you in the cemetery. The captain might be exactly what
you need, in spite of his age."

Chapter 21

CAPTAIN D'IPPOLD

ON A DAY UNCOMMONLY mild for January I'd taken Bimperl on her afternoon walk and was soon joined by Captain d'Ippold. The captain—I now called him Armand—often took a few moments from his duties to step outside the school for a breath of fresh air, and I usually managed to be there when he did. Papa was so distracted that he seemed not to notice my comings and goings. I took advantage of that to meet Armand.

We were walking toward the river, deep in conversation, when a carriage drew up in front of the Tanzmeisterhaus. I stopped, curious to see who might be coming to call, and saw my brother climb out. "It's Wolfgang! He's come home!" I cried and hurried toward the carriage, for the moment forgetting about Armand.

Papa burst out of the house, arms flung wide. He and

Wolfgang embraced long and hard, and I'm sure both were weeping. My own eyes were wet with tears when it was my turn, and then the three of us were laughing and crying, all at once.

Wolfgang had finally come home. It was not the triumphant return we'd hoped for. He had not found a position. He had run up a huge debt. By far the worst, Mama was dead. My brother must have felt uneasy about the reception he'd get at the Tanzmeisterhaus. Who could blame him? But here he was, at last.

In the midst of the excitement I noticed a young woman who had stepped down from the carriage and now stood to one side, smiling uncertainly. It was Maria Anna Thekla, the *Bäsle,* our cousin from Augsburg. Papa may not have been pleased to have someone else at hand for this reunion, but I felt immediately grateful for her presence. She might well prevent the angry explosion that had been building for so long.

That evening we lit every candle in the house. Tresel prepared a special feast—she was so excited by Wolfgang's arrival that she burned the goulash—and the *Bäsle* amused us all with her lighthearted banter. There was no mention of the Weber family or of Aloysia, and Wolfgang seemed happy to indulge his infatuation with our merry little cousin. Papa put up with this diversion for longer than I expected, but after a few days he offered to arrange the *Bäsle*'s trip back to Augsburg. Maria Anna Thekla left with promises for future visits. What remained of the Family Mozart grimly faced the future. The storm had still not broken, but it had been delayed.

We all knew that Papa blamed Wolfgang for Mama's death. "If she had been here in Salzburg, she would not have died!" he'd insisted over and over. I agreed with Katherl— my brother had behaved selfishly, like a spoiled, thought-less child. But Papa, so quick to show anger in his letters to Wolfgang or indirectly with me, did not rage at Wolfgang as I expected. Relief to have his beloved son safely home again must have dissipated his fury. Wolfgang went out of his way to avoid a confrontation. So did I. It might have been better if there *were* an explosion, because resentment and recriminations still simmered just below the surface.

One thing troubling me was that I had nothing of Mama's. "Did you not bring me her amethyst ring? Her watch?"

Wolfgang confessed that he had given the ring, a gift from Madame d'Épinay, to the nurse as payment for caring for Mama in her last days. "I had to sell the watch," he said sheepishly. "We had no money, you see. I sold my own watch, too. The rest—her clothing, her prayer book—are in the trunk with all my music. There isn't much."

He was right: There was little left of poor Mama's life.

WORD QUICKLY SPREAD that the prodigal had returned, and soon friends were flocking to the Tanzmeisterhaus to greet him. Wolfgang submitted to his fate and signed Archbishop Colloredo's contract as organist and Konzert-meister. He hated the idea. "It's like being a horse in harness," he complained. But he had no choice. Papa was deeply in debt, and for once Wolfgang acknowledged his responsibility.

We settled into a familiar pattern. Papa and Wolfgang carried out their duties at the Residenz. When he was at home, Wolfgang composed. I gave lessons every day but one. In our few leisure hours we attended performances in the new theater on Hannibalplatz; sometimes we invited the traveling players to dine with us. There was always music making, with programs three nights a week at court and our Sunday concerts at the Tanzmeisterhaus. The shooting group welcomed Wolfgang back into its midst.

I was fairly content, though my life was nothing as I'd once imagined it would be. I often played at recitals or accompanied other musicians, but these performances came up far short of my early dreams. I lived out those dreams alone at home, playing for my father and brother but mainly for myself. Only in the salon of the Tanzmeister-haus could I truly perform as a virtuoso.

My greatest source of contentment was my friendship with Armand d'Ippold, and I hoped that friendship would soon ripen into love and lead to marriage. *How handsome he is!* I thought. *How kind!* Months earlier I had wanted to invite him to lunch when Wolfgang came home. But even after all this time I was not yet ready to say anything to Papa, who, if he noticed, pretended not to.

Wolfgang caught on quickly. "I have a feeling that my dear sister is developing a bad case of *amour*," he said, striking a theatrical pose. "Am I right? The truth, now! Because I hear it in your music. You're playing with your heart instead of your head. You've always played brilliantly, but now you play passionately—ergo, it must be love. Besides, you have been observed *strolling*."

I blushed to think that my feelings had become so obvious through my music. But I shrugged and tried to pass it off lightly. "Is a lady not permitted to play with passion and to stroll with a gentleman of her acquaintance?"

"Only if her brother approves. Who is this fellow, anyway?"

I told him about Captain Armand d'Ippold, director of the Collegium Virgilianum.

"I know why he's attracted to you—you're more beautiful than ever, one of the best keyboard players in the Holy Roman Empire, and a great wit in the bargain. But tell me—why are you attracted to this particular captain?"

"Because he adores Bimperl. That's enough for me," I said, laughing off Wolfgang's flattery. There was some truth to his observation, though—even Katherl had observed that my eyes seemed brighter and my complexion more glowing. "You are one of those rare women who actually seems to improve with age," she said.

"Then I shall have to take up the matter with Miss Bimperl to see if she approves," Wolfgang said. "A greater question: What does Papa say about this man of war?"

"We haven't spoken of him."

"Unbelievable! Well, I can tell you this—our dearest papa will certainly have a very great deal to say. Be warned. I know from experience."

"You needn't warn me. But for now, *bitte,* say nothing."

"My lips are sealed." He pulled a silly face.

It was so good to have Wolfgang at home again. I had missed his high spirits and his sense of fun. He was still the prankster. When he got the chance, Wolfgang seized my journal in which I carefully listed our activities, names of people who had called on us, where we'd gone and with whom, just as I had for years. Then he proceeded to add something completely absurd, like this entry in April of 1779:

The sun went to sleep in a sack—at ten o'clock it rained with a pleasant stench—the clouds lost themselves, and a fart allowed itself to be heard, a promise of good weather tomorrow.

SOON AFTER ST. MICHAEL'S DAY, the twenty-ninth of September when rents were traditionally due, I found Viktoria reeling from her latest blow: Her stepmother had moved out of the Adlgasser home and gone to live with her father, old Fesemayr. Now Viktoria was all alone to look after her eighteen-year-old half brother, Josef, and her half sister, Anna, thirteen. She had no money to pay the rent. Josef had become so unruly after his father's death that he had to be locked up in the medieval Fortress Hohensalzburg high above the city.

Viktoria was beside herself with worry. The orphans' pittance provided by the archbishop had long since expired, and she was destitute. She had come to the Tanzmeisterhaus to comb my hair two or three times a week—I never could manage my coiffure on my own—and, knowing her straitened circumstances, I tried to pay her. When her pride interfered, I sent her an anonymous gift of money once a month. But those small gifts didn't begin to support her and the younger Adlgassers.

She was allowed a monthly visit to Josef in the fortress, to take him things he needed, and to fetch his clothes for washing and mending. Sometimes I accompanied her up the zigzag path of the Mönchsberg to the fortress. The climb left her so breathless that she could scarcely talk.

"If I were stronger, I could take a situation with a family and earn enough to care for Josef and Anna," she said when we'd stopped for her to catch her breath. "But that's impossible. I've thought of taking in sewing. I'm rather clever with a needle, but I haven't the strength to put in the long hours."

At last a family friend petitioned the archbishop to extend the orphans' pittance, and Colloredo's heart of stone softened enough to keep his former organist's children from starving.

A YEAR PASSED with no significant change in our circumstances. The Mozart family debt had been significantly reduced, due to the hard work of all three of us, but there was little cash on hand. Wolfgang abhorred working for Archbishop Colloredo. He yearned for something—anything!—to happen to release him from bondage. Papa feared I would have no one to support me if he died and if Wolfgang didn't soon grasp the success that always seemed within reach but always eluded him.

But I believed Papa had no need to worry. For a year I had managed to see Armand almost every day—mostly strolling, as Wolfgang called it, but sometimes stopping for an hour at a small inn beyond the city walls, a place so unfashionable and out of the way that we were unlikely to see or be seen by anyone we knew. At first only Viktoria and Katherl knew my secret. Then Wolfgang found out and teased, "If you don't introduce me to your captain, I'm going to tattle to Papa."

I arranged to take Wolfgang with me to our next meeting. As I expected, the two hit it off very well—Wolfgang was his charming self, and Armand pretended to be grave and serious, and we wound up laughing and talking for most of an afternoon. The owner recognized Wolfgang, produced a battered violin, and asked him to play in exchange for a bottle of wine. The instrument had a broken string, but somehow Wolfgang managed to scrape out a lively tune.

"You've got a fiddler, so now you must dance!" Wolfgang commanded.

Armand and I looked at each other. The café was nearly deserted, save for two or three old farmers and a woman with an enormous knapsack who carried goods to country villages. We had never danced together. Armand reached for my hand. The three farmers and the woman watched, grinning, and we danced. I was happy. I was in love.

EARLY IN THE NEW YEAR of 1780 in the presence of the snow-clad figures in the Dwarfs' Garden, Armand d'Ippold took both of my cold hands in his warm ones and said, "I love you, Nannerl. May I ask your father for permission to call on you officially?"

I smiled up at him. These were the words I'd been waiting to hear. "Ja," I replied. "I'd like that."

"And you love me? You consent to be the wife of this old soldier?"

"An old soldier whom I love with all my heart," I said, almost giddy with happiness. "And before these marble witnesses, I pledge myself to be your wife."

We agreed to tell no one until he spoke to Papa. I was

sure Papa would be pleased and relieved, and it was hard not to share the wonderful news, especially with Wolfgang. Two days later the captain came to the Tanzmeisterhaus. I heard Armand's voice and Papa's while I was in the kitchen with Tresel. No one sent for me. I waited until the voices stopped and Armand had gone. Then I went out to speak to Papa.

He looked anything but pleased, and my heart sank. *What could have gone wrong?* "It seems that Captain d'Ippold wishes to marry you and that you have accepted his proposal," Papa said. "But I have refused to grant my permission. Frankly, I'd hoped that your friendship would come to a natural end before it reached this point."

"But *why*, Papa?" I asked, my voice shaking. I gripped the back of a chair to steady myself.

"He's not the right choice, Nannerl. He's too old for you. His father was employed in the salt mines at a low level. He is a member of the imperial army. His position as director of the Virgilianum is not well paid, and he has very little money. But the main reason I object to the match is that Captain d'Ippold serves on the archbishop's war council. His future is entirely in the hands of Colloredo. If Colloredo refused permission for one of his right-hand men to marry a Mozart, it would be humiliating. In short, Nannerl, although I would be pleased to see you comfortably settled, I believe you can do much better than Captain d'Ippold. I know only too well from personal experience the difficulties awaiting one who marries without proper financial backing."

I gasped, groping for words to counter the arguments he had advanced with such chilling logic. I shook my head slowly, tears gathering. *Don't weep,* I warned myself. *This is no time for tears.*

"I will not tell you that you may no longer see your friend," Papa continued. "But I have informed Captain d'Ippold that marriage is out of the question. You are both wasting your time if you choose to continue a friendship that has not the slightest chance of reaching the conclusion you both think you want. Someday, Nannerl, you'll see the wisdom of my decision and thank me for it."

"Thank you for it?" I cried. "Surely you don't expect me to thank you for spoiling my chance at happiness!"

My response shocked him. "Nannerl! Take care how you speak to your father. I've had quite enough of rebellious children."

"*Ja,* Papa, I'm sure you have," I said. I turned away and fled to my room.

When I did not come out for supper, Papa didn't call me. Later he and Wolfgang left for the Residenz. I stayed in and sat at the harpsichord, pouring out my hurt and disappointment, my anger at Papa, and finally my love for Armand, until I felt as dry and empty as a husk.

The next morning when I didn't see Katherl at Mass,

I went to the Lodron Palace and asked to speak to her. The palace was no longer the bustling place it had once been. Count Potbelly had died almost a year earlier, followed within a matter of weeks by his oldest son. Since then the Countess Lodron had lost some—but not all—of her haughtiness, and the surviving children seemed to take their lives and their lessons more seriously.

Katherl came out at once. "We're in the middle of a French lesson," she said. "But they won't mind, since my French is terrible. What's wrong, Nannerl?"

The tears I'd been holding back began to fall. "Armand and I want to marry. He asked Papa for permission, but Papa refused."

I had begun to shiver. Katherl guided me to a bench near a ceramic stove. "Why?" she asked. "What possible reason can your father have to refuse?"

"In short, he believes Armand is too old, too close to Archbishop Colloredo, and has no fortune."

Katherl snorted and squeezed my icy hands. "Your father has been dying to marry you off for years. Then along comes a handsome, well-spoken candidate, and Leopold runs him off!" She shook her head, disbelieving. "Oh, Nannerl, are you truly in love with him?"

"*Ja, ja,* I am," I sobbed.

Katherl put her arms around me. "Have patience. I'll wager a slice of chocolate torte with whipped cream that Leopold Mozart will soon change his mind. He probably just doesn't want to let you go, despite all he's been saying about finding a husband to take care of you." We whispered together a while longer, exchanging comforting words. Then Katherl rose. "I must get back to my charges before they forget everything I just taught them. I'll speak to you again soon. We'll make another pilgrimage to Maria Plain and put it in the hands of the Virgin. Everything will work out just as you wish."

We embraced again, and I stepped out into a world that now seemed drained of every drop of life and color.

Chapter 22

A New Opera

ONE BY ONE the months slipped by, and my captain and I continued to walk together. At times we sat side by side at concerts. Occasionally he came to the Tanzmeisterhaus, supposedly to visit Wolfgang, who winked at me and found an excuse to leave us alone. Katherl and I made another pilgrimage. Nothing changed.

Now that my brother was at home, Wolfgang and I grew close again. He was twenty-four, and I'd turned twenty-nine, but Papa still treated us like helpless, feckless children, unable to make proper decisions. We both resented his attempts to control us and yet we tolerated it—I suppose because we still believed that, as Wolfgang used to say, "After God comes Papa."

One Sunday afternoon in late summer a party of friends made plans to climb the Kapuzinerberg to a beer garden.

Wolfgang and I found ourselves separated from others in the group. He sprawled against a fallen beech log, and I sat down beside him, careful of my skirts. We gazed out over the rooftops and began to talk openly, in a way we never felt free to do within the walls of our home.

"It's been more than two years, and Papa still blames me for Mama's death," Wolfgang said. "It was terrible for me, Nannerl. I don't know what I could have done differently. But whenever Mama is mentioned, Papa reminds me, not at all subtly, that if she'd come home when he wanted her to, and not gone to Paris with me, she would still be alive."

He threw me a look that pleaded for understanding. "It must have been her time," I said. "It wasn't your fault. You must not blame yourself." But I couldn't help adding, "Still, you did behave quite selfishly—running after that Weber girl, wasting precious time and money when you should have been concerned about Papa and me." I was surprised to find I was still angry.

Wolfgang had the grace to look contrite. "I'm sorry, Nannerl." His contrition lasted only for a moment. "But if you only knew her, I know you'd forgive me! She's a lovely girl," he said with a wistful smile, "and her voice is truly magnificent. You've never heard such purity of tone! Her range is almost unbelievable. Her control is perfect. She's an excellent clavier player as well"—he grinned winningly—"though not nearly as accomplished as my dear sister."

He talked about his love for Aloysia and the pain of her rejection: "When I reached Munich, she no longer wanted anything to do with me. I was devastated." Wolfgang picked up a stick and began scratching figures in the dirt. "I wanted to take her to Italy, but Papa said no one would pay the slightest attention to one so young, no matter how large her talent."

"Papa was wrong about that," I said. "The Three Ladies— Madderl Haydn and Anna Adlgasser and Maria Brauenhofer—all trained in Italy before they were twenty and soon had singing careers." I jerked the stick out of his hand and forced him to look at me. "Did it ever occur to you how desperately I yearned to study in Italy when I was a girl of eighteen?"

"You are a superlative clavier player, but you're not a great singer, Nannerl! The archbishop didn't send you to study because he would not have considered hiring a female clavier player, no matter how talented."

"Papa might have persuaded Schrattenbach, if he hadn't always been looking out for you!"

"It's not fair to blame me," Wolfgang argued.

"Have you any idea how much I resented your plans to travel with the Webers?" I demanded, snapping the stick in two. "But I do understand it's Papa who's the real cause of my disappointment. And now he's forbidden me to marry Armand."

"You're really in love with him, aren't you?" he asked, his voice softening.

I nodded. "I'd marry him tomorrow, if Papa would give his consent. But he refuses, and you well know it's not possible for a daughter to marry without it."

"This is ridiculous! Armand should be here with you now! I've got to get away from Salzburg, and so must you. You deserve some happiness, Nannerl. I promise you that as soon as I have a position, I will send for you, and you will have the life you've always wanted."

A noise nearby halted the conversation. Suddenly Abbé Bullinger crashed through the bushes like an affable bear. "Why are you two dawdling here?" he inquired jovially. "The beer will be flat before we get there."

Making an effort to laugh, we rose and followed our friend, trying to forget for a while the painful place in which we found ourselves.

PAPA COMMISSIONED an artist to paint a new family portrait. Wolfgang and I were seated at the harpsichord, our hands crossing as though we were playing one of Wolfgang's duets; Papa leaned on the harpsichord, holding his violin, a quill at his elbow. Mama was represented by her portrait hanging on the wall in an oval frame, a painting within a painting.

My friseur had created a marvelous coiffure tied with a lovely pink ribbon. Papa wore a powdered peruke. Wolfgang had let his light brown hair grow out, and he was very proud of the thick, wavy mane tied with a ribbon at the nape of his neck. That's how he wanted to be portrayed. Papa wouldn't allow it. In the end Wolfgang gave in and wore a peruke as well.

Most of the work on the painting was finished before Wolfgang left for Munich in the autumn. He'd been invited by Elector Karl Theodor to compose an opera for the Carnival season. Archbishop Colloredo grudgingly allowed him a leave of six weeks, beginning in November. "It's not nearly enough time, given the amount of work to be done, but I'm not going to worry about that until I must," Wolfgang said as he packed his music.

He'd already started work on the dramatic opera, *Idomeneo.* "It's going to be an amazing work, Nannerl," he told me. "It's about the king of Crete, who's just defeated the Trojans. His ship is caught in a terrible storm, and he almost drowns. To save his life, he promises Neptune he'll sacrifice the first living creature he sees on shore. That turns out to be his son, Idamante, who's in love with Ilia, daughter of the king of Troy."

I shivered. "Does it end well?"

"It does, just as it will for us, I trust! It's a traditional *opera seria,* but I'm trying all sorts of new things, breaking old conventions. Papa disapproves—he wants me to keep doing the same popular thing. But he'll get used to it."

Wolfgang surveyed his baggage and boxes, and then he

was gone. He had managed to find a way to escape, at least for a while, and I prayed that he would find something permanent and send for me, as he promised.

PAPA BEGAN to make plans to travel to Munich to see the new opera, and I would go with him. Wolfgang wrote regularly, seeking Papa's advice on problems he encountered with the text—the librettist kept making huge changes—and the demands of the singers, some objecting to words with too many repeated vowels that were difficult to sing. He wrote to me, too: "You must not be lazy but practice hard. People are looking forward to hearing you play."

The chance to perform again thrilled me. I played for an hour or two every day for my own satisfaction—music was the one place I could express my pain and frustration at Papa's refusal to accept Armand. But finding extra hours to practice for a performance wasn't easy. Dr. Barisani's daughter Theresia came to the Tanzmeisterhaus three times a week for clavier lessons. She was one of the "favorite mademoiselles" Wolfgang had me visit when he was in Italy. I'd found her profoundly silly then, but she had since matured into a pleasant young woman with a true appreciation for music and the willingness to work hard. Still, I sensed that her interest in music was driven by an even deeper interest in my brother. He apparently thought highly of her, too, sending greetings "to your beautiful and clever pupil." And I had several other pupils as well, all of whom took up my time.

IN AUTUMN I WAS brought low by a heavy catarrh. I lay in bed, drifting in and out of a restless sleep. When I awoke to find Papa waiting with a cup of barley water to hold to my dry lips or sitting quietly by my bed with a book in his lap, I regretted the anger I often felt toward him.

I often dreamed of Armand. I wondered if he knew why he hadn't seen me, if he had inquired about me, if he had decided to give up. Why had he not at least sent me a message?

My fever climbed and my cough worsened, and Papa sent for Dr. Barisani, who pressed his ear to my back, listened to my lungs, and prescribed various medicines and a diet of light, moist foods. "She must be bled," the physician advised. "It's the best way to reduce the fever."

Papa called in the barber-surgeon, Katherl's father. "If your dear mama had been bled in time, and sufficiently, she would be with us to this day," Papa said as the basin filled with my blood and I nearly fainted from weakness.

When I was finally strong enough to leave the house again, I agreed to accompany Katherl to the theater. The play was so dreadful that it drove nearly everyone out, and we left early. Armand d'Ippold was waiting for us. I hadn't seen him for nearly a month.

"I've been so worried about you," he told me. "I've come

by nearly every day. I trust that your father delivered my messages?"

Messages? Papa had not said a word about Armand or his messages, but I couldn't bring myself to betray him. "*Ja, ja,* he did," I lied. "*Danke schön.* Thank you." Later, after Armand had bid us *Gute Nacht,* Katherl and I lingered outside the Tanzmeisterhaus. I confessed I had lied to Armand. "I never got his messages."

Katherl stared at me. "Your father didn't tell you? He has no right to do that to you! My father would never do such a thing!"

"Your father is not Leopold Mozart."

"You must not allow him to treat you like a child. Speak to him, Nannerl!"

"*Ja,* I will," I promised. And I did. Exhausted as I was, still weak from my illness, I went straight to Papa's room. Papa laid aside the book he was reading. "Captain d'Ippold says he came to see me every day," I said. "Why didn't you tell me?"

"What good would it have done you? I thought it best for you not to know, so you could forget him."

I started to tell him *I* would decide if I wanted to forget him, when suddenly I was overcome with weakness, and I stood swaying in the doorway. In the end Papa had to carry me to my own room and put me to bed, as if I were indeed a child.

———

EARLY IN THE MORNING of December 2, a courier rode into Salzburg with the news that Empress Maria Theresia was dead. Every court in Europe would now go into mourning. My first thought (selfishly!) was that her death might interfere with Wolfgang's opera and our journey to Munich. But Wolfgang assured us that the opera would open once the six-week mourning period ended and asked us to send his black suit.

When I heard that mourning dress was to be worn for three months, I ordered a new black gown. I agreed to a high price for it, hoping Wolfgang would pay for it.

The first two acts of *Idomeneo* were in rehearsal, and Wolfgang was writing at breakneck speed to finish the third. "The elector came to a rehearsal, and he's raving to everyone about it." Meanwhile, Wolfgang's six-week leave of absence had expired. Papa decided not to mention it to Colloredo. When the archbishop announced that he was going to Vienna for a few months, the matter was still unsettled.

At the end of January Papa and I set off for Munich. Until the last moment I hoped Katherl might come with us, but she couldn't afford the cost of food and lodging, and we couldn't afford to take her as our guest. What a sad thing, always to have lack of money such a problem! But my disappointment was offset by my excitement: This would be my first journey away from Salzburg in five years, since the performance of Wolfgang's *La finta giardiniera*.

We arrived in time for the dress rehearsal. In Act III the four main characters—Idomeneo; his son Idamante; Ilia, the girl who loves him; and Elettra, her rival—are brought together for a quartet, surely one of Wolfgang's most beautiful pieces. "It's my favorite," he admitted. "It's so moving that I nearly burst into tears every time I hear them sing it."

The audience agreed. During the first performance of *Idomeneo* later, nearly everyone wept. Wolfgang's first serious opera received enthusiastic praise.

"Mozart is the complete master of orchestral color," said the conductor. "His melodies are exquisite. The accompanied recitatives are superlative."

"Such genius!" exclaimed Frau Robinig, who had traveled from Salzburg with the Barisanis. "And to think our Wolfgang is only twenty-five!"

IT WAS CARNIVAL, and we attended countless masked balls and entertainments and spent time with friends, but by far the best part for me was the chance to perform with my brother. On several occasions we played concertos on two harpsichords and duets on one. For so many months after Papa's refusal to allow my marriage, my days had passed in a muffled fog. But now I felt truly alive again, transported by the beauty and excitement of the music, acutely aware of every sensation. It was the way it had been when we were children, *Wunderkinder*—a perfect intuition of how the music should be played. Wolfgang praised me to the stars, and I was glad I'd put in all those hours of practice. If only Armand had been there to hear us. His absence was a dull ache. I supposed it always would be.

Then Wolfgang received painful news of his own. "Aloysia won a position with the Burgtheater in Vienna a year and a half ago," he told me, his face very pale. "The family moved there with her, but a month after her debut her father died." His lips trembled. "Aloysia has married an actor, Josef Lange. She's expecting a child."

He looked completely crushed. I took his hand. I understood now, as I had not before, what it was to lose the one you loved and hoped to marry. "Ah, my poor Wolfgang," I said sympathetically. "What is there to say?"

"Nothing," he whispered and stumbled away.

After the last performance of *Idomeneo* we traveled to Augsburg for a family visit. The *Bäsle* was just what my brother needed. Wolfgang and our dear little cousin behaved with great decorum, although they did manage to slip off together quietly more often than I thought proper. *Has the girl no morals?* I wondered. *Has he?*

We had several more opportunities to perform together in the city of Papa's birth, repeating the two concertos we'd played in Munich. The usual grayness of my life disappeared, and I felt bathed in color—dazzling at times, becoming muted with a change in key, darkening in a minor mode, brightening again as the tempo quickened.

Among those in the audience was Theobald Marchand, director of the court theater in Augsburg, with his wife and children. They were utterly enchanted by our playing. *If only our lives could be like this always,* I thought as Wolfgang and I took our bows and the young Marchands gazed at us worshipfully.

We returned to Munich. There was no offer from the elector, a severe disappointment to all of us. Instead, Wolfgang found a summons from Colloredo, ordering him to Vienna. The archbishop intended to remain there for some time and expected a group of his musicians to entertain him and his friends until he returned to Salzburg.

This was not what Wolfgang wanted to hear, but he had long overstayed his six-week leave, and he packed up his belongings and his music. With cries of *Bravo!* still ringing in his ears, he was on his way to Vienna.

Meanwhile, Papa and I traveled back to Salzburg, taking with us Herr Marchand's eleven-year-old son, Heinrich. Hennerle, as he was called, would live at the Tanzmeisterhaus and study music with us. It seemed like a good idea, for it guaranteed us a small but steady income.

Papa still had his duties at the Residenz in addition to his private pupils, and I was charged with running the household, despite Tresel's best efforts to thwart me, and attending to my own pupils. More than ever I needed time to escape into my music to renew myself. But now, on top of all, we were expected to educate Hennerle in the classics, teach him a foreign language or two, and, of course, provide musical training. Although he was a sweet-tempered boy, he was lazy and practiced only if one of us stood over him.

We needed Wolfgang's help. But we had no idea when he was coming home.

Part 4

MOZART
1781

Chapter 23

COLLOREDO

WOLFGANG ARRIVED IN VIENNA, "tired as a dog," and
started complaining. He'd been put up in a palace near the
cathedral with other members of the archbishop's staff
and was being treated as a servant. His place at the lunch
table was somewhat lower than the men whose duties
were to light chandeliers and open doors and only a little
higher than the cooks, an obvious insult. He disliked the
early hour at which lunch was served: noon. The food was
wretched. Worst of all, he was forbidden to give concerts
for noble Viennese families. Not only was he underpaid
and disrespected, but he was also denied the chance to
earn a few extra florins.

"I can see how this is going," Papa said, scowling at Wolfgang's letter. "Without me to rein him in, Wolfgang is sure
to enrage Colloredo. And then there will be the devil to pay."

In his next letter Wolfgang referred to the archbishop as "the arch-booby," calling him a "malevolent prince who plagues me daily and pays me the most miserable salary." He wrote this without bothering to use the family cipher. The archbishop's censors had undoubtedly read every word and reported to him.

Papa clutched his head and groaned. "Has Wolfgang lost his senses? This cannot continue." He snatched up his quill and poured out another letter in an effort to control my unruly brother.

We still didn't know if or when Wolfgang was coming home. In one letter he debated his preference for one kind of transportation to Salzburg over another—by mail coach, ordinaire, or post chaise—and the relative costs. Then in the next letter he sang sweet praises of Viennese life, convinced he could easily find work there. If only he could persuade Emperor Josef to hire him! If only he would be appointed music teacher to some member of the imperial family!

In May he wrote, "I am seething with rage!"

He and Colloredo had gotten into a shouting match. Wolfgang described the scene, the archbishop blazing away "like a fire," calling Wolfgang a rascal and a dissolute fellow, a scoundrel and a vagabond. Wolfgang, his blood beginning to boil, could scarcely get in a word.

"I'll have nothing more to do with you!" Colloredo shouted.

"Nor I with you!" Wolfgang shouted back.

"Then be off with you!" the archbishop roared.

Wolfgang took him at his word, shoved everything into his trunk, and rushed out into the streets and from there into a pretty little room rented from none other than "old Madame Weber." Papa's face was dangerously flushed when he read this. His worst fears were being realized. What would happen next?

LETTERS ARRIVED from Wolfgang, promising sums of money that were never sent. We could certainly have used it, but I suspected that our circumstances at the time were not nearly as dire as my brother's. The Viennese court had retired to the country for the summer, taking Wolfgang's potential pupils. He had to find a way to survive until the court returned in autumn. Yet even with such poor prospects, Wolfgang seemed determined to make his separation from the archbishop's court permanent and official.

"He cannot resign from his position with the archbishop without my permission. And I will not give it!" Papa was shouting now, forgetting that Hennerle, only eleven, was standing wide-eyed in the doorway.

I steered Hennerle to the little room we used for his study. "Come, let us work on Latin conjugations," I whispered. Papa had already flung himself down at his writing table to begin his reply.

———

ONE DAY IN EARLY summer I encountered Katherl at the mercer's shop. "Just the person I wanted to see!" she cried. "I have a letter from my brother Franz!" Franz Wenzel Gilowsky was a physician struggling to establish a practice in Vienna. "He's written me all about Madame Lange," she said as we waited for the mercer's assistant to fill our orders. "It's quite a tale. What would you like to know?" she asked with an arch smile.

Madame Lange, I thought; *formerly Aloysia Weber.* "All of it, of course," I said.

"Well," she said, "there's truth and there's rumor, and it's not always easy to tell them apart. Franz says Josef Lange was widowed two years ago. He's a fine actor and a talented painter as well. He met Aloysia Weber at the Burgtheater, where she made a sensation with her singing debut. They were married on the thirty-first of this past October." Katherl leaned close and whispered, "She was already four months gone. He's said to be mad about her and a jealous fool. Surely Wolfgang knows all about this by now. I wonder how he feels?"

It had started to rain, and Katherl and I huddled together in the shelter of a doorway with our shopping baskets. "I think it hurt him, but I can say truthfully that my brother is as fickle as a honeybee, flitting from flower to flower," I admitted. "He'll forget Madame Lange soon enough and lose his heart to someone new."

"He has plenty to choose from," said Katherl. "Frau

Weber has three more daughters, each talented and beautiful, although none as talented or as beautiful as Madame Lange. The problem is Frau Weber. Franz says that since her husband died she's become a bit too fond of drink, and she can be awfully unpleasant."

When the shower passed, Katherl and I went our separate ways, promising to meet soon again. I was still thinking about the Webers, with whom Wolfgang was now living. There was a great deal I was not going to tell Papa. He'd have to hear it from someone else, which of course he would.

MAMA HAD BEEN DEAD for three years. I missed her, and I'm sure Papa did, too, although he rarely spoke of her—perhaps it was too painful. Often, I'm afraid, I took out my own frustration on poor Tresel, shouting at her over trifles, calling her a stupid ox, until both of us collapsed in tears. But I had one pillar of strength during that difficult summer, when it seemed that Wolfgang was doing everything imaginable to enrage the archbishop and drive Papa to the point of apoplexy. That pillar was Armand d'Ippold. He visited me as often as he dared, in spite of Papa's continued opposition to a marriage and his stiff formality whenever Armand was around.

"You must not take everything so to heart, dear Nannerl," Armand said soothingly when he'd found me in a state of nervous exhaustion over Wolfgang's latest letter and Papa's ensuing storm. "Come, sit down and play something for me. That will cheer you."

He was right. Playing always cheered me, especially when Armand was my audience. I was able to pour into the music all the tender sentiments I was forbidden to express. Since I'd fallen in love with Armand, the kind of music I most liked to play had changed, almost without my realizing it. It wasn't just that I played with my heart instead of my head, as Wolfgang had once pointed out. When I was young and dreaming of a career, I loved to play bravura pieces, the faster the better, to show off my virtuosity, dazzling large audiences with speed and precision. But I'd come to prefer the andante movements that spoke intimately of longing, one soul for another. And so I sat down and played for Armand, caressing the wooden keys as I desired to caress *him*. I poured out my heart, and he listened, his love for me shining in his eyes.

I pleaded again with my father to reconsider. "Papa, I beg you," I said, kneeling by his side. "Armand is devoted to me. He is not wealthy, but he earns enough to support me, and you as well, when you decide to retire. We would welcome you into our home. And I love him!"

Papa regarded me coldly. "I shall never consent to your marriage to Captain d'Ippold," Papa reminded me.

"But—," I began.

"I have given you my reasons," he interrupted. "All the pleading in the world will not change my mind. I will not forbid you to see him, but it would be wise of you to see less of him."

When I repeated this latest exchange to Armand, he smiled and said, "We must have patience, my dearest. I believe your father is testing us, to be sure our affections are steadfast. And I intend to see you as often as I'm permitted."

My own outlook was much darker. I believed Papa meant what he said, and if I could not persuade him to change his mind, I also could not oppose him. To marry without a parent's consent was unthinkable—I could not name one respectable person who had done so.

One day, when I had finished my lessons for the morning and the Lodron children had been sent off to the country to visit their cousins, Katherl and I decided to climb the Kapuzinerberg to the monastery above the city.

"There's a new rumor about Wolfgang," I told her when we reached the crest and stopped to rest. "He admits now that he was a fool about Aloysia—she's just given birth to a son—but a musician from Vienna informed Papa that Wolfgang is involved with another of the Weber sisters, Constanze. Wolfgang denies everything, of course."

Katherl laughed. "And you believe him?"

I shook my head. "I know him too well. Then last week he wrote Papa a letter swearing that the whole business with the archbishop is a matter of honor, which he prizes 'more than life itself.' Those are his words. He'll do anything to stay in Vienna. He insists that Papa and I, and Armand, too, would prosper there. But Papa still refuses to allow Wolfgang to resign officially. He's as stubborn about that as he is about allowing me to marry Armand."

"Take Wolfgang's advice, Nannerl, and go to Vienna," Katherl said. "Armand d'Ippold is the perfect match for you, despite his age. Your father wants to control you, because he can no longer control your brother. Wolfgang has broken away, your dear mother is dead, and your father is terrified of losing you, too. You're all he has left."

"You may be right," I replied. "And that makes it doubly difficult to go against his wishes. But if Wolfgang offered me the opportunity to go to Vienna, I think I would seize it." Below us a bell struck the hour, and we started down. "Whether I go or stay, Katherl, you owe me a slice of chocolate torte. Papa is not going to change his mind about Armand."

THE DAY CAME when there was no turning back for Wolfgang. The archbishop's assistant, Count Arco, summoned him for a meeting, and the two got into a noisy quarrel. The count called Wolfgang a knave and a clown and kicked him—literally booted him in the behind—out of the antechamber and down the stairs. Wolfgang's pride and honor were severely wounded. He considered the matter finished. And now Archbishop Colloredo was on his way back to Salzburg—without Wolfgang.

We had begun to hear unpleasant tales about my brother and his affairs with various women. Maybe the rumors were the mischief of one of the archbishop's staff members, but they were enough to ignite Papa's smoldering temper. "He must leave that Weber household at once!" he bellowed, and began another letter.

AROUND THE TIME of my name day and my thirtieth birthday Wolfgang sent me a gift of several pretty ribbons and a letter inquiring about Armand. I wrote to thank him and described Papa's unshakable opposition to a marriage. "He's absolutely set against it. Advise me, if you can." I hoped for my brother's support and counsel, but I didn't hear from him for a long time. Apparently he was too busy to reply. I was more disappointed than angry. Wolfgang had shown repeatedly that his heart was in the right place and his intentions were good—noble, even—but he could not be counted on for help when I needed him.

By the end of summer I had fallen ill again, and once more Papa cared for me. The strain of his work at the Residenz and of his numerous pupils, especially Hennerle, complicated by my own poor health, took its toll. Papa complained of dizzy spells and faintness.

This time Wolfgang responded, suggesting a common remedy for Papa's ailments: cart grease wrapped in paper and worn on one's chest, a veal bone wrapped in paper with the bright yellow petals of leopard's-bane and carried in one's pocket. And he was quick to diagnose my malady as well. "The best cure for you would be a husband," he wrote. "Marriage would have a profound influence on your health."

He made several suggestions: Armand d'Ippold should come to Vienna and find work—Wolfgang would make contacts for him. "And you could teach and give concerts. There are many distinguished families who hesitate to engage a man to teach their children but would be happy to pay handsomely for a woman." Between the three of us, he said, we could support Papa in a proper retirement.

"Lovely idea, isn't it?" I told Armand, who'd been permitted a short visit.

"But not easily accomplished by a man of fifty-two," he pointed out. "What would I do there? My work is here, at the school and with the archbishop. Not in Vienna." We sat in silence, not even daring to hold hands in my father's house, lest we be forbidden to meet at all.

WITH THE RETURN of the nobility to Vienna for the autumn season, Wolfgang's fortunes improved. Vienna buzzed with the news of a royal engagement. Grand Duke Paul of Russia, son of Catherine the Great, was coming for the betrothal of his wife's fourteen-year-old sister, Princess Elisabeth of Württemberg, to Emperor Josef's nephew. Having all this royalty present meant more opportunities for Wolfgang to perform. At the emperor's request, he was composing a comic opera, and he had the chance to play for the royal visitors, perhaps even to be appointed the young princess's keyboard teacher. Things would work out well after all.

Then we learned that Wolfgang had fallen in love again. The object of his affections was Constanze Weber, Aloysia's younger sister. When her name was first mentioned, Wolfgang had denied everything. Now he was not just in love with her. He was determined to marry her.

Chapter 24

IN LOVE

WOLFGANG BEGAN his letter of December 15 as he always did, "Dearest, best beloved father," and ended it, as he always did, "Ever your most obedient son, W. A. Mozart." Between beginning and end my brother revealed his love for Constanze and set forth his reasons for wanting to marry her. His honor was at stake, he explained fervently. He must marry Constanze Weber!

This touched off another round of fireworks.

I sympathized with my brother's desire to lead his life without Papa's interference, but I also understood Papa's reasoning: Why couldn't Wolfgang recognize how much we depended on him to find work that would support an aging father and an unmarried sister? He could barely support himself, and now he intended to support a wife as well.

Aloysia Weber had once spurned my brother's affections and almost immediately given herself to the first handsome actor who flattered her. It wouldn't have surprised me if this younger sister was also lacking in virtue and had spun a web of deceit and seduction to lure my brother into marriage. I was prepared to scorn Constanze Weber.

Papa saved all of the family's letters, keeping them in a series of handsome wooden cases on a shelf by his writing table. I often found Papa with tears in his eyes, rereading Mama's letters. Now I saw him with the letters Wolfgang had written to Mama and me from Italy and Vienna when he was still our Wolferl and eager to please—not this rebellious and often arrogant young man determined to have his own way at all costs. The collection of letters, numbering in the hundreds, made up a recorded history of our family life.

While Papa was out, I searched for the letter in which Wolfgang had had quite a lot to say about his views on love and marriage. I found what I was looking for: Only five months earlier he had replied to gossip regarding his supposed plan to marry a daughter of the Weber household. He denied the rumor. "If ever there was a time when I thought less of getting married, it is most certainly now! My mind is fixed on very different matters." He was polite to all the young women in the house where he rented a room, he claimed, and to Constanze in particular, "but I am not in love with her."

Now it seemed the earth had reversed its direction, the sun rising in the west and setting in the east. He had decided to marry Constanze, and he rushed on to demonstrate just how *logical,* how *well thought out* his decision was, how *well founded* his reasons. It made me want to scream!

His first reason was physical: "The voice of nature speaks as loud in me as in others." But, he assured Papa, he was too honorable to seduce an innocent girl and too fearful of disease to fool about with whores.

His second reason was practical: He needed someone to take care of him. A wife was necessary, since he'd never learned to look after himself.

If his first reason made me blush, the second made me laugh. He all but blamed his parents (and me) for the fact that he was badly spoiled! He listed two more reasons: his preference for a peaceful domestic situation, and—the one most likely to provoke Papa—his desire to save his beloved from her wretched family. It provoked me, too. He was more concerned about rescuing the Weber girl than he'd ever been about rescuing *me.*

I read Wolfgang's letter so many times that I could have recited it from memory. "She is not ugly, but at the same time far from beautiful. Her whole beauty consists in two little black eyes and a pretty figure." I had learned not to trust my brother's descriptions of women. They were never accurate, and they changed according to his whim. I tried to imagine what Constanze Weber must really be like.

"Wolfgang wants to marry," I told Armand the next time he came for a brief visit. Papa was drilling Hennerle the Lazy from his violin book, and we had a few moments alone. "My brother promises that Papa will receive one-half of his fixed income, once he's secured it. At that time he will ask Papa to give his consent to the marriage."

"And what does Leopold Mozart say about that?" Armand asked with a faint smile. "One-half of zero is always zero, as I teach my students. Your father is no more likely to consent to that marriage than he is to ours."

I didn't need Armand to tell me how hopeless it seemed for all of us, including poor little Fräulein Weber.

THE EXPLOSIVE LETTER of December 15 arrived in Salzburg at about the same time as a musician named Peter Winter, who was traveling from Vienna to Munich. Herr Winter stayed just long enough to poison Papa's mind entirely and to plant further suspicions in mine.

Winter claimed there was more to the story than Wolfgang admitted. The Weber girls' guardian had forced him to sign a formal agreement, promising to marry Constanze within three years, with or without Papa's consent, or to pay her an annual sum of three hundred florins. And Herr Winter stated plainly that Fräulein Weber was a trollop.

"A slut!" Papa cried, repeating their conversation to me.

My brother, contracted to marry a slut—was it possible? Wolfgang had been infatuated with any number of "mademoiselles," all from good families. With the exception of the *Bäsle*, they had all behaved like proper young ladies. I might have expected Papa to throw Herr Winter out of the house, for this accusation was as much an insult to my brother as it was to Fräulein Weber.

But instead all of Papa's fury was directed at Wolfgang. The door had scarcely closed behind Herr Winter before Papa was at work on another letter. I didn't see his reply before he posted it—Papa often refused to let me read his intemperate letters to Wolfgang—but I could guess at the contents.

Days passed. My nerves, always taut, were now completely frayed. At last the post arrived from Vienna. Wolfgang begged Papa not to believe ill of his beloved.

"*Basta!*" Papa roared. "Your brother is a fool! He's throwing away his life—as well as mine and yours!"

I'm not sure which infuriated Papa more: Wolfgang's decision to marry this particular girl, his intent to marry without a secure and settled income, or the marriage contract he'd apparently been induced to sign.

Wolfgang tried to explain it away. The Weber daughters' guardian, Johann von Thorwart, had put it to him plainly: Sign a contract or stop seeing the girl. "What choice did I have?" Wolfgang wrote plaintively. So he'd drawn up the contract, signed it, and presented it to Frau Weber.

But at that crucial moment Constanze stepped into the scene. "Dear Mozart," said our heroine, "I don't need such assurances from you. I trust you." With that, she ripped up the contract, the pieces fluttering to the floor around the happy lovers, exactly as Wolfgang might have written it in an opera.

Now, my brother said, he was certain that his most beloved father would consent to the marriage to this perfect girl, "a girl who has everything but money."

Papa snorted. "Money is the whole point, does the idiot not understand that? That's why her mother opened her house to him, gave him the run of it, and allowed him every opportunity to be seduced by the daughter, all in the mistaken belief that my son would be their financial salvation."

Herr Winter had also told Papa—I learned this later—that Wolfgang had come to be despised at court and by the aristocracy, so that he had little chance of being offered a permanent position by any of them. Papa repeated the slanderous remarks to Wolfgang, who responded by providing names of those at the highest levels who admired his music and paid him extravagant compliments. (But didn't think to pay him cash, apparently!) At the top of the list was the wealthy Baroness von Waldstätten, herself an excellent performer on the harpsichord. The baroness had become his friend and patroness.

Wolfgang dealt with most of this quite calmly, considering, but then he got to his final point: "Of all the despicable things Herr Winter said, the one that truly infuriates me, and that I cannot forgive, is that he called my dear Constanze a trollop."

And those were the last words we had from my brother in the year 1781.

As the new year progressed, Wolfgang wrote less frequently, claiming he was very busy. He described his days: awakened by the friseur who came to dress his hair at six; composing until nine; giving lessons until one; lunch, sometimes not until quite late; composing again from six o'clock until nine, unless there was a concert; an evening visit to his dear Constanze; composing until bedtime, which was often not until one o'clock; up again at six. It sounded exhausting, but also exhilarating, compared to my dull life that began with Mass every morning and continued with a round of lessons and household duties, and an afternoon walk with the dog, with an hour or perhaps two to escape into my music.

Late in January Papa left for Munich, to take Hennerle for a reunion with his parents—he hadn't seen them for a year—and to bring back with them Hennerle's older sister. Margarethe, called Gretl, would now join our household as a pupil. It was Carnival, and I'd assumed that I, too, would be making the trip. But Papa quickly put an end to that notion.

"It would cost too much," Papa said. I flinched—how many times had I heard that excuse! "Then there is the matter of finding you suitable accommodations. And without Wolfgang to make arrangements, there would be no opportunities for you to play. Surely you understand this, Nannerl."

I *did* understand that without my brother no one was interested in my music. I was ready to protest that I, too, deserved the pleasure of a visit to Munich. But then I realized there would be compensation: Papa's absence meant that Armand and I were free to be together, if only for a brief time.

For more than three years Armand had been my devoted friend and, later, my suitor, but Papa did not budge from his position. He knew Armand and liked him as a man, but not as a husband for me. And Armand never challenged Papa.

"I am a soldier," Armand explained, "raised from childhood to respect authority—whether that authority is an archbishop or a father—and to obey without question. And I am not a hotheaded twenty-year-old youth, prepared to snatch you up and carry you off on my horse." Then he added with a smile, "As much as I would like to do that."

Armand also knew, as I did, that if we defied my father and married without his permission, Archbishop Colloredo would very likely remove the captain from the council and from his position at the Virgilianum. We would have nothing on which to live.

I made up my mind to enjoy the time we would have together while Papa was away. People were accustomed to
seeing us sitting side by side at concerts and plays. We
must have appeared to be the most casual of friends, even
as we danced together at the Carnival balls—nothing for
the gossips to whisper about. When Armand walked me
home from these events, I was careful to keep a proper
distance, not even to tuck my hand in the crook of his arm.
Our behavior was always above reproach.

But one starry night with fresh snow glittering beneath
a bright yellow moon, Armand suddenly pulled me close
and kissed me full on the mouth. It was the first time he
had kissed me passionately, and I was startled. My breath
came faster and my own desires welled up to match his.

"Darling Nannerl," he whispered, "how I wish that we
could always enjoy this kind of happiness together. You
know that I adore you."

"And I, you, dearest Armand," I murmured.

It was as if a dam had burst in our hearts. Armand held
me tighter, kissed my lips again, and spoke eagerly of his
love for me. I responded just as ardently. I knew I should
push him away; what if someone saw us and passed on a
distorted story to the archbishop? Instead, I clung to him
helplessly and began to weep, my face pressed against the
rough wool of his cloak.

Finally, I wrenched myself from his arms and rushed

into the house. For an hour or more I pounded my pillow and sobbed.

By morning my grief and disappointment had turned to cold anger. Wolfgang had quit a position he detested with a man he despised, left a town he disliked, fallen in love with a girl many disapproved of, and, I had no doubt, would defy Papa and marry her with or without his consent, no matter what the consequences. My brother—the virtuoso performer, the genius composer—would do exactly as he well pleased, just as he always had! But my life would go on as it had been, with no possibility of the kind of happiness I wanted, Armand as the beloved husband with whom to share my life and my love of music and children who could come to love it, too. Only a miracle could change that.

While Papa was away in Munich, Armand and I continued to see each other, but only in public. He could not visit me at the Tanzmeisterhaus—that would have been highly improper. And we did not permit ourselves the fervent kisses that had threatened to sweep us away—that was just too painful. Instead, I poured all of my passion into my music, sitting alone at the harpsichord night after night, hour after hour, letting my love for Armand find its outlet in my playing until I was too exhausted to continue.

PAPA RETURNED to Salzburg with both Hennerle the Lazy and his sister, Gretl. We now had two resident pupils and some needed additional income, but I resented the loss of time for my own precious music. And of course, my stolen time with Armand was over.

Gretl Marchand could not have been more unlike her brother. She practiced gladly, happy to learn whatever we wished to teach her, and eagerly lapped up lessons in French and Italian, drawing and arithmetic—all the things Wolfgang and I had studied when we were children. Gretl spent a great deal of time with me, often helping with the work of the household. She took over the care of Herr Canary and the finches and got them to sing again. She had more patience than I did with Tresel. And she began to show considerable talent as a singer. I enjoyed watching her bloom.

Both children fitted in well with our Salzburg life. They attended morning Mass with me, joined in our weekly shooting parties, and were always ready to make music with us and our friends. Papa grew fond of these "turbulent creatures," as he called them. They filled the Tanzmeisterhaus with their good cheer, which had been missing from our household since Mama's death. Their lively presence often pulled me back from the edge of hopelessness and despair.

Chapter 25

CONSTANZE

LETTERS FROM WOLFGANG were rare after he'd announced his determination to marry Mademoiselle Weber, but he did send me a gift of two delicately pretty caps and some rather extravagant fringes for my dresses, the handiwork of his beloved.

Then Constanze herself wrote:

I should never have been so bold as to write to you, esteemed friend, had not your brother promised that you would not be offended that I am being so bold as to write to one who, though never met, is yet very precious, as she carries the name of Mozart. . . .

It was enough to set my teeth on edge.

There were rumors that a crisis had nearly ended

the engagement. A parlor game in which Mademoiselle Weber unblushingly allowed one of the young male party guests to measure the calf of her leg shocked my brother. He rebuked her, and she fled to the home of Wolfgang's patroness, Baroness von Waldstätten, who took in the heartbroken girl until matters could be smoothed over. This tale did nothing to reassure us of the young lady's respectability.

More important to me than the ups and downs of Wolfgang's love life was the fate of his new opera, *The Abduction from the Seraglio,* composed to honor the visit from the Russian grand duke. Described as "lighthearted," it was the story of a young lady named Constanze (imagine!) who'd been kidnapped by pirates from her betrothed, sold to a Turkish pasha for his harem, and of course eventually rescued.

For various reasons *Il Seraglio* was not performed for the first time until July of 1782, long after the Russians had left. The theater was crowded and there were calls for repeated encores, but there were also mishaps. When the singers lost their places in the trio at the end of the first act, Wolfgang was in such a rage that he was beside himself. "And the emperor had a complaint, too," Wolfgang told us. "'There are too many notes, my dear Mozart, too many notes!' And I said to him, 'Excellency, there are just as many notes as there should be!'"

Then in the very next sentence he returned to the subject uppermost in his mind, begging Papa to consent to his marriage to Constanze.

My heart is restless and my head confused. Your advice is well-meaning, but it no longer applies to a man who has gone so far with his beloved. Nothing can be postponed. Most beloved Father, I long to have your consent.

"He can barely support himself, let alone a wife and the inevitable children," Papa fumed. "Why does he insist upon putting himself, and therefore us, in such jeopardy?"

She has seduced him, I thought; *and he has compromised her.* "Give him your consent, Papa," I said calmly. "I'm sure you will live to regret it if you don't. Your refusal will not stop him. It will only turn him away from you."

How ironic, that I could not use this argument for myself. The difference was that Wolfgang was capable of supporting himself, and I, now thirty-one, was dependent on Papa. The possible effect on Armand's position at court and the inevitable disgrace stopped me from doing what my heart most desired; Papa's refusal would not stop Wolfgang.

Papa gazed at me, absently unfolding and refolding Wolfgang's letter. "Very well," he said at last, sighing deeply and reaching for his quill. "I shall give him my fatherly blessing."

THEY WERE MARRIED on Sunday, the fourth of August, in a shadowy side chapel at Stephansdom, Vienna's great cathedral. Constanze was twenty; Wolfgang was twenty-six. Katherl's brother Franz Gilowsky served as best man; Constanze's younger sister Sophie stood up for her; her mother and Thorwart, the guardian, were the witnesses; the district councilor gave the bride away. Wolfgang described the ceremony, but I have no idea what she wore— probably a dress done up with some of those silly fringes that seemed to please her. She probably wore a hat as well—he didn't say. Wolfgang was no doubt dressed more elegantly than Constanze; he had managed to persuade Baroness von Waldstätten to buy him the opulent red silk coat with mother-of-pearl buttons he had long admired.

"When at last we were united as husband and wife, everyone present burst into tears, so deeply were their hearts touched," he wrote. I read this and burst into tears as well, joy for my brother's happiness mingled with my own heartache. After the ceremony they drove to the baroness's luxurious home for a wedding supper with platters of boiled beef and roast pheasant, several bottles of wine from vineyards outside the city, and an elegant Linzer torte made with almonds and raspberry jam.

I wished I'd been there. I hadn't seen my brother for many months, and I missed him.

PAPA HAD GIVEN UP the battle. There was nothing to do now but make peace with the situation. Wolfgang promised that he and his "dear little wife" would visit us, but practical matters always intervened, one thing after another.

First, Grand Duke Paul might be returning to Vienna, and that would mean a special presentation of *Il Seraglio*. Then the nobility began to move back from their summer homes in the country, increasing the possibility of paid concerts and paying students. This source of income was more necessary than ever; the position Wolfgang had been counting on, music teacher to young Princess Elisabeth of Württemberg, had gone to another musician, one who could teach her singing as well as the clavier.

Wolfgang brushed off his disappointment. "I won't have to drive all the way out to the convent where the princess is living until her marriage, only to discover that she doesn't feel like taking a lesson that day."

Wolfgang assured us that he and Constanze would be in Salzburg by Papa's name day; obligations forced another postponement. The weather turned so dreadful that even carriages with eight horses could not get through the drifts. His "dear little wife" was suffering from an acute headache. His pupils "absolutely refused" to let him go.

The news that Constanze was expecting a child in June brought another delay and a new promise of a visit before her confinement. Each excuse was accompanied by an expression of their deep desire to see us.

"I don't believe they have the slightest intention of coming," Papa complained sadly. "Do you?"

I did not.

ONE DAY WAS MUCH like the next, and one week flowed into another. We took in a third pupil, the Marchand children's eight-year-old cousin, little Johanna Brochard, called Hanchen. Armand remained my devoted friend, but we no longer discussed the possibility of marriage. He calmly accepted the situation as it was, and I was hurt and angry, but we both realized that nothing would change. My temper had grown short; regrettably Tresel, our cook, often took the brunt of it.

On a cold and cheerless day just after I'd again shouted at Tresel, driving poor old Bimperl into hiding, and felt even more miserable myself, Katherl happened by. She brought a letter from her brother Franz, describing the Carnival ball Wolfgang and Constanze had given in their large apartment.

"It sounds as though they're having a merry time of it," Katherl said. "Franz says they're deeply in love. Constanze is growing plumper by the day, and so is Wolfgang, but Franz thinks he works much harder than is good for him."

Wolfgang did seem to be working too hard—teaching, preparing for a series of concerts he would give during Lent, and composing concertos for the fortepiano and arias for Aloysia, with whom he had somehow forged a musical partnership. But I was working hard as well and *not* having a merry time of it. No private balls for me, no deeply rewarding love affair. I handed the letter back to Katherl with a grimace.

"Perhaps we should make another pilgrimage to the church of Maria Plain," she said. "And petition the Virgin for something different."

"Perhaps," I agreed. But somehow I was always too busy to arrange it.

DESPITE OUR MISGIVINGS about Wolfgang's marriage and his choice of a bride, Papa and I were gladdened by news of the birth of their son, Raimund Leopold, on June 17, 1783. The renewed promises to visit seemed sincere. Papa and I made cautious plans for their arrival.

They arrived at the end of July. I'd been watching for them for days, hurrying often to the window hoping to see their carriage. Nevertheless, I was caught unprepared when I heard Hennerle's shout, "They're here! The coach is below!"

Papa rushed down to greet them, but my hair was untidy and I hesitated by the window and watched the scene from behind a shutter. Papa and Wolfgang embraced; Wolfgang took his wife's arm and drew her forward; Papa grasped her hand and raised it to his lips; there was animated conversation; the coachman lifted down their trunks and boxes; Constanze glanced up toward the window where I stood, gazing down at her. *Not beautiful, but pretty enough,* I thought, and stepped back.

"Aren't you going down?" Gretl asked from behind me.

"*Ja,*" I said, helplessly patting my hair. "I'm going."

I started down the stairs, a smile fixed on my lips and a determination in my heart to behave well toward my brother's wife, no matter how I felt. Wolferl and I embraced wholeheartedly, but he broke away quickly, eager to present his bride. She insisted on embracing me, which I found a bit forward of her; this time I was the one to pull away.

Constanze tried hard—a little too hard—to be pleasant and agreeable. One day I found her gazing at the family portrait that hung in the salon. "Tell me about your mother," she said. "I would like to have known her."

"She was warm and witty, and everyone loved her," I replied.

"I know I would have loved her, too," said Constanze.

"And she would have loved you," I said, adding, "she loved everyone."

We settled into a routine, attending Mass together every day, usually in the Mirabell Palace chapel, and talking about many things—even Armand, whom she met on several occasions.

"He worships you," she whispered.

"And I, him. But the situation is hopeless."

"You must never say that," she counseled.

Most on her mind and dearest to her heart, naturally, was her two-month-old son Raimund, left behind in Vienna. "Wolfgang wanted him brought up on barley water, as you both were as infants," she confided, "but my mother and I believe that infants are better fed on the breast, as my sisters and I were. Eventually we won him over and hired a nurse. It's the more modern way and by far the best, don't you agree?"

I nodded, although I had no experience and no opinion. "And where is Raimund now?" I asked.

"With my mother and the nurse," Constanze said. "I do miss him so. I wonder if we shouldn't have arranged to bring him with us—the nurse, too, of course. But my mother persuaded us it was better to leave him. Travel is hard in the best of circumstances, and she believes infants should not be subjected to it."

"We traveled constantly when we were children," I said. "It was difficult, I can tell you that." *And wonderful, too,* I thought, remembering.

DURING THE WEEKS Wolfgang and Constanze were with us, we entertained guests, played cards, attended the theater, went sightseeing, and set off on pilgrimages. Joachim von Schiedenhofen and his wife called several times, as did

Katherl, Abbé Bullinger, and the members of the shooting company, and our old landlord, Hagenauer. Armand
stopped by often. The Marchand parents made the trip
from Munich for Gretl's performance in an opera. Every
day without fail we made music—we had a houseful of
musicians ready at every moment! Mostly we played Wolfgang's music, and I was struck again and again by the brilliance of it.

There was only one truly uncomfortable moment during the visit. Wolfgang was showing Constanze Papa's
collection of the gifts we'd received on our grand tour—
toothpick holders and the like. Constanze turned to Papa.
"Herr Mozart, I should so like to have something from
this collection as a souvenir of our visit," she said, her eye
on a pretty gold snuffbox.

"I beg your pardon, Frau Mozart," Papa said stiffly, "but
I am unwilling to remove anything from the collection."

She colored deeply, clearly embarrassed. "*Ja,* I understand," she murmured, moving away from the cabinet, and
the moment passed.

SOMEHOW, IN THE MIDST of all this activity, Wolfgang
found time to compose. Late one night after everyone else
had retired, I found him seated at his old writing desk. He
was writing the Mass in C Minor he intended to perform
before he and Constanze returned to Vienna. "It's a gift

for Constanze," he told me. "She's to have the solos. I've written it for her, and to the glory of God for the birth of our son."

"I see that you still compose the way you always did," I commented. "It's all in your head, and then you write it down."

"Exactly right, Horseface," he said with a laugh.

Suddenly it was the end of October, and Wolfgang and Constanze prepared to leave. The night before they left, and the high point of their visit, was the performance of Wolfgang's new Mass in C Minor at St. Peter's Church. Wolfgang conducted in his red silk coat with the mother-of-pearl buttons, and Constanze's glorious soprano voice soared among the sumptuous stucco and frescoes to the vaulted ceiling. The mass was a deeply religious master-piece. By its extraordinary length and ornate style and the sublime solos, Wolfgang deliberately flouted the rules for church music set forth by the emperor and the arch-bishop: no more than forty-five minutes, no fugues, no solo singing. "I'm not getting paid for this one," he said. "I'll write whatever I like."

Knowing he had composed this mass as a gift of love for his wife, I felt a sharp stab of envy. "I shall always love you best," he had promised me long ago, but I could see plainly that was no longer true.

They left the next day. Constanze wept during our

farewells, urging us to visit them in Vienna and promising to return soon with little Raimund. "I am so eager to see him—the journey home will seem extremely long," she said. She rushed back to embrace me again. "Don't forget to write to me, dear Nannerl," she begged. I assured her I would.

There were more kisses, more promises. *"Auf Wiedersehen!"* we cried. "Until we meet again!"

"We can be glad *that's* over," Papa exclaimed as we waved them out of sight. "The girl has a lovely voice, but Wolfgang has done himself no good at all by marrying her."

I said nothing. Maybe Papa was right. Or maybe he wasn't.

ALL OUR VISITORS had gone, and Papa and I were alone again with our three pupils. Wolfgang wrote from Linz, where they stopped on their way to Vienna so he could give a concert. "As I haven't brought a single symphony with me, I am writing a new one at top speed," he said. He had four days. I had no doubt he'd finish the piece in time.

But his next letter, written after they were back in Vienna, was nearly incomprehensible in the grief that spilled from the page. Wolfgang and Constanze had arrived home to discover little Raimund Leopold had died on the nineteenth of August of *frais,* a cramp in his belly. It happened shortly after they'd left for Salzburg, and for three whole months Frau Weber and Constanze's sisters had kept the terrible news from them. I suppose the women believed there was nothing to be done.

Papa shook his head sadly. "It's God's will," he said. "Our first child, a son, lived just six months. Our second died after only a few days, the third after just eleven weeks. Two more infants—a boy and a girl—lived only a short time. You were the first of our children to survive, Nannerl, and then Wolfgang was born. We were never sure how long the Almighty would allow us to keep either one of you. So I know how Wolfgang and his wife must feel."

Together we walked to Holy Trinity Church and lit a candle for the soul of Raimund Leopold, Papa's first grandchild. I knelt before the high altar and prayed that Wolfgang and Constanze would find consolation in each other and in their faith, and that God would soon bless them with another child. Then I added a prayer that I, too, would someday experience the incomparable joys— and the inevitable sorrows—of marriage and motherhood. But as I murmured "Amen" and made the sign of the cross, I understood that at the age of thirty-two my time had likely already passed.

Chapter 26

BERCHTOLD

ON A HOT DAY after a long, bleak winter and a brief, wet spring, Katherl and I stole an hour at a café near Hannibalplatz. As we sat eating our ices, Katherl tapped my arm, her eyes fixed on the entrance.

"Don't look now," she whispered, "but I think that's Herr Berchtold von Sonnenburg who just came in. He's the magistrate in St. Gilgen. His second wife died in childbirth last year, poor thing. He's got a house full of children, and I'll wager he's looking for a new wife." She smiled winningly at the newcomer. "He's good-looking," Katherl murmured. "A little older than we are, but not too much."

I turned my head to catch a glimpse. The man's face was half hidden by a newspaper. "*Ja,* I do know of him. By coincidence, he lives in the house by the lake where my mother was born, and he holds the position my grand-father once held. I've never been to St. Gilgen, but Papa has always said it's beautiful."

"Beautiful," Katherl agreed, "but also quite isolated, especially in winter. Still, it might not be too bad to be snowed in with the likes of him." She was gazing dreamily in Herr Berchtold's direction.

I smothered a laugh. "With him and his houseful of children in need of a mother! Are you sure that's what you'd want?"

"If that's the only way to get a husband, then I'd accept the bargain," she said. "Wouldn't you?"

I shook my head. "I doubt that I'll ever marry," I replied. "I could crawl to Maria Plain on my knees every day for a month and not find a man who suited my father." I spooned up the last of my lemon ice. "I must go," I said. "It's time for Hanchen's lessons."

As I rose to leave, the man from St. Gilgen peered over the top of his newspaper. He lowered the paper and smiled warmly, his hazel eyes crinkling. *In his late forties,* I thought. *Katherl's right—he's not at all bad-looking.* I stood rooted to the floor, feeling my cheeks color. Then, ducking my head, I hurried out of the café.

Katherl rushed after me and grabbed my arm. "I saw how he smiled at you!" she exclaimed. "He's *interested* in you, Nannerl, that's plain to see."

I pulled away from her. "I'm going," I said and fled, overwhelmed by a flood of confused feelings. It had been a long time since a man—other than Armand—had looked at me with such frank interest.

Only one day later Papa informed me that he'd received a note from Johann Baptist Franz Berchtold von Sonnenburg. "He's asked permission to call on you," Papa said. "I know of this man. He has a good reputation. Are you willing, Nannerl?"

I was silent for a moment, recalling the man's warm smile and hazel eyes. "Tell him—," I began, and then stopped, remembering another man's smile, another man's eyes. The memory made my heart ache. "Tell him I'd welcome his visit," I said.

"I WOULD BE honored if you would play something for me," Herr Berchtold said the first time he came to call. "I am especially fond of your brother's music." I played one of Wolfgang's sonatas and a rondo, and when I finished, he stood and applauded. I was flattered by his attention. And I did like his smile. He asked me to call him Johann Baptist.

Official business kept Johann Baptist in Salzburg for a week. Each day he arrived at the Tanzmeisterhaus and kissed my hand. On the third day we went walking. As we passed the Virgilianum I wondered if Armand happened to see us. Thinking of him now was painful. I often went alone to the Mirabell Gardens, where I had pledged my love for Armand, witnessed by the marble dwarfs, but I could not bear to go there now with Johann Baptist. Instead we strolled along the Salzach. For the next three mornings he accompanied me and my pupils to Mass; in the afternoons he returned to the Tanzmeisterhaus and again asked me to play for him. He treated me with gravity and respect, smiled, and gently touched my cheek.

At the end of the week as he finished his official business and prepared to return to St. Gilgen, Johann Baptist made a formal proposal of marriage. "I've come to ask you to be my wife," he said directly. "I have five children. The eldest is a girl who will soon be thirteen. She shares your name—Nannerl. The others are boys, the youngest just two years old. My second wife, Jeanette, died in childbirth a year ago."

I murmured a few words of condolence, my mind racing. I was stunned by the speed of this development.

"I take it as a good omen that your future home— should you accept my offer of marriage—was once the home of your grandparents. Your mother was born there. I believe you'll find the village to your liking," he continued. "The house is on the shore of the Abersee, and the rooms are comfortable. Your father will be welcome to visit as often as he likes. Your brother as well." He reached for my hand. "Well, what do you say, Fräulein Mozart? Will you marry me?"

I pleaded that I needed a little time to think about it. "I'll expect your answer in a week, Fräulein," he said, bowed and left. I watched him go, wishing he had swept me into his arms and kissed me, or that something had been said about love. No doubt he was just being honest.

I brooded, turning the matter over and over in my mind. Papa urged me to accept his offer. "Berchtold von Sonnenburg is a decent man of good background. His income is secure. At last I can rest easy about your future."

I needed to talk with someone about this. I already knew what Katherl would say. The next morning after Mass I sent my three pupils home without me and walked quickly to the Adlgasser apartment near St. Sebastian's. I'd seen little of Viktoria since her stepmother had abandoned them. Now my friend struggled to care for the disturbed Josef and sickly Anna on her own. Viktoria answered my knock and let me in. The shabby apartment smelled of camphor used to relieve her sister's ailing lungs. Viktoria clutched a faded shawl around her thin shoulders.

"You're looking well," she said when we were seated on a threadbare sofa. "Have you come to tell me that you are at last to marry Captain d'Ippold?"

I stared down at my hands. "*Nein,* I have not. Papa refused to consent. But I have had another offer. His name is Johann Baptist Berchtold von Sonnenburg, and he's the magistrate of St. Gilgen. He's a widower with five children."

I glanced up. Viktoria was regarding me intently with bright, feverish eyes. "And have you accepted his offer, Nannerl?"

"Not yet." I suppressed a sigh. "Papa believes the marriage will provide me with security. I'll soon be thirty-three and not likely to have another opportunity. He has a nice smile, and he enjoys music. I think I can learn to care for him."

"What do you know about the children?" she asked.

I repeated the little I knew: Maria Anna, called Nannerl, soon to be thirteen; Wolfgang, ten; Josef, seven; Johann, four; and the baby, Karl, barely two.

Viktoria shook her head slowly. "They will not make it easy for you, Nannerl. I can tell you that from experience. I'm afraid it's a bad bargain."

"That's why I came to talk with you, dear friend."

"If you decide to marry him, the best thing is to have a baby of your own as soon as possible. The children may resent the little intruder, but at least you'll have one you can love and train up as it should be."

We sat in uneasy silence for a time, while I considered Viktoria's advice. *Maybe she's just been unlucky,* I thought as I rose to leave. "Papa will wonder what kept me."

At the door Viktoria and I embraced. "I wish you—," she began and stopped. "I wish you contentment," she finished.

I hurried home. My talk with Viktoria had done nothing to make my heart lighter or my decision easier.

FOR SIX LONG TURBULENT days and six sleepless nights I pondered. I begged off from my pupils' lessons and spent hours at the harpsichord, playing mostly Wolfgang's compositions and hoping the music would calm me and help me make the right decision.

I did not love Johann Baptist, certainly not the way I'd loved Armand—and still did! Nor did Johann Baptist pretend to love me. Long ago, when I was a young girl, I believed I'd marry only for love. I was no longer young. Perhaps I should accept what was being offered. With God's grace, I would have a child, perhaps more than one. And I would be leaving Salzburg, not for a city as exciting as Vienna or Munich, but someplace new. Johann Baptist did not strike me as the sort of man who would insist on making every decision for me. I would no longer be under my father's thumb. I would have a life of my own. Perhaps in time I'd learn to love him—I had to believe that. I played on.

On my name day, the twenty-sixth of July, I wrote to Johann Baptist and accepted his offer of marriage. The wedding would take place on the twenty-third of August, a date that suited his schedule. I'd hoped to be married in Dom St. Rupert, but my future husband was too busy to return to Salzburg. I would make the journey to St. Gilgen with Papa and a few friends.

I wrote to Wolfgang, inviting him and Constanze. He replied enthusiastically, joking rather crudely, "Your days as a vestal virgin are at an end!" But Constanze was pregnant again and due to give birth in September. They could not attend the wedding. I was disappointed, but I agreed that she should not travel, and he could not leave her alone.

I had much to do and little time in which to do it. Tresel and I unpacked the large wooden marriage chest where I'd long ago placed linens and other household items, as well as a set of silver spoons Mama had once given me. Tresel bleached the bed linens in the sun, Gretl ironed them as I'd taught her, and I sprinkled them with lavender and packed them again in the chest. I went through the motions, keeping thoughts of Armand at bay.

Katherl popped in and out, torn between being happy for me and desolate that I was moving so far away. "I'm sure you're doing the right thing, Nannerl. It's high time you had a husband and family, although how you'll survive out there without a friseur is beyond imagining. Now what are you planning to wear for your wedding?"

I hadn't given it much thought. Everything in my clothes chest seemed worn and out of style, and there wasn't time to order a dress from the seamstress.

Katherl took over. "I have a lovely blue silk in my chest that I had made a few years ago, when I thought I was about to marry—oh, I don't even remember who, maybe it was the court chemist, but I was very hopeful!" Katherl laughed. "It would be perfect for you."

I tried on her blue silk dress with wide skirts and a low neck. She pronounced it almost perfect. "We can ask our little Viktoria to make a few adjustments," Katherl proposed. "She's clever with needle and thread."

Although Viktoria plainly thought I was making a mistake to enter into this union, she agreed to help. I paid a last visit to the friseur and sacrificed my elaborate coiffure for a simpler style more appropriate for life in the country. With a lace fichu, new stockings, and some buckles for my shoes, I was ready for the wedding, if not for the marriage. I scarcely knew the man who was about to become my husband, and there were five children I'd never even met. On some days I felt I could not go through with it, but on others I told myself that going forward was the best choice.

The week before we were to leave for my new home, Papa tied a handkerchief over my eyes and led me into the salon where he kept a number of musical instruments for sale. "Remove the handkerchief," he ordered. I did, and found myself standing in front of a handsome fortepiano. "Your wedding present, dear Nannerl," he explained. "We'll take it with us to St. Gilgen."

I threw my arms around my father's neck and kissed him soundly on both cheeks. "Oh, my dear papa!" I cried. "With that beautiful instrument and copies of Wolfgang's music, I know I shall be content!" If I could have music, I thought, everything else would surely work out. But that may have been wishful thinking.

MY LAST DAYS in Salzburg were a round of dinners and farewell parties. Armand was present at many of these events, always correct and smiling. If he had any regrets, his military discipline prevented them from showing. Then, on the day before I was to leave, he came to the Tanz-meisterhaus to wish me well.

"I shall always be your devoted friend," he promised stiffly. "Know that you can rely on me."

"Oh, Armand," I began, my voice trembling. I wanted to tell him that I still loved him, that I would always love him, that I was marrying this man because it seemed the only possibility.

But Armand placed a finger on my lips and shook his head. "Perhaps you could play something for me?" he asked. "Just one last time."

I nodded and sat down at my new fortepiano that had not yet been packed for the journey to St. Gilgen and considered what I might play. Finally I settled on an adagio from a sonata Wolfgang had composed years ear-lier. For the next few minutes I poured out my love for

Armand through a melody that seemed to express my yearning.

As I played the last notes, I felt Armand's lips brush the back of my neck. "Farewell, my love," he whispered.

I buried my face in my hands. How could I go through with this? I turned, ready to beg him to stay. But Armand had already gone.

Chapter 27

MARRIAGE

WE SET OUT FOR St. Gilgen beneath a lowering sky. Papa, Katherl, Gretl, Hanchen, and I rode in one carriage with my baggage, including Herr Canary in his pretty little cage. In a second carriage were various friends looking forward to a summer outing by the lake. A wagon rumbled along behind with the fortepiano packed in straw. The trip would take six hours.

Heavy rains had left the road through the mountains in such bad condition that several times our carriage nearly toppled over. When the sun broke through at last, we stopped for a picnic lunch in a meadow where wildflowers bloomed riotously—delicate edelweiss, bright pink Turk's-cap lilies, and fiery alpenroses. Sure-footed steinbocks leaped from rock to rock, coveys of wood grouse took flight, foxes darted for cover, and a lone eagle soared over-head. "A good sign," everyone agreed.

As we approached St. Gilgen, the road descended steeply toward the lake. Our carriages rattled through the village, past the tiny parish church where I supposed I would be married, and drew up in front of a large building on the lakeshore. This had once been my grandparents' home, and my mother's, and now it would be mine. Four un-kempt little boys and a tall young girl burst out of the front door and stared at us glumly. Their father, my husband-to-be, followed.

I climbed out of the carriage and greeted each child, be-ginning with the eldest. The girl called Nannerl accepted my handshake properly, although I did notice that her hands as well as her dress were not quite clean. The older boys glared at me, and the youngest wailed and reached for his sister. I tried to smile.

Johann Baptist kissed my hand and welcomed our guests, who hastily retreated to a nearby inn. Papa stayed to see to the unloading of my fortepiano. Johann Baptist took the opportunity to lead me through my new home. The chil-dren trailed behind, banging doors and interrupting rudely. Their father didn't correct them. The littlest sucked his thumb and stared at me from the shelter of his sister's arms.

I will have to win them over slowly, I thought.

Administrative offices occupied the ground floor; the

living quarters above had a number of large rooms, mostly bare and uninviting. I peered into the kitchen where a slatternly cook and housemaid bobbed their heads without meeting my eye.

Suddenly I felt very tired. "I beg you to pardon me, Johann Baptist," I said, "but I really must go to the inn and rest. Otherwise, I'm afraid I'll become quite ill." In truth, I wanted to get away from this disorderly brood.

Papa had already gone on with the others; I assured Johann Baptist that I could make my own way—walking alone would help to clear my head. Katherl was waiting when I reached the room I was to share with her that night.

"Those children act like wild creatures," Katherl said, as I collapsed onto the feather bed. "Except the girl. She might be old enough to behave for you. But the boys! Whatever are you going to do with them?"

"I have no idea," I confessed, near tears. "But I hope their father will be of some help in the matter."

"He should have started before you got here," Katherl said severely. She was silent for a while and then spoke again. "Nannerl," she said, "I know that I urged you to marry this man. But I may have advised you badly. It's still not too late, you know. You don't have to go through with it. You can call it off."

I stared at her. Katherl rarely wept, but she was weeping now. "Don't blame yourself, dear friend, I beg you," I said. "But it *is* too late."

I hadn't slept well in weeks, I was exhausted from packing, and the journey from Salzburg had further wearied me, but still I couldn't fall asleep. Thoughts of Armand would not leave me.

THE NEXT AFTERNOON, while our friends went for walks along the shore of the lake, its calm waters flat as a looking glass, Katherl and I conferred with the cooks at the inn who would prepare the wedding lunch. Gretl and Hanchen appeared, pink-cheeked and breathless, carrying armloads of wildflowers to decorate the little church.

On Monday morning, the twenty-third of August, Katherl helped me to dress in the blue silk gown and arrange the lace fichu. It had rained again during the night and turned the streets of St. Gilgen to thick mud that threatened to ruin my satin slippers. Gretl fastened a few wildflowers to the brim of my velvet hat.

"You are more beautiful than ever," Katherl said, holding up a looking glass. "I just hope those blue eyes and that porcelain skin aren't completely wasted in this godforsaken wilderness."

By ten o'clock Papa, my Salzburg friends, and Johann Baptist's brother and his wife from Strobl, a village at the other end of the lake, had gathered at St. Aegidius, the same church where my grandparents were married and my mother was baptized. Dear Mama! She'd been often in my thoughts as I prepared for my wedding. What would she think of my decision to marry Johann Baptist? Would she have agreed with Papa that Armand was not a suitable husband, but Johann Baptist was? In any event, she would not have opposed Papa, any more than I did. But I wished she were with me now, on my wedding day.

A flock of small white clouds scudded past the church steeple shaped like two onions, one set atop the other. Katherl and I walked from the inn in silence and entered the church together. Johann Baptist and the priest waited by the altar. A few candles flickered.

The ceremony was brief, and almost before I knew it, I had pledged myself to honor and obey someone who was a complete stranger to me. The sexton pulled on a rope and the bell in the steeple rang out, a mournful sound. This was Johann Baptist's third marriage, and he appeared unmoved. I wondered how he felt. I felt neither joy nor sorrow, only numbness.

We stepped outside and picked our way through the mud to the inn. Platters of boiled beef tongue, smoked sausages, trout fresh caught from the lake, and roast duck were laid out on a long wooden table; Gretl and Hanchen had strewn flowers here, too. Several bottles of good wine had survived the trip from Salzburg, and after toasts were drunk and everyone had eaten their fill, my husband and I returned to the house by the lake, followed by a wine-mellowed procession. Papa had brought his violin, I sat down at my fortepiano, and for an hour or two we made music together, the most pleasant part of my day. I would have gladly continued it even longer. My stepchildren crept into the room and listened, if not exactly politely, then at least without being disruptive.

Soon after the sun had disappeared behind the mountain peaks, our guests said *Gute Nacht* and retired to the inn. Papa kissed me on the forehead, gave me his blessing, and left with the others. The boys regarded me with hostility until young Nannerl coaxed them away. I was alone with my husband.

Johann Baptist opened a bottle of aged brandy and poured us each a glass. "Drink this," he said, not unkindly. "It will go easier for you." I had been dreading this, but I did as he told me, and I endured it.

The next morning I found a purse containing five hundred florins by my pillow. It was my *Morgengabe*, a "morning gift" to reward my virginity. I thanked him, but the only reward I wanted was to conceive quickly. I badly wanted a child of my own.

Later that day Papa and Katherl and my two dear pupils and the rest of our friends embraced me and wished me much happiness before they began their journey home. Wishing I were going with them, I watched the horses labor up the hill toward the road to Salzburg and handkerchiefs flutter from the carriage windows, and somehow I managed not to weep.

As I turned back to the house—my new home—I heard a sickening discordant racket coming from my fortepiano. I rushed inside and found the two older boys, Wolfgang and Josef, pounding gleefully on the keyboard.

"Stop it! Stop it at once!" I screamed, furiously dragging at their shirt collars and yanking them away. "Don't you dare touch this instrument ever again! Do you understand?"

"We were just making music," Wolfgang growled. "Papa didn't say we couldn't," he added defiantly, and gave the keyboard another vicious thump.

"*I* said you could not," I told him fiercely.

Josef thrust out his lower lip. "*You* can't tell us what to do." But the two moved carefully away from me.

When I reported the incident to Johann Baptist, he said, "I'll speak to them. They're only children, after all, and they've never seen such an instrument before."

I stood openmouthed, expecting more, and silently vowed to call in a locksmith.

MY NEW ROLE as wife and stepmother demanded all my attention. My husband showed more interest in his professional duties than in his family. The children were utterly without supervision or discipline. Their manners were disgraceful. Their schooling had been neglected; the village school was makeshift, and their father declined to spend the money for a private tutor. At the age of thirteen, young Nannerl could barely read or write. The boys did not know how to do sums or brush their teeth. They paid no attention to personal cleanliness. I scarcely knew where to begin.

"You must wash your hands and face before coming to the table," I told them repeatedly.

"We don't have to obey you," said Wolfgang, the eldest boy and spokesman for his brothers.

I sent him away without dinner. He went to the cook, who felt sorry for him and fed him.

Not only the children defied me. The cook, the chambermaid, and the undermaid were used to doing as they pleased and would not tolerate any sort of correction. They all promptly quit and had to be coaxed back.

There were never enough hours in the days to accomplish all that had to be done. Between managing the household and supervising the children, I needed to spend time on my fortepiano. I had piles of music sent by Wolfgang I wanted to learn, and his keyboard compositions had become much more difficult, demanding the highest level of technical skill. Music had always been my refuge and my joy; now it was my salvation. All my cares were erased when I played. I was free to think of nothing but the music and the challenges it presented.

When things didn't go smoothly—and very often they did not—my husband spoke sharply to me, reducing me to tears. "*Must* you spend so many hours practicing?" he asked. "I should think an hour a day is sufficient."

"I've always needed three," I insisted.

"You're not at the Tanzmeisterhaus," he said, and I felt as though I'd been slapped. I settled for two when I could squeeze them in, and nothing more was said.

One day when I was unpacking some of my things, I found the wire contrivance the friseur had used to prop up some of my more extravagant coiffures, and I burst into tears.

Papa and I fell into a pattern of writing once a week, sending our letters with the courier who carried documents between my husband's office and the court in Salzburg, or with a woman who made the trip on foot with a rucksack loaded with items from the St. Gilgen glass factory. Papa's letters often contained news of Wolfgang, such as the birth of their new baby, Karl Thomas. Mine were filled mostly with the trials of managing a disorganized household and requests for things I needed but couldn't buy in the village. These letters became my lifeline.

I was determined to replace the cook and at least one of the maids with others who were not so coarse or stupid. At Michaelmas when new servants were customarily hired, Papa sent us a new cook, better than the old one but unhappy at living in such a remote place. I knew she wouldn't stay long. Autumn winds swept in a damp chill from the lake that penetrated every corner. The keys on my forte-piano began to stick, and within a matter of weeks it was unplayable. I wrote desperately to Papa, but it was not a simple matter to get the court tuner to come out to St. Gilgen. Herr Canary sickened and died, and I mourned him like a lost friend. My life had sunk to its lowest point.

I longed to visit Salzburg, and at Christmastime I persuaded Johann Baptist to make the journey in order to see a performance of *Il Seraglio*. For a blessed week I felt as though I was back where I belonged, attending the theater, seeing friends, and making music. When the time came for us to leave again, I went reluctantly, only because it was my duty. *What had I been thinking?* I wondered as the carriage lurched toward St. Gilgen.

THAT FIRST WINTER I arose each morning questioning how I would survive until spring. Heavy clouds often cloaked the towering mountain peaks surrounding the lake, and even on a clear day the sun reached our valley for only a few short hours. The ice on the Abersee was thick enough to support horse-drawn sledges. Dressed in rough woolen petticoats and thick stockings, I found the water buckets frozen solid each morning. My chapped hands cracked and bled—I could not have played my fortepiano, even if it had been playable. The servants grumbled. The boys shouted and slammed through the house and ignored my pleas to use knives and forks instead of fingers to tear at their meat.

I tried hard to win the respect, if not the affection, of my stepchildren, but mostly I failed. The boys had been left to run wild with only their sister to exercise any influence over them. Young Nannerl, now turning into a buxom thirteen-year-old, had never been given any training or discipline of her own.

I couldn't help comparing this family with the one in which my brother and I had been raised. Our father had provided us with a superb education equal to any given the wealthiest nobility. We had grown up performing for the Holy Roman Empress and the electors of Bavaria. We had dined with the king and queen of France. But my stepchildren were not fit to sit at the same table with our narrow-minded parish priest or his uneducated sexton, who also served as schoolmaster.

The children's father usually took their part. "You are too hard on them, Nannerl," he said coldly. "They've been deprived of a mother, and for two years they've had no one to guide them. You can't expect them to change overnight."

But I had been there, living in that godforsaken wilderness, as Katherl so aptly called it, for six months—certainly more than "overnight"—and nothing had improved. I felt immensely frustrated.

I also felt very lonely. We did receive occasional visits from my husband's brother and sister-in-law, who lived in Strobl on the other side of the lake. The brewmaster and his wife sometimes came to play cards in the evening. Johann Schmauss, the owner of the glassworks, occasionally brought his viola, but once I'd heard him muddle through a few tunes, I decided it was not a good idea to encourage him. Not all music brought joy.

But I did have something wonderful to look forward to: God had answered my prayer, and I was expecting a child.

Chapter 28

LEOPOLDL

IN THE DEPTHS of the dark St. Gilgen winter Papa's letters began to arrive from Vienna.

Papa was staying at my brother's splendid apartment behind Stephansdom, around the corner from the palace where Colloredo's secretary had once kicked Wolfgang down the stairs. Wolfgang and Constanze had moved numerous times since their marriage, but this, their newest home, caused our father's jaw to drop—especially the yearly rent of 480 florins, more than five times what Papa was paying for the Tanzmeisterhaus. He described Wolfgang's wonderful fortepiano being carried out of their apartment to one elegant concert after another. I read this while my own beautiful instrument sat silent in the drafty hall of my freezing house.

One detail after another aroused my envy. The Mozarts

dined out frequently, enjoying champagne and oysters, meat dishes and fancy glazed fruits, as though every day were a feast day. It was Lent, but no one in that Viennese circle observed the fast. Friends clamored to entertain Papa. Even Frau Weber, Constanze's mother, about whom we had heard so many unflattering comments, went to great lengths to please him. She prepared an exquisite lunch that included a plump roast pheasant with cabbage and several side dishes. The Baroness von Waldstätten sent her coach and horses to bring him to her country home.

"I never get to bed before one in the morning or rise before nine or lunch before two," Papa wrote. "And the concerts are endless!"

Mozart—and everyone called him that, Papa said, even his wife—had become one of the most sought-after musicians and composers in the city, his genius attracting the recognition it deserved, now that he'd made friends with the right people. Even Emperor Josef waved his hat and cheered, "Bravo, Mozart!" Papa was pleased at the income Wolfgang earned from the concerts, but he worried that expenses were also high and confessed to me his fear that my brother borrowed heavily from friends and had debts he wasn't talking about.

Papa remained with Wolfgang and Constanze and enchanting little Karl Thomas for ten weeks. The archbishop denied him leave to stay away any longer, and at the end of April, Papa left Vienna and arrived to an empty house, now that the Marchand children were back in Munich. I'd persuaded Johann Baptist to travel to Salzburg to greet him, intending to stay for only a week, but when I saw how melancholy my father became at the thought of being left alone, we extended the visit for another few days. By then I was large in my pregnancy, and my husband insisted that we return home.

"Your father should have stayed in Vienna with your brother," Johann Baptist said.

We'd scarcely arrived in St. Gilgen before Papa began urging me to come back to Salzburg to await my confinement. It was what I wanted, but Johann Baptist said, "I can't afford the expense of this constant running back and forth."

"You've lost two wives in childbirth," I reminded him. "Surely you don't want to risk losing a third."

He could scarcely argue with that, and in the end he agreed. But, claiming he had too much work to leave in the hands of his assistant, he would not accompany me, even though I was in my eighth month. I wrote to Papa, who wrote back, "Then I shall come and fetch you myself."

I was embarrassed to have my father see how I was living, how badly the children behaved, how plain the food was that we put on the table. And I knew that I looked a fright. Our new chambermaid, who was supposed to be able to dress hair, turned out to be utterly worthless. My hair, now touched with the first strands of gray, was tucked under a cap. The first thing I planned to do when I arrived in Salzburg without my husband was to call on my friseur.

SALZBURG WAS HOT and miserable, and I didn't mind at all. I was happy to be there, among friends, to await the birth of my baby.

My son was born at the Tanzmeisterhaus at noon on the twenty-seventh of July 1785, the Feast of St. Pantaleon. At five o'clock Papa carried him to the church of St. Andrä across from Mirabell Palace to be christened Leopold Alois Pantaleon. We called him Leopoldl—little Leopold. Whatever resentment I'd felt toward my domineering father and my stern husband was washed away by the arrival in my life of this precious baby.

Johann Baptist brought young Nannerl to Salzburg to meet the new addition to the family. "I was hoping for a sister," the girl muttered sullenly. "We have enough boys." But Johann Baptist seemed pleased to have a fifth son. He and his daughter stayed less than a week before returning to St. Gilgen; Leopoldl and I stayed on at the Tanzmeisterhaus.

For the next few weeks I allowed myself to be coddled and spoiled. I spent hours simply gazing at this miraculous child, marveling that such happiness was mine at last. I examined his tiny fingers, wondering if someday he, too, would become a fine musician, maybe even a great one. As soon as my strength returned, I played for him, beginning with his uncle's earliest pieces, and composed my own songs to sing to him. Papa hovered over his new grandson and namesake. Tresel could scarcely keep her hands off the infant, hugging and kissing him whenever she could.

Eventually, though, at Johann Baptist's constant urging, I had to prepare to return to St. Gilgen. The thought of all the problems awaiting me with my ill-behaved step-children and my wretched servants plunged me into the blackest of moods. How could I take my darling Leopoldl into such a dismal setting?

Papa observed my state of mind and laid out a proposal. "Why not leave Leopoldl in my care?" he suggested. "Only temporarily, of course—just through the winter. It will give you more time to settle the unruly situation you face with your husband's other children, and your infant son will have the benefit of a number of devoted servants to watch over him. Not to forget a doting grandfather," he added with a smile. "And before you know it, spring will be here and your son will be ready to join his new family."

At first I found the idea unthinkable. *I cannot leave my precious son! This child is all that I have!* But as the time to leave drew near, I began to see the advantages of Papa's suggestion. Leopoldl would certainly be better off here, and it would be for only a short time, I felt sure. I would submit to the pain of the separation for the baby's own welfare. An exchange of letters between Papa and Johann Baptist assured my husband not only that the child would receive the best of care, but also that Papa would bear all the expenses. That was the winning argument for Johann Baptist. He agreed to the arrangement, and early in September I tore myself away from my child and rode back to St. Gilgen, alone and weeping.

Almost immediately I regretted my decision. In less than two weeks Papa wrote that Leopoldl was ill with *frais*—cramps in his belly—and an infection in his mouth. The doctor was summoned and various treatments tried—spirit of hartshorn on the soles of the feet was thought to draw the cramps out of his body—but for days it seemed that Leopoldl might not survive.

I cursed myself for leaving him, although I recognized he was receiving better care in Salzburg than could have been provided in St. Gilgen. If only I were with him! But Johann Baptist insisted we must wait. I wept and prayed, and finally, by the end of the month, Papa assured us the danger was past. Now I could turn my full attention to my stepchildren, who were behaving more and more like the untutored barbarians they were. And their father seemed not to care.

EARLY IN THE NEW YEAR of 1786 Papa accepted the Marchands' invitation to visit Munich for Carnival and suggested that Johann Baptist and I come to Salzburg to care for Leopoldl while he was away. I leaped at the suggestion. I had not seen my child in five months, and I was aching to hold him in my arms once more. But my husband would not agree. "I'm much too busy," he said.

I wept, pleaded, coaxed, and finally I raged at him, "You care nothing about our son or about me but only about yourself!" When he still would not give in, I informed Papa we would not be able to come.

Papa wrote back scathingly, "I salute my son-in-law and ask him, 'What do you believe people must think of a man who can hold out for months without seeing his child?'" At the end of this letter he added, less harshly, "Don't worry about a thing. There's no child in Salzburg more carefully cared for. And our friend Captain d'Ippold will come every day. He's entirely devoted to the boy."

I dropped the letter, stunned. Armand d'Ippold seemed more concerned about my child than his own father was! *He's entirely devoted to the boy.* I believed it was because Armand remained entirely devoted to *me,* and I wondered if it even once entered Papa's mind that he had made a grave error in forbidding me to marry Armand and pushing me instead to marry Johann Baptist. But Papa never admitted he was wrong, and besides, what difference did it make now? I was simply grateful Armand was there and Leopoldl was well looked after.

SOMEHOW I GOT THROUGH another winter at St. Gilgen, another discouraging struggle with servants and stepchildren, all the while longing for my little one. Not until

June—ten months after Leopoldl was born—did I succeed in convincing Johann Baptist to visit Salzburg. There I found a whole collection of people completely dedicated to our little man. Heinrich Marchand, now a tall and talented sixteen-year-old violinist, had returned from Munich to live at the Tanzmeisterhaus and work for Archbishop Colloredo, and he seemed entranced by Leopoldl's big blue eyes and winning smile.

Armand d'Ippold came by nearly every day and patiently allowed the child to clamber all over him. Katherl, who also visited us often, got me alone one day while Armand played with my son and Johann Baptist had managed to find business of some sort that needed attending.

"I don't know who angers me most," she huffed. "Johann Baptist, who seems not to pay attention to anything but his 'business,' Leopold, who forced you into this situation, or Armand, who didn't simply carry you away when he had the chance. Anyone can see that you're not happy, Nannerl, so don't bother to deny it."

Her words stung, and I replied heatedly, "And who are you to judge? You, still unmarried and likely to remain so with that sharp tongue of yours!" But then my defenses crumbled. "Oh, Katherl," I said, sighing. "You always speak the truth. Perhaps you should be angry with *me*. I allowed it, didn't I? But you can't deny I have a beautiful child, and that's worth everything."

Katherl put her arms around me and embraced me. "*Ja,* you're right. The boy is a treasure—I can't deny it. Forgive me for speaking so candidly. Now let's join the others. I'm sure Captain d'Ippold doesn't want to miss a single minute of your presence."

JOHANN BAPTIST AND I prepared to return to St. Gilgen. I had every intention of taking Leopoldl with me, but when I saw how much Papa adored him and how that love was returned, and balanced that against what he would receive at our home in the village, I could not bring myself to take the child away from his grandfather.

If I had to sacrifice my happiness for his, so be it. Leopoldl stayed in Salzburg, and I prayed that I would again conceive. I yearned for a child that would be wholly mine.

Chapter 29

PAPA

IT WAS SEPTEMBER and Leopoldl was fourteen months old when I again held my darling child in my arms. I more easily persuaded Johann Baptist to make this trip to Salzburg, for young Nannerl was being confirmed. This was a glorious time, with chances to participate in music making and a visit from the Marchand family, who'd come to hear Gretl sing parts of Mozart's new comic opera, *The Marriage of Figaro*. Now that he'd become famous, everyone in Salzburg was calling him Mozart, as they did in Vienna, and because everyone else did, I found myself sometimes slipping into the habit, too.

Figaro had had its premiere at the Vienna Burgtheater on May first. The opera, with a libretto in Italian, recounts the events of a single day of mix-ups and mistaken identity among the count and countess, the count's valet—

Figaro—and his beloved, Susanna, and several others. It was enormously popular, with so many calls for encores that the four-act opera, already running nearly four hours, sometimes went on for twice that long, until Emperor Josef issued a decree restricting the number of encores.

When *Figaro* opened a few weeks later in Prague, audiences went mad over it. Everybody in the city was singing the arias, or playing them, or whistling them. Mozart's name, like his music, was on everyone's lips, and when he and Constanze left the old Bohemian city, he took with him a commission for another opera, *Don Giovanni,* based on the legend of Don Juan, a seducer who refuses to repent.

Even with all this acclaim, Wolfgang still had not been offered a salaried position. He was working frantically to meet expenses. The family moved out of their splendid apartment and into cheaper rooms.

Most disheartening to me, my brother had long ago stopped writing to me—I didn't even know of the birth and death of another son—and I didn't write to him. Our lives had taken us in opposite directions. Once, long ago, I'd felt that we were two halves of the same person, but now we seemed to have almost nothing in common. There was no argument, no falling-out—it simply happened, the letters getting further apart until there were no more. Papa kept me informed and continued to send me my brother's music. I, too, immediately loved the arias from *Figaro* and taught myself to sing them. The countess's beautiful lament, *Porgi amor qualche ristoro*—"Oh love, bring me comfort"—touched me so deeply I wept. What was Wolfgang feeling that allowed him to write with such compassion?

After the September visit to Salzburg, I let myself be persuaded again to leave Leopoldl with his grandfather. Johann Baptist didn't object. My stepchildren were more troublesome than ever, and my husband and I often argued about them, and about other matters as well.

Then in March Papa fell ill. I struggled through snow-choked mountain passes to reach Salzburg and stayed for two months, caring for him. During the hours I sat by Papa's bedside, we talked quietly together. We shared our tender memories of Mama, gone from us now for more than eight years. We spoke of our years touring Europe, musical prodigies giving concerts before royal audiences. We didn't talk about the disappointments—only the triumphs. Especially Wolfgang's.

"No one knows how much time one has left in this earthly life," he said, his voice barely above a whisper. "But it is my fond hope that both my children will prosper. I'm satisfied that you're taken care of, Nannerl. Johann Baptist is an honest man, though I know you must find him difficult at times."

Difficult indeed! I nodded, adjusted his pillow, and waited for him to continue.

"But I worry about Wolfgang. He has no sense about money. I've changed my mind about the Weber family," he said with a faint smile. "Constanze is a good woman, and very practical. If there's one thing Wolfgang needs, it's a practical wife!"

"And you've become fond of her?" I asked.

"I have, and of her sisters, too. They're all very talented. The eldest, Josefa, has a magnificent voice. So does Aloysia, though I'm surprised she and Wolfgang have worked so well together after her unforgivable treatment of him. Sophie, the youngest, is a dear, sweet girl. Even Frau Weber has much to recommend her." His voice had become weaker.

"Do you need anything, Papa?" I asked.

"Rest," he sighed. "Just let me rest."

MY LITTLE SON scarcely knew me. I felt the pangs any mother would as Leopoldl lifted his chubby arms to Tresel and saved his sweetest chatter for his ailing grandfather, and I set about wooing the affections of my own child with music, the language of love that I knew best. I was making progress when I received a letter from Johann Baptist, urging me to come home. Since my father seemed to be holding his own, I left in mid-May for St. Gilgen, promising Papa to return as soon as I could.

I found my husband in a dour mood, my stepchildren rebellious, the servants undisciplined. I longed for Leopoldl more than ever, and I worried about my father.

Ten days after I left Salzburg, as I was supervising some

late planting in the garden, I observed a tall figure striding down the path from the coach road. Both the figure and the stride were familiar to me; it was Armand d'Ippold. Not stopping to think how I must have looked in my old dress and stained apron, I rushed to greet him. But when I saw the sorrow etched in his face, I stopped short and my hands flew to my mouth. "My father is dead, isn't he?" I asked. I felt faint and began to sway.

Armand nodded, reaching out to steady me. "Two days ago, on the twenty-eighth of May, early in the morning. It happened quickly, before the priest could come. We buried your father in the cemetery of St. Sebastian that same evening. I've already written to Wolfgang. I started to write to you, but then I decided to come here myself."

I tried to speak, could not, and collapsed sobbing into Armand's waiting arms.

When I was calmer, I led him into the house, called Johann Baptist from his work, and gave him the news. The next morning the three of us left for Salzburg by mail coach. *How will I manage now, without Papa?* I had depended on him for so much—his weekly letters, his advice, his support. His love.

I was so caught up in my sorrow that I gave no thought to the oddity of traveling with the man I'd once loved— and, if I'd allowed myself to admit it, still did. Beside me sat the man I'd married, a man, I realized now, who resembled Papa in many ways. I was simply glad for Armand's comforting presence.

THERE WAS A great deal to be done to settle my father's estate. But first, we had to return to St. Gilgen, taking with us Leopoldl and Johann Baptist's eldest son, Wolfgang. The boy had been attending school in Salzburg—Papa had kept an eye on him there—and had fallen dangerously ill. After three years with the Berchtold family I had grown fond of the boy. For more than a month we hovered by his bedside. Then we lost him.

Our lively two-year-old was a helpful distraction. My stepdaughter, young Nannerl, adored Leopoldl from the first, and he, dear little soul, seemed to fall deeply in love with her. He followed her everywhere, and she was soon his closest companion.

Young Nannerl had developed into a good-natured and competent sixteen-year-old, for which I took some credit. I discovered how much I'd come to rely on her when Leopoldl and two of the younger boys were stricken with smallpox. Only by the grace of God and Nannerl's devotion in caring for them did all the children survive. It reminded me of the terrible days long ago in Vienna and Olmütz when Wolfgang had suffered from that same scourge and still bore the scars to prove it.

———

I RETURNED TO SALZBURG to prepare my father's goods for auction. During that trying time I received a letter from my brother, the first in at least a year. He expressed displeasure at hearing the news of our father's death from Captain d'Ippold and not from me. Then he discussed how Papa's bequests were to be made. I was shocked that Wolfgang refused the personal items Papa had expressly noted were to be given to him, the snuffboxes and watches and ceremonial swords Papa had kept on display in the Tanzmeisterhaus for all these years. Wolfgang wanted only his share of the proceeds. He wanted nothing but the money!

He offered no help in handling the countless details. Had it not been for Armand, I don't know what I would have done. How strange, I thought; the man who stood by me and helped me most in settling my father's affairs was neither my brother nor my husband but the man my father had refused to let me marry.

Armand tried to help me understand why Wolfgang behaved as he did. "There are rumors, of course," he said gently, attempting to cushion the truth. "Some say your brother has lost considerable amounts to gambling. I believe he has fallen deeply into debt because of his high expenses. Certainly he needs to maintain a certain standard to impress his patrons and supporters. It wouldn't do for Mozart to go about with frayed cuffs and live in squalid rooms. He's had to borrow constantly just to pay his bills."

"Papa suspected this was so," I said.

"There were some things about which your father was right. But not everything," he said, reaching for my hand.

"Dear Armand," I said, allowing my hand to rest in his, "have you ever thought of how our lives might have turned out so differently?" I thought, but didn't say, *The sole reason we did not marry now lies dead and buried.*

Armand smiled. "Every time I looked at your beautiful Leopoldl, I wished he were our child and you were my wife."

He raised my hand to his lips and kissed it.

THIS WAS A SAD TIME for me, but my friends—and not just Armand—were a great comfort. Katherl came nearly every day as I sorted through Leopold Mozart's vast library of books, music, pictures, and mementos. She was most interested in the collection of items Papa had kept on display from our grand tour and Wolfgang's journeys to Italy. It gave me pleasure to recall the circumstances in which we'd acquired the various gifts.

Katherl sipped coffee as I sat at the small clavichord and played through a few of Wolfgang's early compositions. Later, as I was locking the instrument with the same key Papa had once mistakenly carried with him to Italy, Katherl said suddenly, "Who would have thought it would end like this?"

"What do you mean?"

"You and Wolfgang were once inseparable, and now you hardly hear from him. Once we all believed that you'd have a brilliant career, and now you're buried alive in St. Gilgen. I was sure you'd marry Armand d'Ippold, who still adores you, but instead you've ended up with a man who's just as overbearing as Leopold Mozart ever was."

I gasped, shocked by her blunt words. "You should not speak so," I told her. "You *must* not speak so. And when you look at your own life—"

"At least it's my own life," she interrupted. "And I make my own decisions. Nannerl, it's about time *someone* speaks to you like this, frankly and honestly. You should leave Berchtold to sit on his own dung heap and move back to Salzburg with Leopoldl. Your father has surely left you enough money, and you can give lessons and live your own life among people who care deeply for you. I beg you to give yourself a chance for happiness!"

"I cannot do that," I said.

"Cannot or will not?" Katherl demanded. "Give me a reason."

"Because I'm expecting another child."

Chapter 30

REQUIEM

THE TANZMEISTERHAUS stood empty, everything sold or given away except for a few things I couldn't bear to part with. I returned to St. Gilgen with Leopoldl, Katherl's words still ringing in my ears. But the strain of all I'd been through in the past months and the difficulties of those last good-byes, knowing I'd never again sleep in the Dancing-Master's House, was too much, and I lost the infant in my womb. For weeks I grieved: Papa and Mama were dead, my brother estranged, the promise of a new child gone. But I picked up the pieces and went on.

I can't say that I ever enjoyed living in St. Gilgen, but that's where my life was, and I accepted it. My fortepiano had gradually improved during the warm summer months. Johann Baptist at last understood my need to practice for at least two hours a day. In the evenings I often played for him, and these were our best times together.

My prayers were answered when I conceived again. Johanna, whom we called Jeanette, was born in March of 1789 and thrived. But Maria Babette, born a year and a half later, lived only a few months; her death was another heartache. I finally persuaded Johann Baptist to send the three oldest boys to school in Salzburg. He resisted—he always resisted my suggestions—until I convinced him that if they were to make their way in the world, they must not be brought up like uneducated peasants. And so, in November of 1791, off they went—protesting and on the verge of open rebellion, but they went. There were now only two little ones in our household, Leopoldl and Jeanette, plus my good right hand, young Nannerl. I had finally made peace with the cook and housemaids. I was neither unhappy nor happy but simply lived my life from one day to the next.

One afternoon when young Nannerl was helping me clean out an old trunk, I found a stocking with something knotted in the toe. "It's a seashell," I explained to Nannerl, who'd never seen one. "It was given to me long ago by a boy in England. Hold it to your ear, and you'll hear the sound of the sea."

She did, smiling delightedly.

"Keep it," I told her. "And dream that someday you'll

travel far and wide, and stand on the shore to watch how the sea runs away and comes back again."

I HAD NOT SEEN Wolfgang since he and Constanze visited Salzburg in 1783. When Papa died in 1787, our only remaining link was broken. I relied on friends—Katherl, Armand, travelers from Vienna—to keep me informed. We'd become virtual strangers, but I was still very proud of my brother. I would love to have been present that autumn at the opening of *Don Giovanni* in Prague with Aloysia Weber Lange singing one of the major roles. Wolfgang was at the peak of his creativity. One brilliant composition after another poured out in a seemingly endless stream. After half a dozen years in Vienna, he was named Imperial and Royal Chamber Composer. At last, a permanent position! Papa would have been so pleased.

The furious pace of his composing continued with three more symphonies, the most dazzling yet. Another hugely successful opera, *Così fan tutte,* was staged in 1790. I heard of the triumphs but less of the disappointments, the debts, the illnesses, the slights: When Emperor Josef died and his successor, Emperor Leopold II, was crowned in Frankfurt, other Viennese musicians were invited to be part of the celebration, but Mozart was snubbed. I don't know why.

During the summer of 1791, while I was immersed in the rustic life of St. Gilgen, Wolfgang completed two more operas, *The Magic Flute* and *La clemenza di Tito*—"The Clemency of Titus." He was up to his eyes in work, rising at four thirty each morning and never going to bed before midnight. In July Constanze gave birth to another baby, a boy they named Franz Xavier. Wolfgang and Constanze traveled to Prague for the openings of both operas.

A killing pace, I thought when I learned of what came to pass during the last months of that year.

Wolfgang received another commission, and it was a strange one, to be undertaken in secret. A wealthy count whose young wife had died at the age of twenty wanted a requiem mass written for her. Because the old count was a music lover and something of a composer himself, he wanted people to believe *he* had written it. Mozart would not be recognized as the composer, but the patron paid well and my brother needed the money. Wolfgang had a talented pupil, Franz Xavier Süssmayr, who could help him with his monumental workload.

In autumn my brother's health began to decline. He was utterly exhausted, yet in spite of his weariness he continued to work. The mass for the dead had to be finished. He seemed weak, but he would not leave the requiem alone. In a moment of despair he told Constanze he thought the requiem was really for himself.

"Don't say that!" she begged, but he could not be dissuaded.

Constanze tried to persuade him to work on something else, but he returned to the requiem again and again. Soon he had fallen seriously ill, and by the twentieth of November he could not leave his bed. His body swelled, and he was too weak to hold a pen. His life seemed to be draining away.

Constanze did all she could to help him. Süssmayr sat by his bedside, writing down as Wolfgang dictated. His friends came every day to sing through what had been written, so that he could hear it. As the days ticked by, his condition worsened. Still he kept working. On the fourth of December, Constanze sent for her younger sister, Sophie. He knew he was dying. He told Sophie when she arrived, "I have the taste of death on my tongue already," and begged her to stay. He wanted Sophie to be with Constanze when his last moment came.

It was Sophie who would tell me all this much later, when it was all over.

That evening Sophie was dispatched on errands—to bring a priest, who, not understanding the urgency, at first refused to come, and then to the theater to fetch the doctor, who came in his own good time, after the play was over. Even in his last hours Wolfgang was trying to explain to Süssmayr how he wanted the requiem to be finished. He was working on a middle section, the *Lacrimosa,* "Tearful that day on which will rise from ashes the guilty man for judgment." He wanted to be sure the timpani were included. I remembered when we were children in London, forced to be quiet during Papa's illness, and he had dictated one of his first symphonies to me: *I have a great fondness for the kettledrum,* he said.

The doctor belatedly arrived and prescribed cold compresses, but it was too late. Wolfgang slipped into unconsciousness, never to awaken, his Requiem in D Minor unfinished. I wonder now if he saw death's black angels with their great iridescent wings, and if they were singing to him as they bore him away.

Constanze, or perhaps her sister Sophie, sent me the briefest of messages several days later.

Wolfgang Amadeus Mozart died soon after midnight on the fifth of December 1791. His body was consecrated in the Crucifix Chapel of Stephansdom and then carried through snow and sleet for burial in the cemetery of St. Marx in an unmarked grave. *Requiescat in Pace.* May he rest in peace.

IT CAN'T BE TRUE! I thought as I read that brief, terrible message.

I sat for a long time, holding the note in my hands, reading it again and again, as if the words might be different this time, the ending changed. At first there were no tears—the shock was too great for such a simple response. I thought about the austere funeral; the emperor had ordered all funerals to be as plain as possible. It seemed an unfitting farewell for a man of such brilliance, such genius. But there was neither the resolve nor the money to bury my brother any differently.

Dry-eyed, I took the note to Johann Baptist. "We must go to Salzburg," I said. "I want to be with people who knew him."

My husband tried to discourage me. "The weather is very bad," he said. "The journey is too dangerous."

"Then I shall go alone," I said.

He gave in, and we went together.

Everyone in Salzburg was talking about Mozart's death. Archbishop Colloredo came to offer condolences. "It was God's will," he said. I merely nodded. *If you had treated him as he deserved, he would not have died this way.*

There were some who suspected foul play. "My brother says many musicians were jealous of him," Katherl said. "But he believes that Wolfgang worked himself to death."

And in the end, that's what I believed, too.

Whatever the reason, my brother was gone—not merely out of touch, but gone forever. I felt as though I had lost a part of myself and might never be whole again.

Wolfgang was thirty-five when he died. One can only wonder what great works he might have created had God granted him a longer life. But then I thought of his music—his magnificent music. I would always have that, and so would the rest of the world.

———

JOHANN BAPTIST AND I returned to St. Gilgen. I went alone into the music room, starkly empty except for my fortepiano, a small stove, and a rough wooden cabinet stacked with music. I was pleased that young Nannerl had kept the room at the proper temperature. I closed the door, sat down, and tried a few keys. None of them stuck, and the tuning, while not perfect, was good enough. From the piles of Wolfgang's music that I'd accumulated over the years, I pulled out the concertos Papa had had copied for me in the months before he died, and the most recent sonatas, and I set to work.

The music was challenging. It had been years since I had performed for a real audience, but I attacked the concertos as I had when I was a young girl, eager for approval. Every day throughout the long winter I rushed through my chores, left orders for the servants, and shut myself up with the music. Young Nannerl sensed my need and took over most of the running of the household without being asked. Johann Baptist said nothing, only offering to bring me more candles if I chose to practice after dark, as I often did.

Slowly the music came back to me. My fingers regained their dexterity. The constant use seemed to improve the tone of the fortepiano. I ate and slept Mozart's music, breathed it, lived it, digging through the piles of music, slowly and painfully mastering it and making it mine.

One evening toward spring I glanced up and saw that young Nannerl had crept into the room, bringing a chair for herself. A few nights later she came back with the two youngest children, who sat on the floor, wide-eyed and silent as their mother played. Then Johann Baptist joined them. When I'd finished a particularly difficult concerto, he began to applaud. The little ones turned to look at their father. Is this the proper thing to do? What will Mama think? Young Nannerl whispered something, and the children began to clap, too.

"Bravo!" Johann Baptist said.

"Bravo!" my children echoed.

Mozart and I are in Munich, or Vienna, or any one of a dozen great cities. We are seated side by side at a harpsichord, our hands poised above the keys. The audience is utterly silent, breath drawn and held, waiting. There's no signal—Mozart and I simply sense when the moment is right, and our fingers begin to fly over the keys. Every note is perfect. We are lost in our music, possessed by it. At that moment we're one person, not two.

We come to the final note and lift our hands from the keys. The silent breath is released, and the applause surges, rises, fills our ears. Bravo! the audience cries. Bravissimo!

Back in the present, I rose, acknowledging my family's applause with a deep curtsy.

Tears streamed down my cheeks. I let them fall.

A Note from the Author

MOZART WOULD HAVE been astonished.

Musicians and music lovers worldwide celebrated the year 2006 as the 250th anniversary of his birth. There were countless performances of his music in cities large and small throughout Europe and the United States. Thousands upon thousands of tourists (I was among them) flocked to Vienna and Salzburg to visit his birthplace, wander through the streets where he once walked, gaze at the instruments he played, sit in the churches where he performed, listen to his sublime music, and buy souvenirs with his likeness on music boxes, T-shirts, chocolates.

But there are no souvenirs of his sister, Nannerl.

For ten years after Wolfgang's death, Nannerl and her family lived on in St. Gilgen. When Johann Baptist died in

1801 at the age of sixty-five, Nannerl, then nearly fifty, moved back to Salzburg with her two children, Leopold (at sixteen too old to be called Leopoldl—"little Leopold"— any longer) and Jeanette, eleven, who was already blossoming into a fine singer and harpsichordist. Her stepdaughter, young Nannerl, chose to move to the village of Mondsee, taking her brother Josef with her.

But Salzburg was no longer the same. Armand d'Ippold, Nannerl's old love and faithful friend for so many years, had died a few months earlier. Jeanette died not long after her sixteenth birthday. When Leopold finished his schooling, he went into the army, then into government work, finally settling in Innsbruck. Nannerl was alone.

She kept in occasional contact with Constanze and the two boys; Karl Thomas was just six and Franz Xavier only four months old when their father died. Constanze, to her credit, took control of the family's tangled finances and managed to save herself and her children from destitution. It can't have been easy.

Eighteen years after Mozart's death, Constanze married a Danish diplomat, Georg Nissen, and moved to Copenhagen. When Nissen retired, they returned to live in Salzburg, where they spent the rest of their days.

By the end of her life, Nannerl was nearly blind. She hadn't touched the clavier in years. She died October 29, 1829, at the age of seventy-eight.

Mozart's final resting place in a cemetery outside of

Vienna is still not known exactly. But one day in Salzburg
I wandered away from the crowds and tour buses and
found my way to St. Peter's Cemetery, outside the church
where Mozart's Mass in C Minor had its first performance. The cemetery was a lovely, peaceful garden with
pansies, begonias, and sunflowers blooming among dense
green ivy. There near the entrance to the catacombs,
carved long ago into the rock of the Mönchsberg, I found
Nannerl's grave, shared—oddly, I think—with Michael
Haydn, the organist, who died in 1805, her name and his
incised on the tombstone.

*What must it have been like to be the highly talented sister of a
genius?* I wondered. *What was it like to live in Mozart's shadow?*

To answer my own questions, I decided to write this
book.